DC SUPER HERO GIRLS

WRITTEN BY
Shea Fontana

ART BY
**Marcelo DiChiara,
Agnes Garbowska,**
AND **Mirka Andolfo**

COLORS BY
Silvana Brys
AND **Jeremy Lawson**

LETTERING BY
Janice Chiang

COVER BY
Yancey Labat and Monica Kubina

SUPERGIRL BASED ON THE CHARACTERS CREATED
BY JERRY SIEGEL AND JOE SHUSTER.
BY SPECIAL ARRANGEMENT WITH
THE JERRY SIEGEL FAMILY.

MARIE JAVINS Group Editor
BRITTANY HOLZHERR Editor
DIEGO LOPEZ Assistant Editor
STEVE COOK Design Director - Books
AMIE BROCKWAY-METCALF Publication Design

BOB HARRAS Senior VP - Editor-in-Chief, DC Comics
BOBBIE CHASE Executive Editor, Young Reader & Talent Development

DIANE NELSON President
DAN DiDIO Publisher
JIM LEE Publisher
GEOFF JOHNS President & Chief Creative Officer
AMIT DESAI Executive VP - Business & Marketing Strategy, Direct to
Consumer & Global Franchise Management
SAM ADES Senior VP & General Manager, Digital Services
MARK CHIARELLO Senior VP - Art, Design & Collected Editions
JOHN CUNNINGHAM Senior VP - Sales & Trade Marketing
ANNE DePIES Senior VP - Business Strategy, Finance & Administration
DON FALLETTI VP - Manufacturing Operations
LAWRENCE GANEM VP - Editorial Administration & Talent Relations
ALISON GILL Senior VP - Manufacturing & Operations
HANK KANALZ Senior VP - Editorial Strategy & Administration
JAY KOGAN VP - Legal Affairs
JACK MAHAN VP - Business Affairs
NICK J. NAPOLITANO VP - Manufacturing Administration
EDDIE SCANNELL VP - Consumer Marketing
COURTNEY SIMMONS Senior VP - Publicity & Communications
JIM (SKI) SOKOLOWSKI VP - Comic Book Specialty Sales & Trade Marketing
NANCY SPEARS VP - Mass, Book, Digital Sales & Trade Marketing
MICHELE R. WELLS VP - Content Strategy

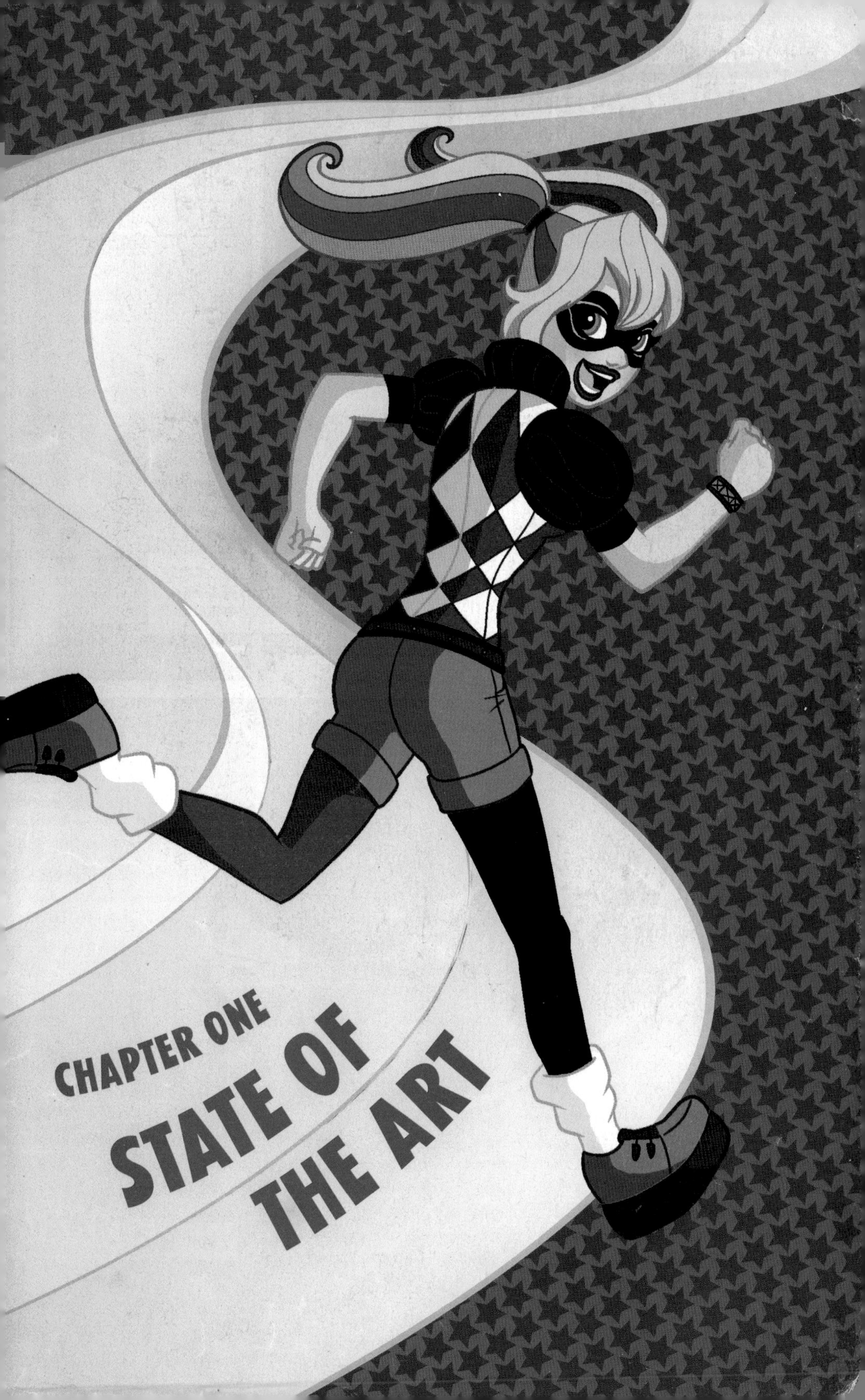

CHAPTER ONE

STATE OF THE ART

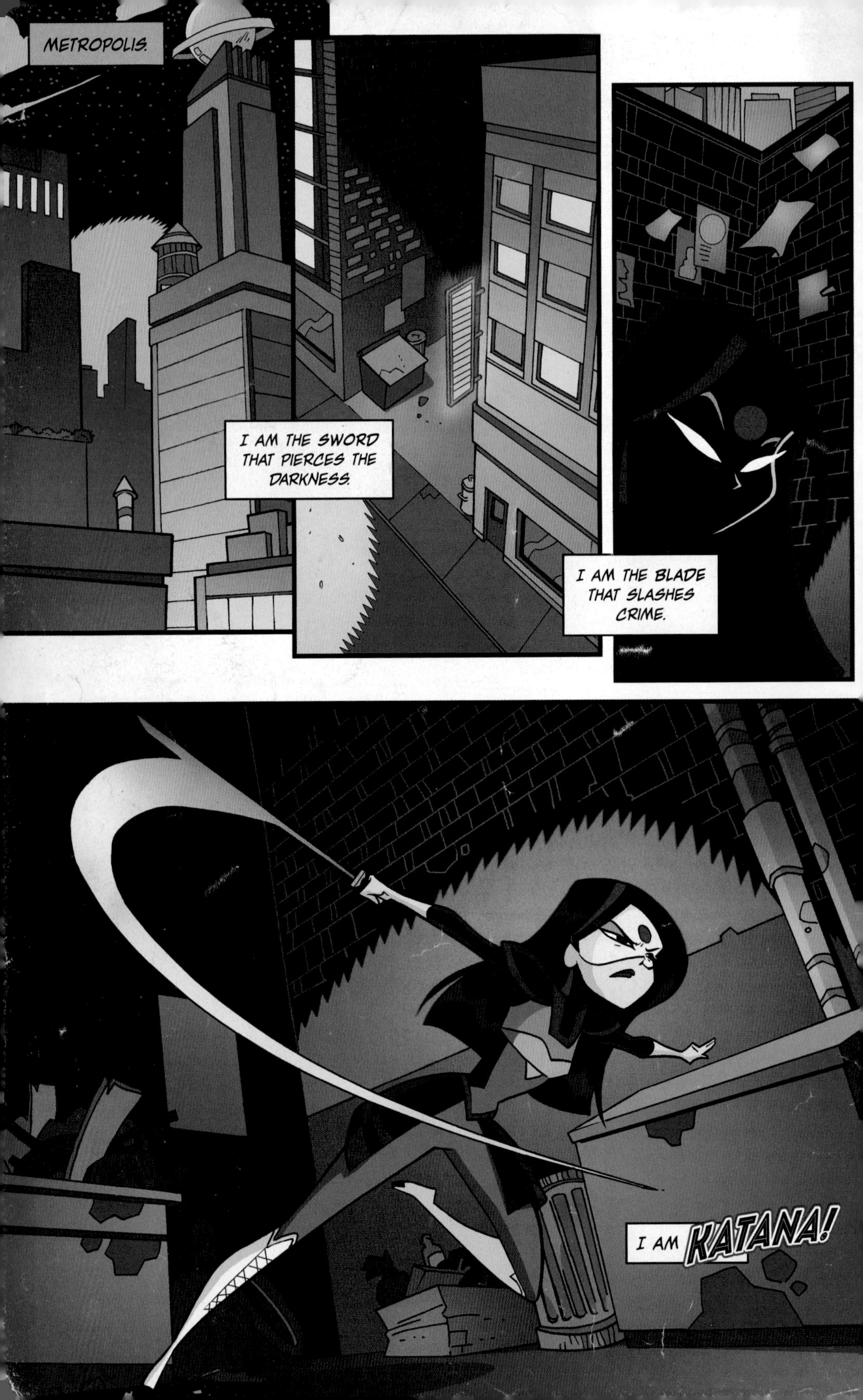
METROPOLIS.
I AM THE SWORD THAT PIERCES THE DARKNESS.
I AM THE BLADE THAT SLASHES CRIME.
I AM KATANA!

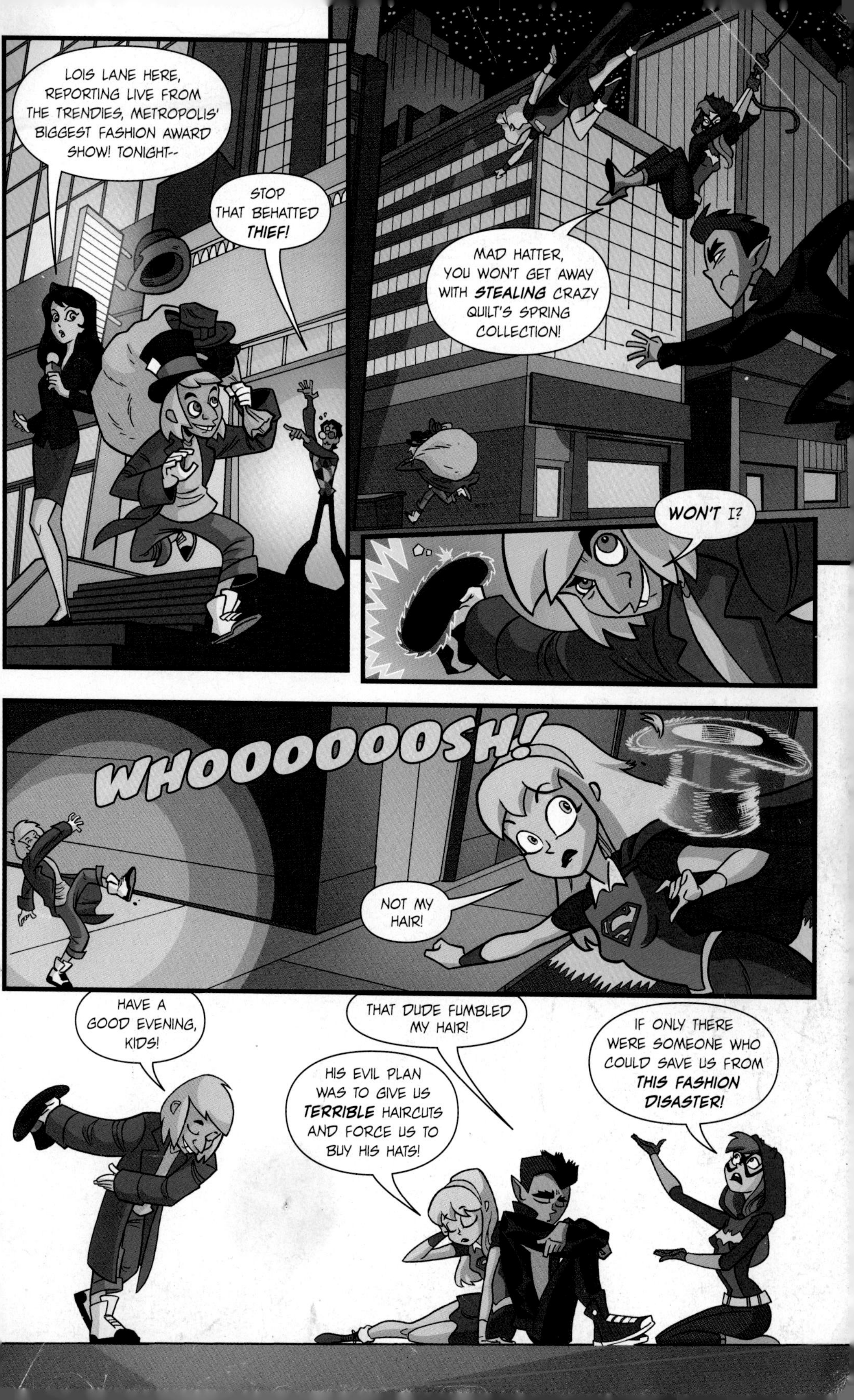
LOIS LANE HERE, REPORTING LIVE FROM THE TRENDIES, METROPOLIS' BIGGEST FASHION AWARD SHOW! TONIGHT--
STOP THAT BEHATTED THIEF!
MAD HATTER, YOU WON'T GET AWAY WITH STEALING CRAZY QUILT'S SPRING COLLECTION!
WON'T I?
WHOOOOOOOSH!
NOT MY HAIR!
HAVE A GOOD EVENING, KIDS!
THAT DUDE FUMBLED MY HAIR!
HIS EVIL PLAN WAS TO GIVE US TERRIBLE HAIRCUTS AND FORCE US TO BUY HIS HATS!
IF ONLY THERE WERE SOMEONE WHO COULD SAVE US FROM THIS FASHION DISASTER!

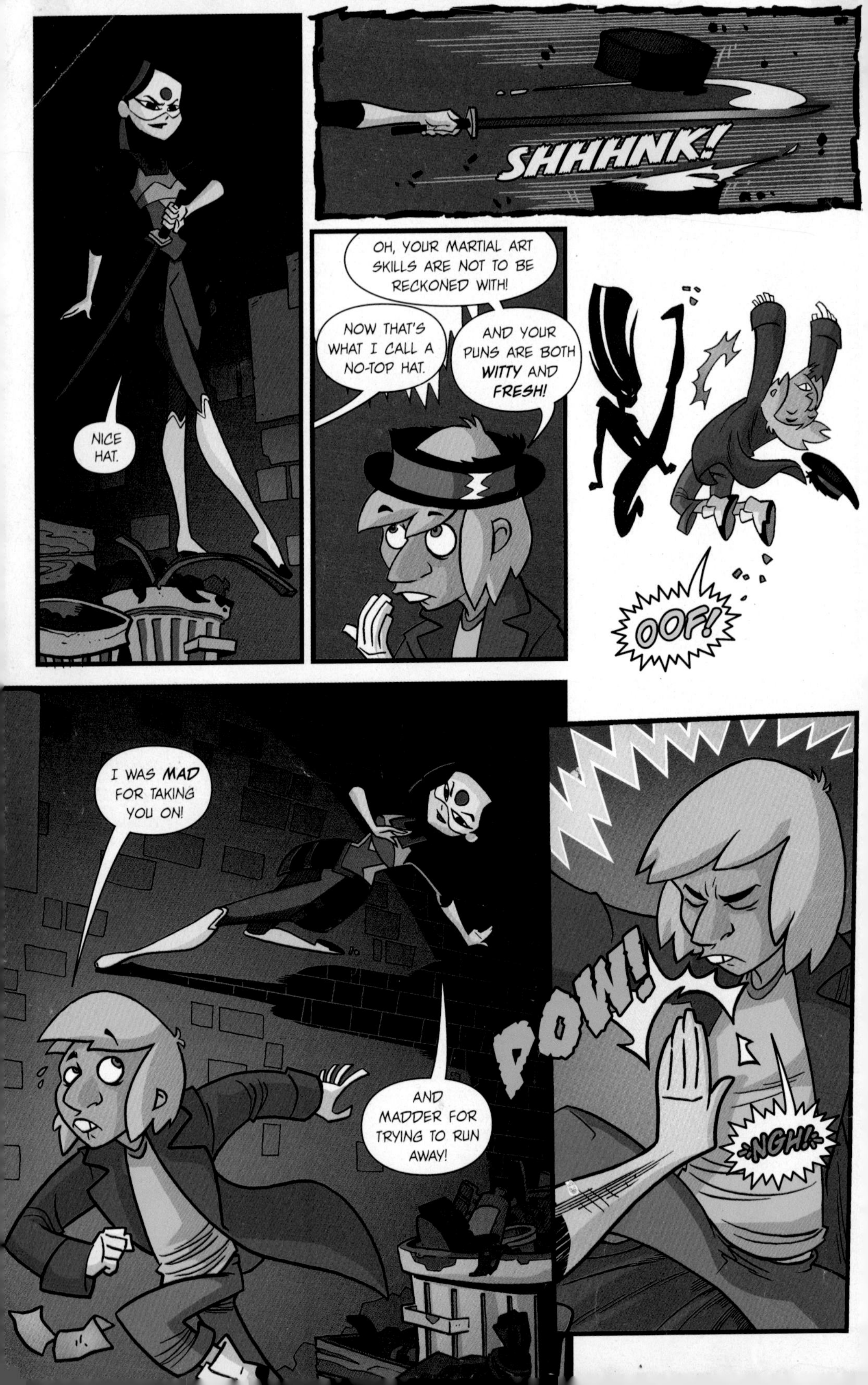

SHHHNK!
NICE HAT.
OH, YOUR MARTIAL ART SKILLS ARE NOT TO BE RECKONED WITH!
NOW THAT'S WHAT I CALL A NO-TOP HAT.
AND YOUR PUNS ARE BOTH WITTY AND FRESH!
OOF!
I WAS MAD FOR TAKING YOU ON!
AND MADDER FOR TRYING TO RUN AWAY!
POW!
NGH!

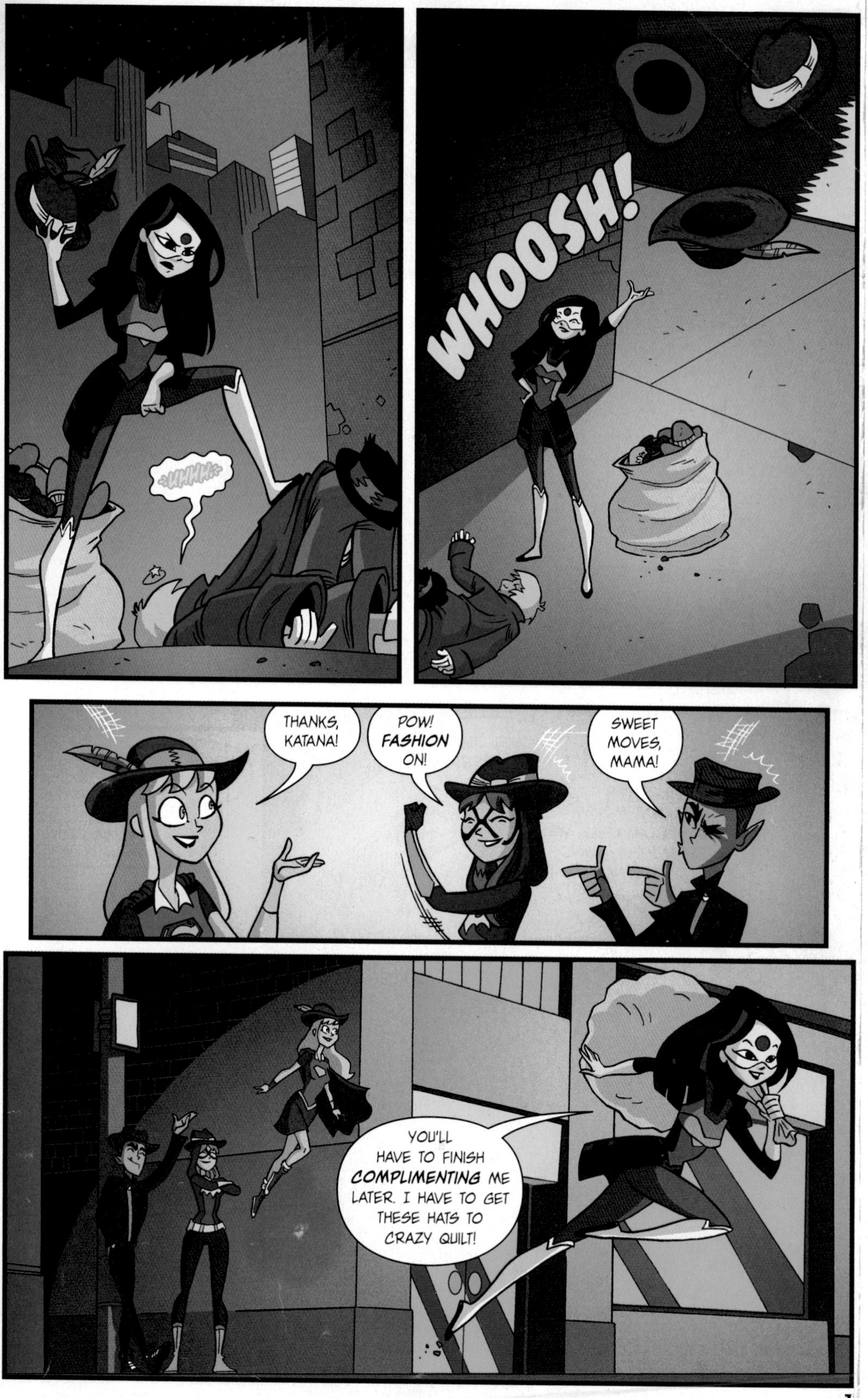
WHOOSH!
THANKS, KATANA!
POW! FASHION ON!
SWEET MOVES, MAMA!
YOU'LL HAVE TO FINISH COMPLIMENTING ME LATER. I HAVE TO GET THESE HATS TO CRAZY QUILT!

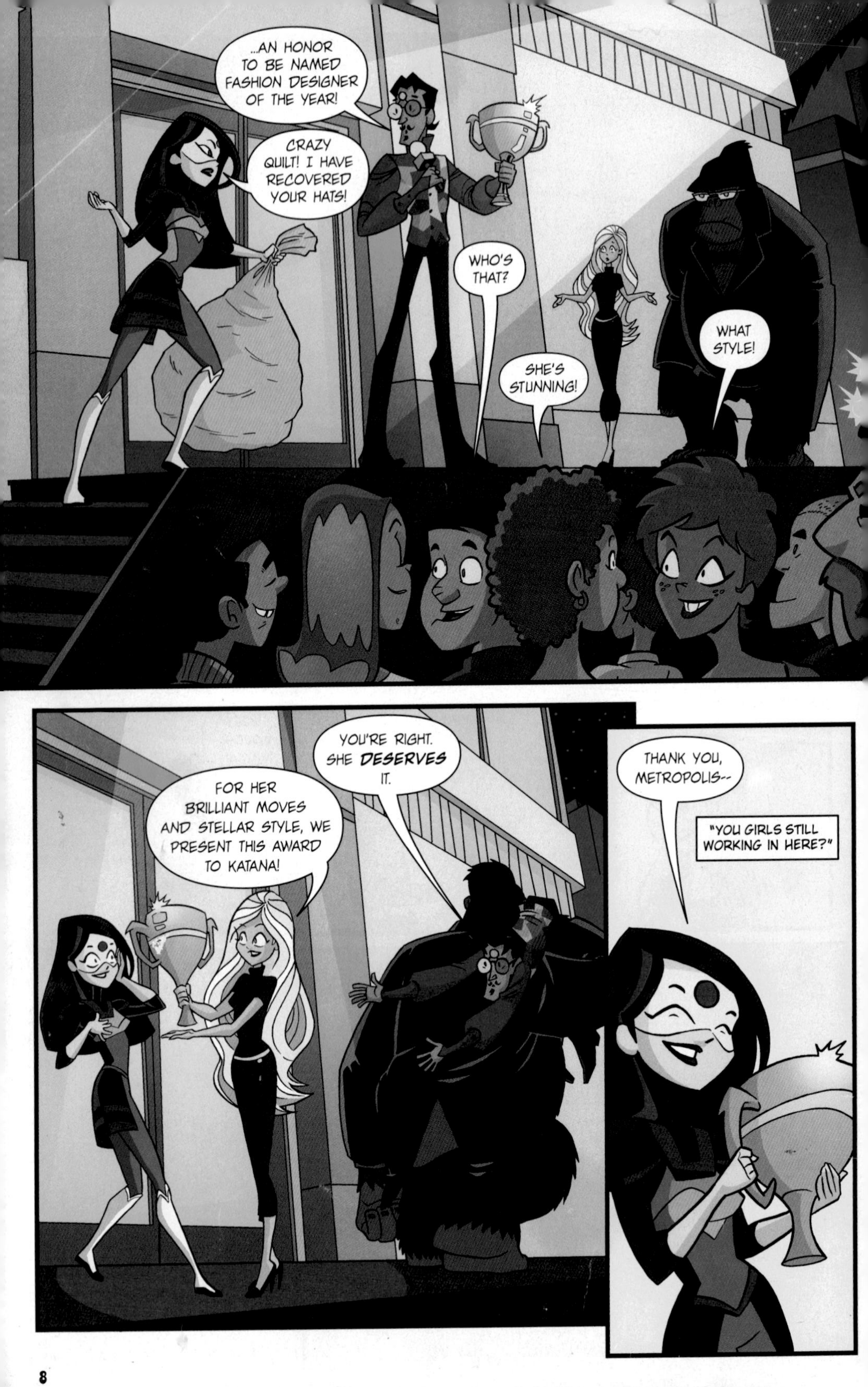
...AN HONOR TO BE NAMED FASHION DESIGNER OF THE YEAR!
CRAZY QUILT! I HAVE RECOVERED YOUR HATS!
WHO'S THAT?
SHE'S STUNNING!
WHAT STYLE!
FOR HER BRILLIANT MOVES AND STELLAR STYLE, WE PRESENT THIS AWARD TO KATANA!
YOU'RE RIGHT. SHE DESERVES IT.
THANK YOU, METROPOLIS--
"YOU GIRLS STILL WORKING IN HERE?"

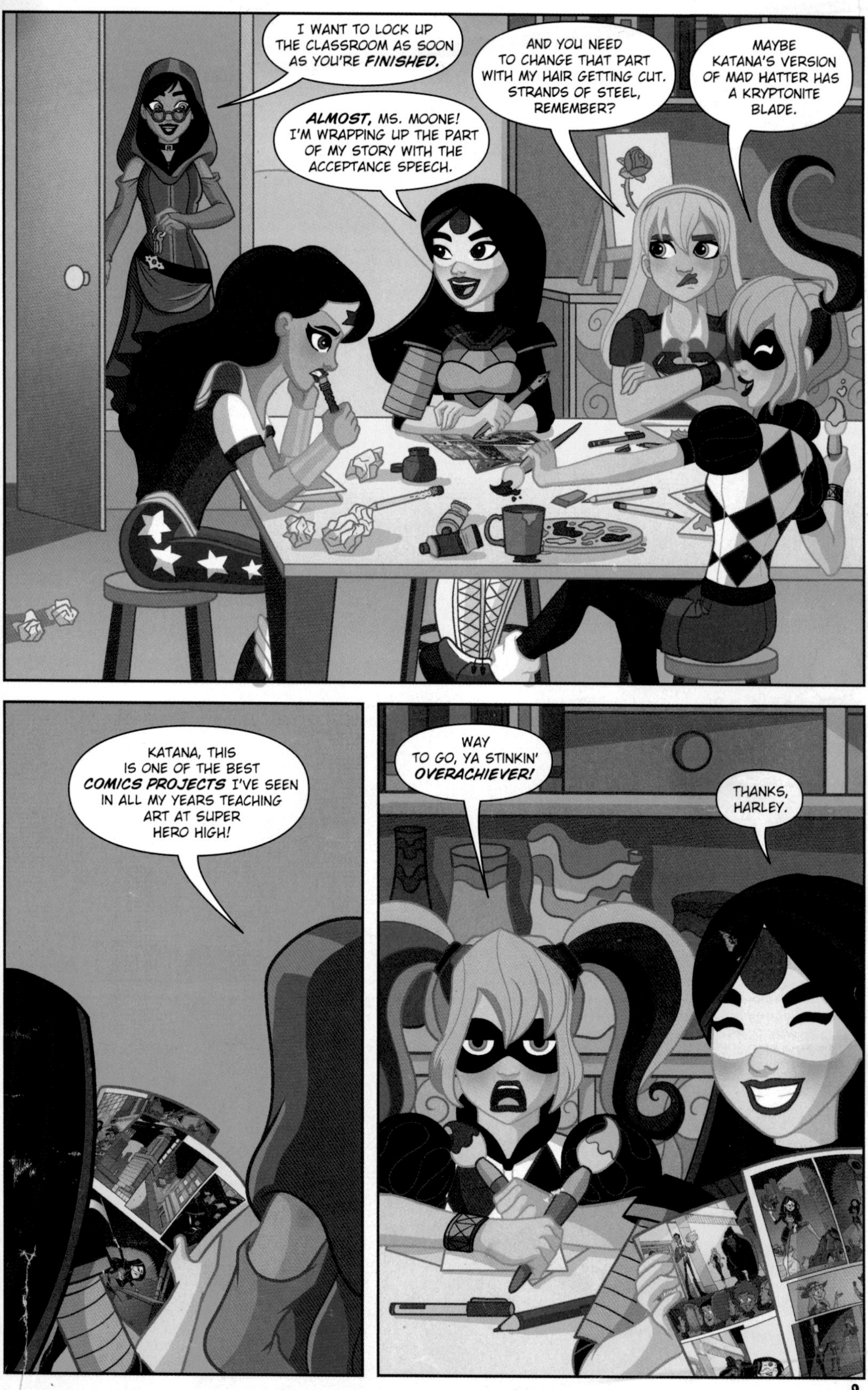
I WANT TO LOCK UP THE CLASSROOM AS SOON AS YOU'RE ***FINISHED.***
ALMOST, MS. MOONE! I'M WRAPPING UP THE PART OF MY STORY WITH THE ACCEPTANCE SPEECH.
AND YOU NEED TO CHANGE THAT PART WITH MY HAIR GETTING CUT. STRANDS OF STEEL, REMEMBER?
MAYBE KATANA'S VERSION OF MAD HATTER HAS A KRYPTONITE BLADE.
KATANA, THIS IS ONE OF THE BEST ***COMICS PROJECTS*** I'VE SEEN IN ALL MY YEARS TEACHING ART AT SUPER HERO HIGH!
WAY TO GO, YA STINKIN' ***OVERACHIEVER!***
THANKS, HARLEY.

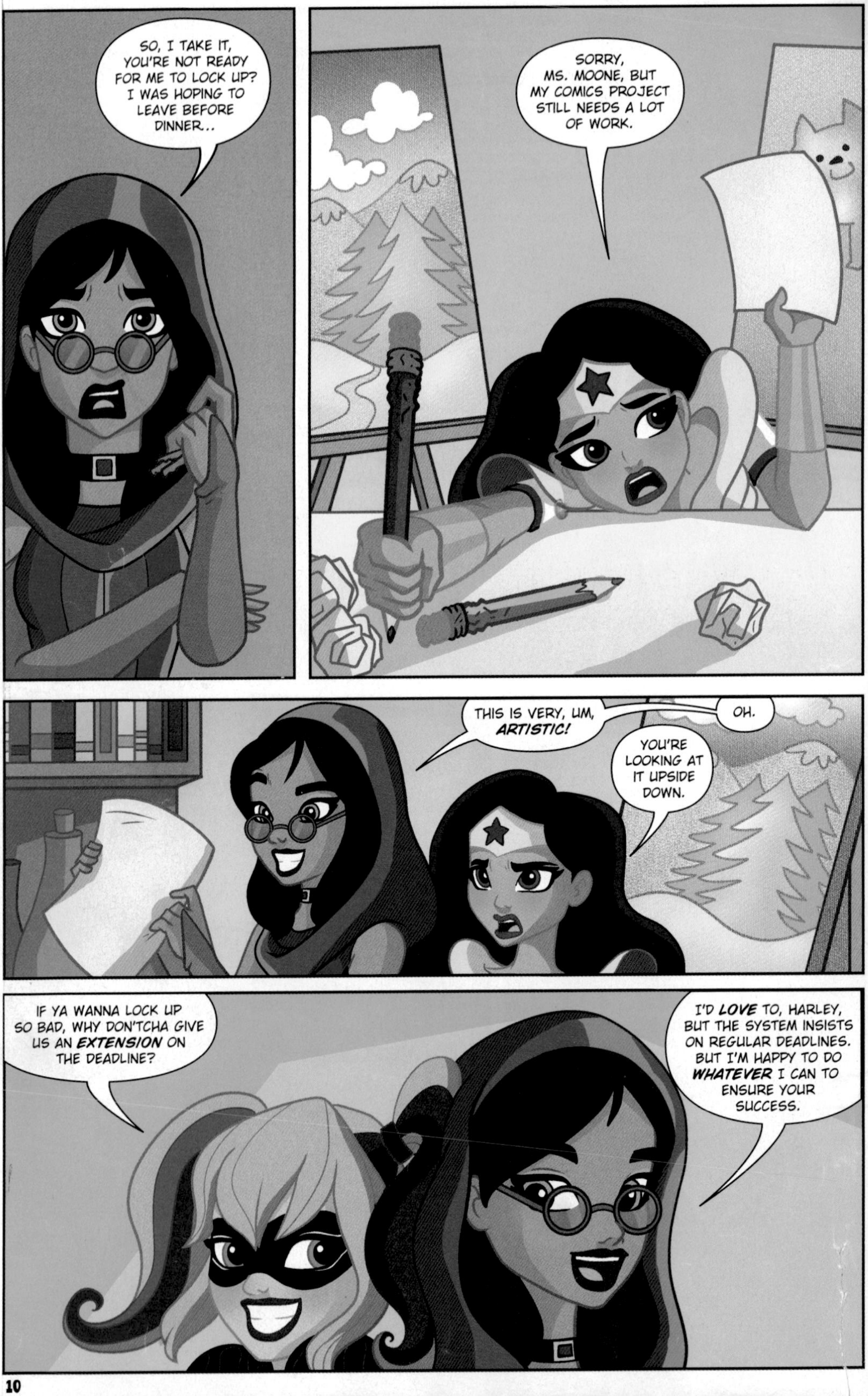
SO, I TAKE IT, YOU'RE NOT READY FOR ME TO LOCK UP? I WAS HOPING TO LEAVE BEFORE DINNER...
SORRY, MS. MOONE, BUT MY COMICS PROJECT STILL NEEDS A LOT OF WORK.
THIS IS VERY, UM, ***ARTISTIC!***
OH.
YOU'RE LOOKING AT IT UPSIDE DOWN.
IF YA WANNA LOCK UP SO BAD, WHY DON'TCHA GIVE US AN ***EXTENSION*** ON THE DEADLINE?
I'D ***LOVE*** TO, HARLEY, BUT THE SYSTEM INSISTS ON REGULAR DEADLINES. BUT I'M HAPPY TO DO ***WHATEVER*** I CAN TO ENSURE YOUR SUCCESS.

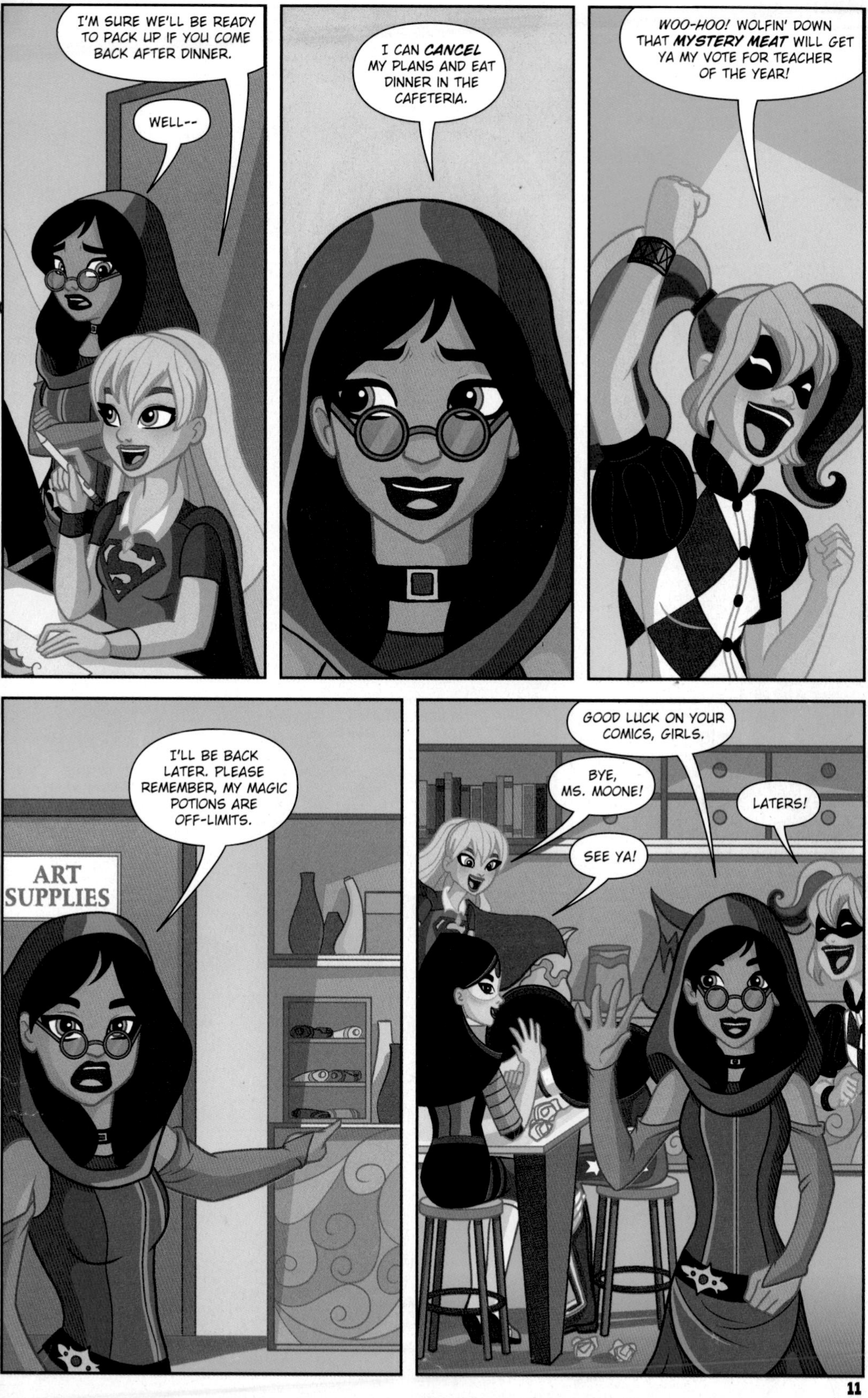
I'M SURE WE'LL BE READY TO PACK UP IF YOU COME BACK AFTER DINNER.
WELL--
I CAN CANCEL MY PLANS AND EAT DINNER IN THE CAFETERIA.
WOO-HOO! WOLFIN' DOWN THAT MYSTERY MEAT WILL GET YA MY VOTE FOR TEACHER OF THE YEAR!
I'LL BE BACK LATER. PLEASE REMEMBER, MY MAGIC POTIONS ARE OFF-LIMITS.
ART SUPPLIES
GOOD LUCK ON YOUR COMICS, GIRLS.
BYE, MS. MOONE!
SEE YA!
LATERS!

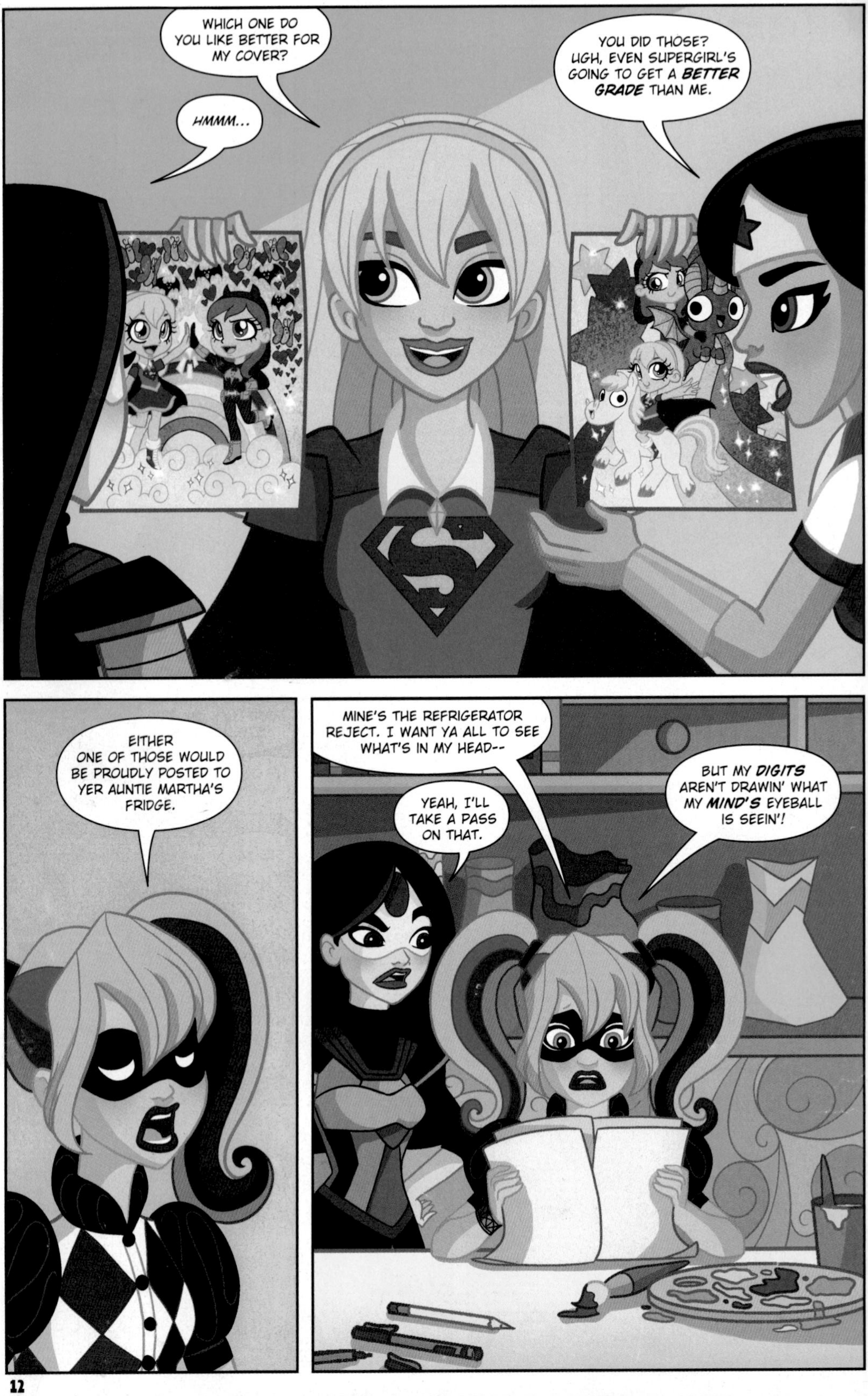

WHICH ONE DO YOU LIKE BETTER FOR MY COVER?
HMMM...
YOU DID THOSE? UGH, EVEN SUPERGIRL'S GOING TO GET A **BETTER GRADE** THAN ME.
EITHER ONE OF THOSE WOULD BE PROUDLY POSTED TO YER AUNTIE MARTHA'S FRIDGE.
MINE'S THE REFRIGERATOR REJECT. I WANT YA ALL TO SEE WHAT'S IN MY HEAD--
YEAH, I'LL TAKE A PASS ON THAT.
BUT MY ***DIGITS*** AREN'T DRAWIN' WHAT MY ***MIND'S*** EYEBALL IS SEEIN'!

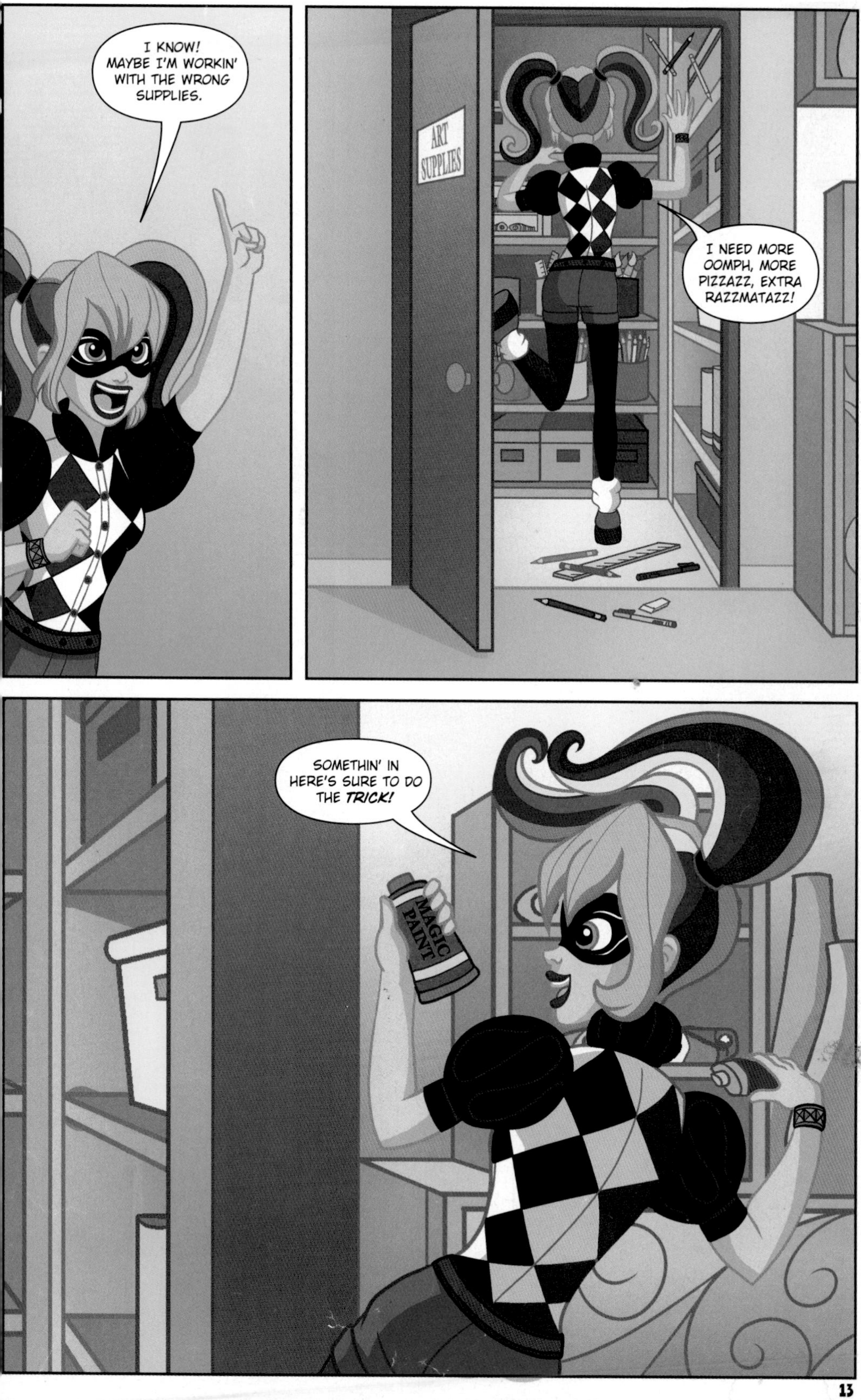
I KNOW! MAYBE I'M WORKIN' WITH THE WRONG SUPPLIES.
ART SUPPLIES
I NEED MORE OOMPH, MORE PIZZAZZ, EXTRA RAZZMATAZZ!
SOMETHIN' IN HERE'S SURE TO DO THE *TRICK!*
MAGIC PAINT

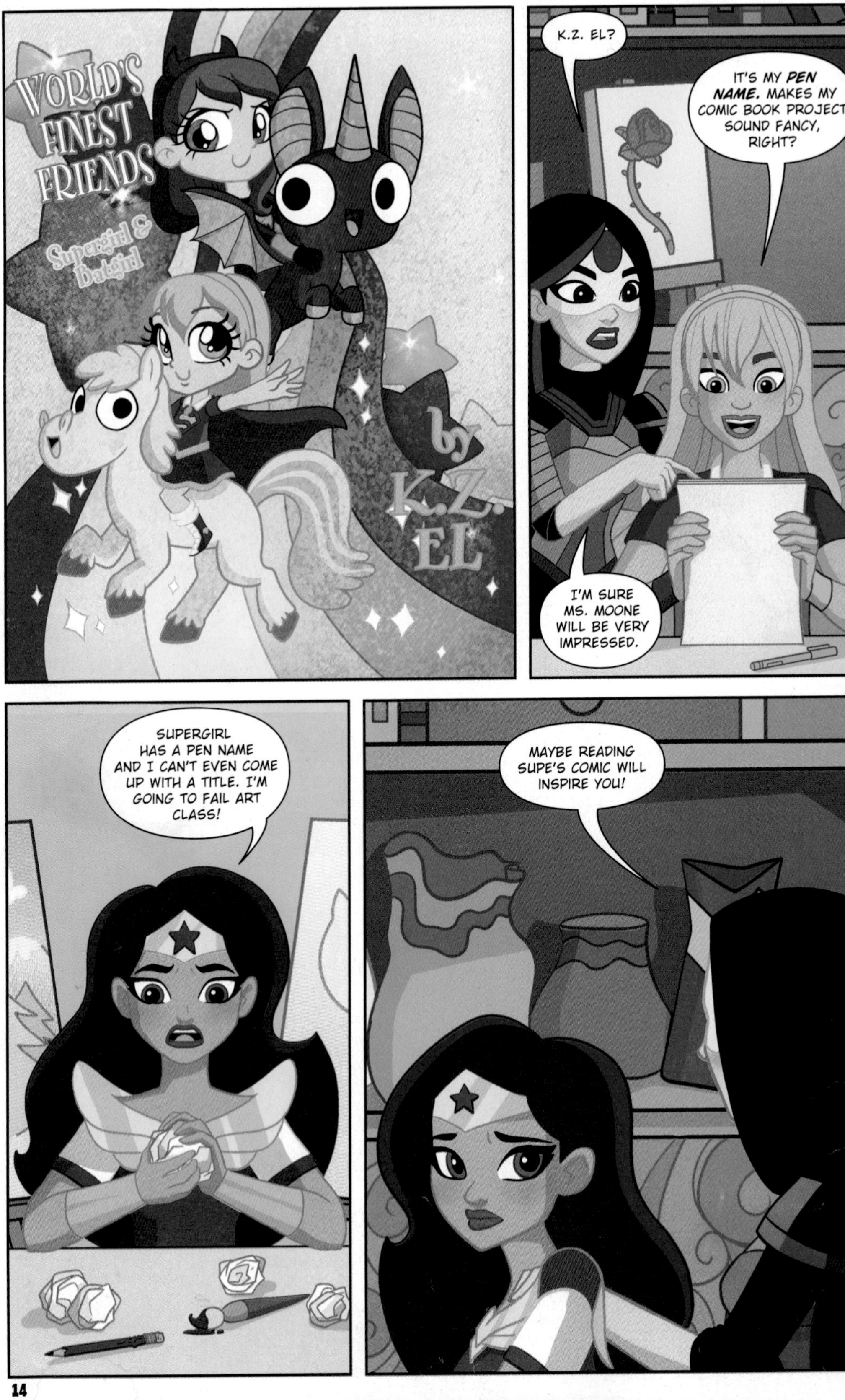
WORLD'S FINEST FRIENDS
Supergirl & Batgirl
by K.Z. EL
K.Z. EL?
IT'S MY **PEN NAME.** MAKES MY COMIC BOOK PROJECT SOUND FANCY, RIGHT?
I'M SURE MS. MOONE WILL BE VERY IMPRESSED.
SUPERGIRL HAS A PEN NAME AND I CAN'T EVEN COME UP WITH A TITLE. I'M GOING TO FAIL ART CLASS!
MAYBE READING SUPE'S COMIC WILL INSPIRE YOU!

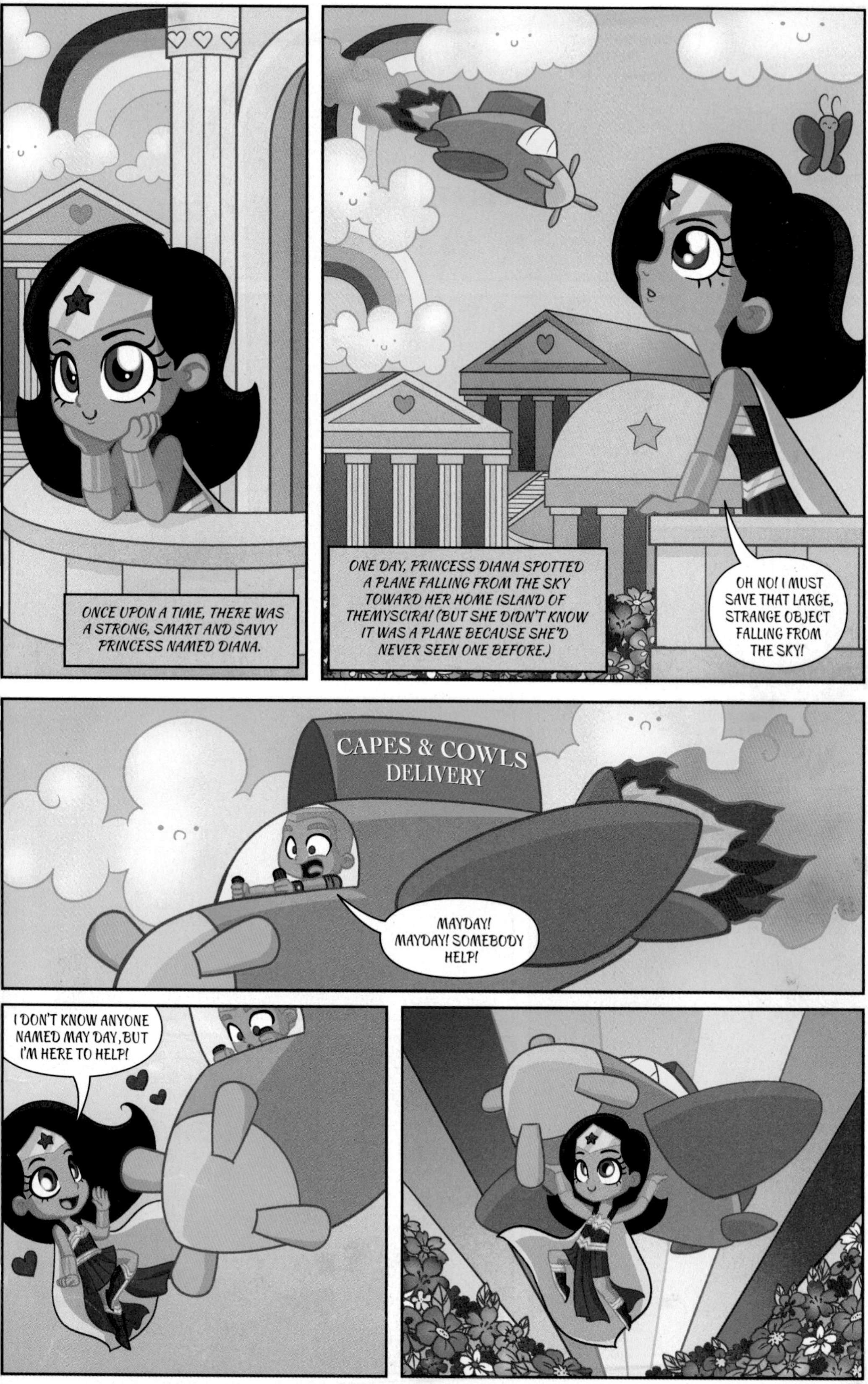
ONCE UPON A TIME, THERE WAS A STRONG, SMART AND SAVVY PRINCESS NAMED DIANA.
ONE DAY, PRINCESS DIANA SPOTTED A PLANE FALLING FROM THE SKY TOWARD HER HOME ISLAND OF THEMYSCIRA! (BUT SHE DIDN'T KNOW IT WAS A PLANE BECAUSE SHE'D NEVER SEEN ONE BEFORE.)
OH NO! I MUST SAVE THAT LARGE, STRANGE OBJECT FALLING FROM THE SKY!
CAPES & COWLS DELIVERY
MAYDAY! MAYDAY! SOMEBODY HELP!
I DON'T KNOW ANYONE NAMED MAY DAY, BUT I'M HERE TO HELP!

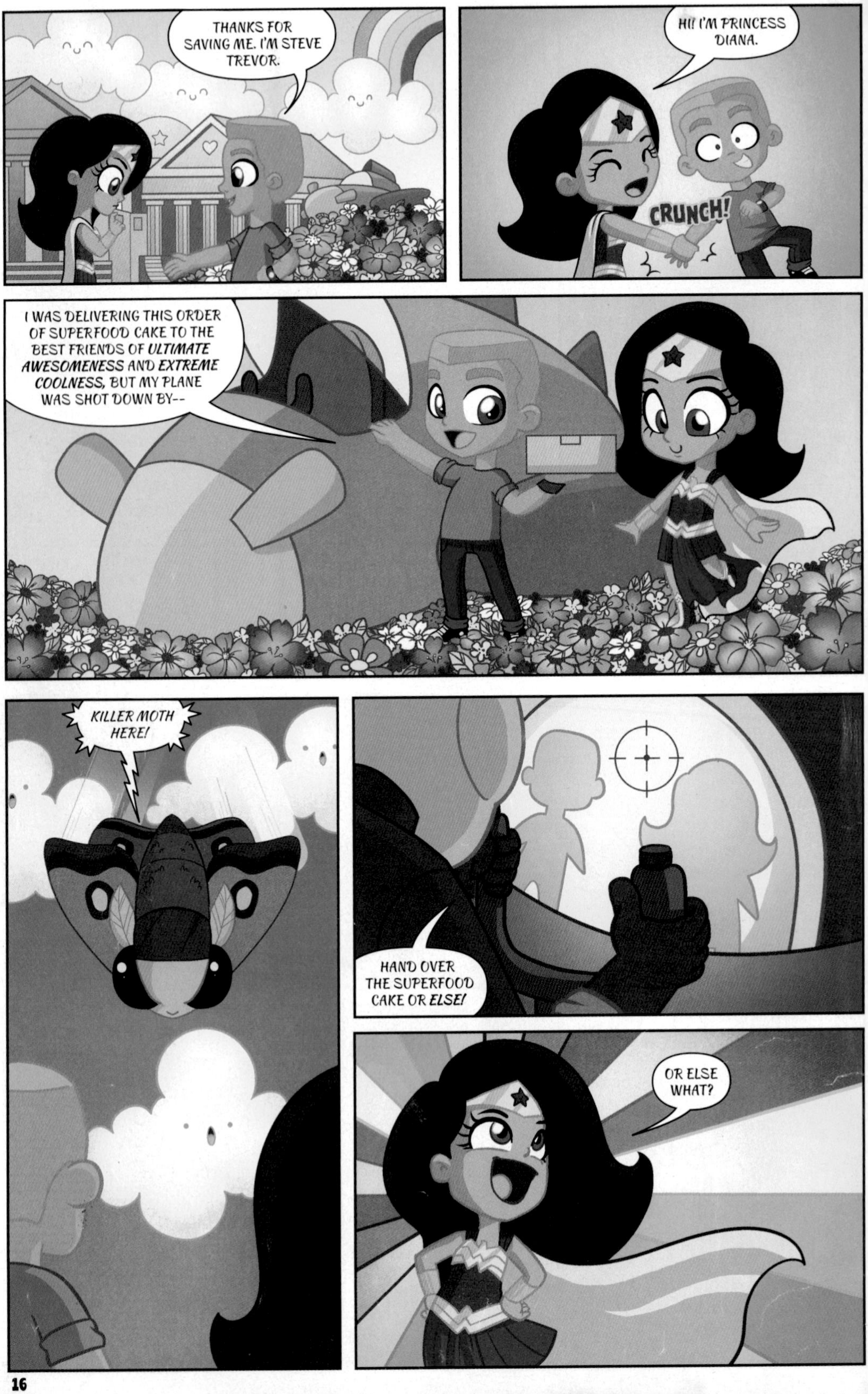
THANKS FOR SAVING ME. I'M STEVE TREVOR.
HI! I'M PRINCESS DIANA.
CRUNCH!
I WAS DELIVERING THIS ORDER OF SUPERFOOD CAKE TO THE BEST FRIENDS OF *ULTIMATE AWESOMENESS* AND *EXTREME COOLNESS*, BUT MY PLANE WAS SHOT DOWN BY--
KILLER MOTH HERE!
HAND OVER THE SUPERFOOD CAKE OR *ELSE!*
OR ELSE WHAT?

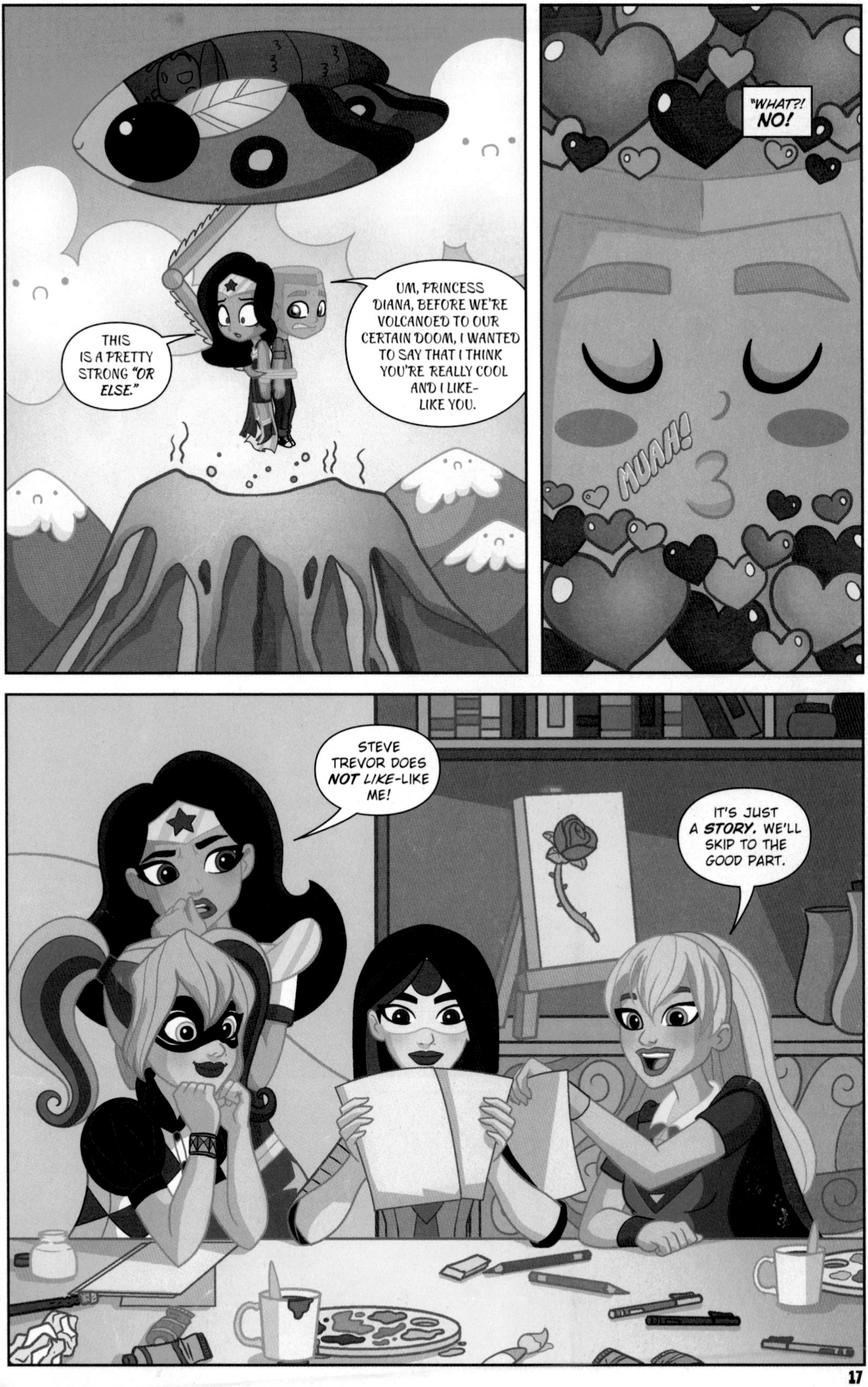
THIS IS A PRETTY STRONG "OR ELSE."
UM, PRINCESS DIANA, BEFORE WE'RE VOLCANOED TO OUR CERTAIN DOOM, I WANTED TO SAY THAT I THINK YOU'RE REALLY COOL AND I LIKE-LIKE YOU.
"WHAT?! NO!
MUAH!
STEVE TREVOR DOES NOT LIKE-LIKE ME!
IT'S JUST A STORY. WE'LL SKIP TO THE GOOD PART.

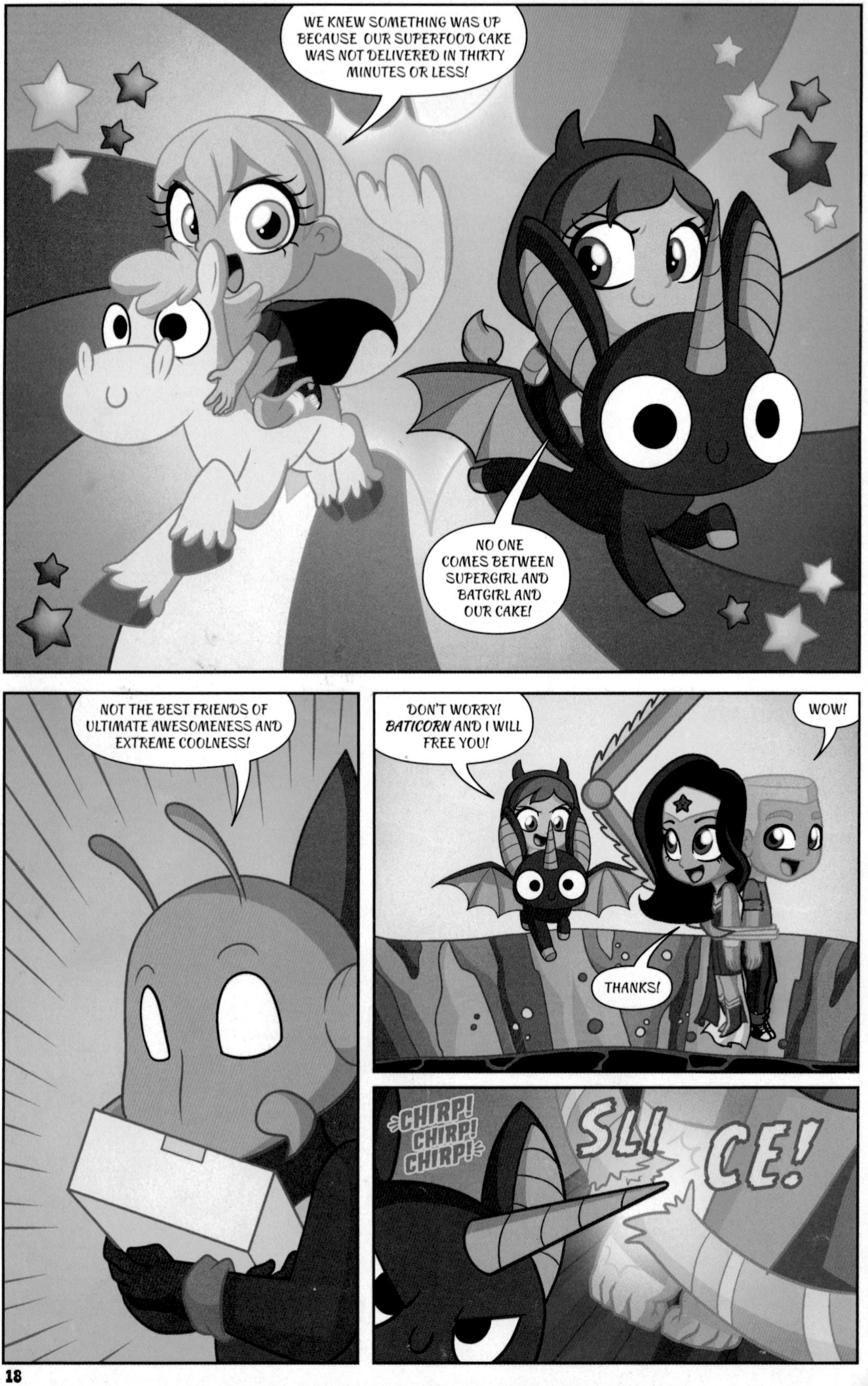

WE KNEW SOMETHING WAS UP BECAUSE OUR SUPERFOOD CAKE WAS NOT DELIVERED IN THIRTY MINUTES OR LESS!
NO ONE COMES BETWEEN SUPERGIRL AND BATGIRL AND OUR CAKE!
NOT THE BEST FRIENDS OF ULTIMATE AWESOMENESS AND EXTREME COOLNESS!
DON'T WORRY! *BATICORN* AND I WILL FREE YOU!
WOW!
THANKS!
CHIRP! CHIRP! CHIRP!
SLI CE!

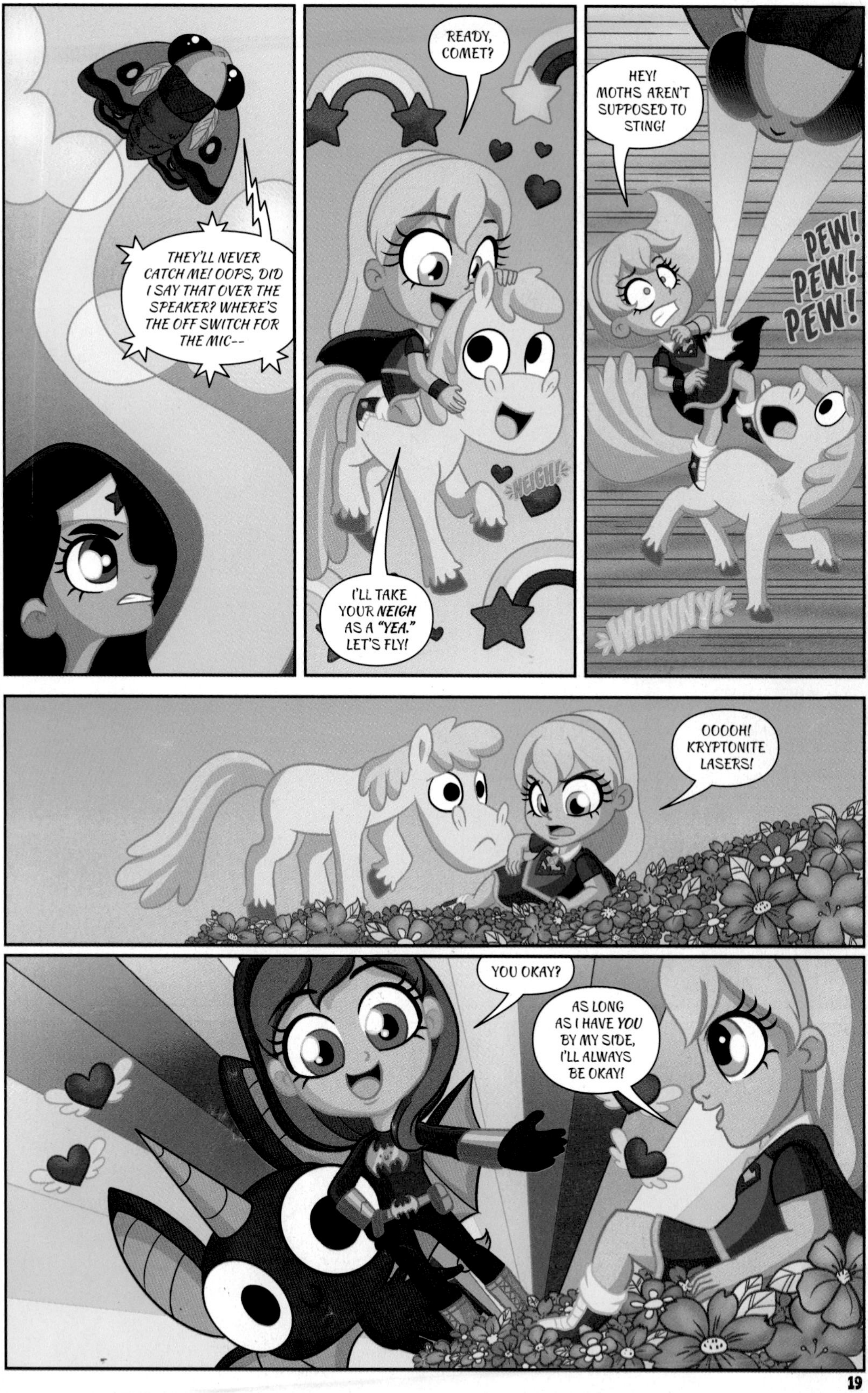
THEY'LL NEVER CATCH ME! OOPS, DID I SAY THAT OVER THE SPEAKER? WHERE'S THE OFF SWITCH FOR THE MIC--
READY, COMET?
NEIGH!
I'LL TAKE YOUR *NEIGH* AS A *"YEA."* LET'S FLY!
HEY! MOTHS AREN'T SUPPOSED TO STING!
PEW! PEW! PEW!
WHINNY!
OOOOH! KRYPTONITE LASERS!
YOU OKAY?
AS LONG AS I HAVE *YOU* BY MY SIDE, I'LL ALWAYS BE OKAY!

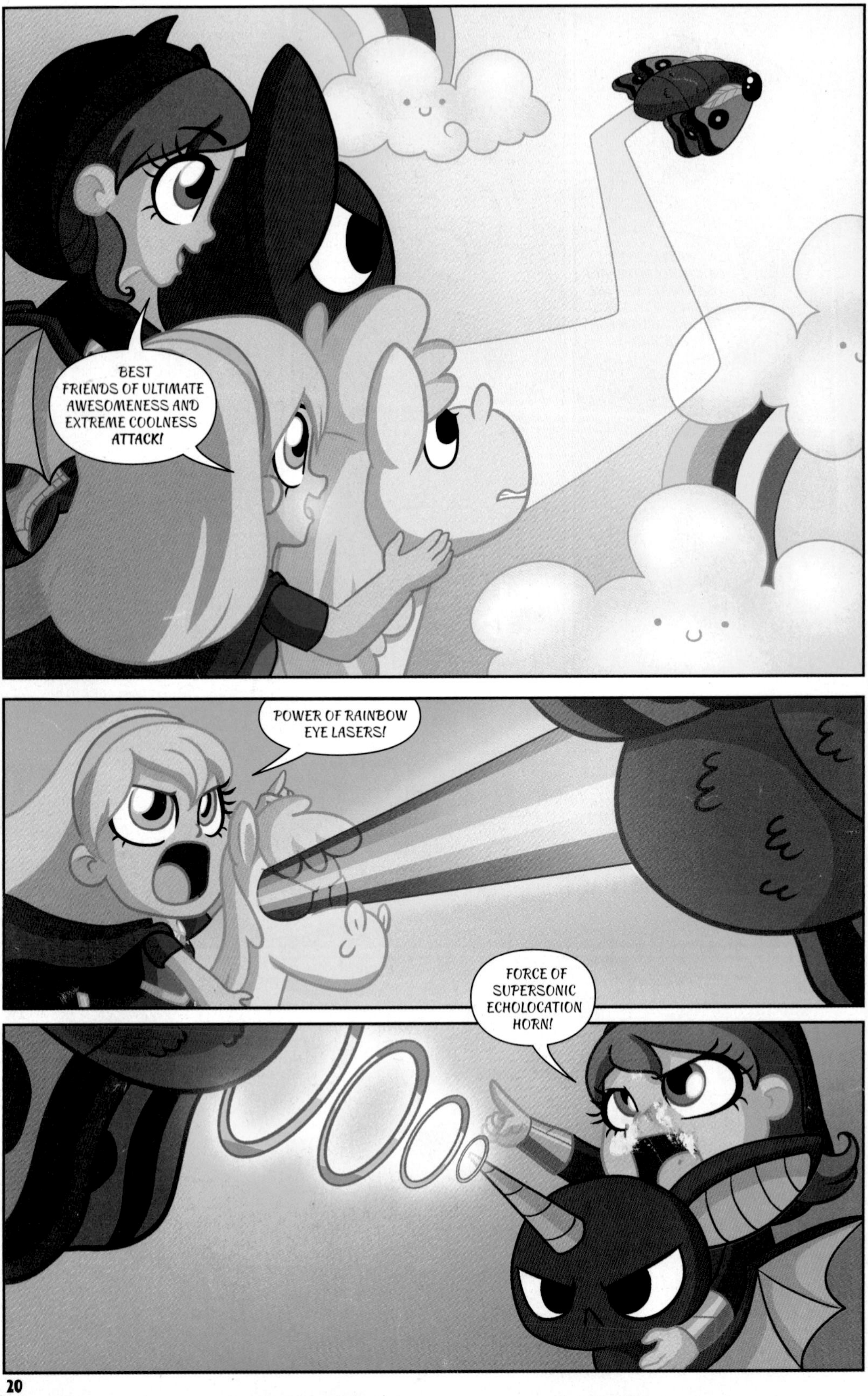
BEST FRIENDS OF ULTIMATE AWESOMENESS AND EXTREME COOLNESS ATTACK!
POWER OF RAINBOW EYE LASERS!
FORCE OF SUPERSONIC ECHOLOCATION HORN!

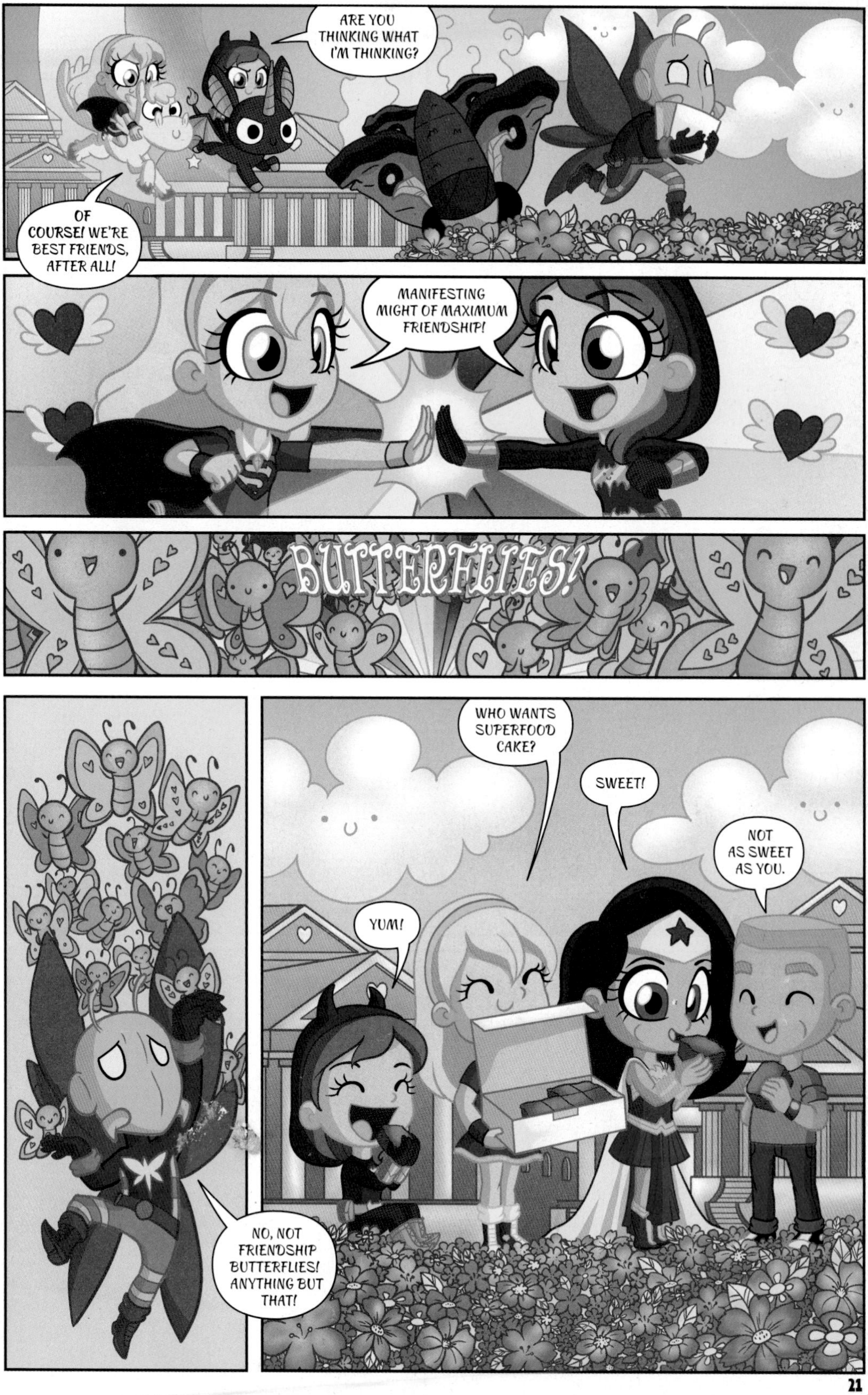
ARE YOU THINKING WHAT I'M THINKING?
OF COURSE! WE'RE BEST FRIENDS, AFTER ALL!
MANIFESTING MIGHT OF MAXIMUM FRIENDSHIP!
BUTTERFLIES!
NO, NOT FRIENDSHIP BUTTERFLIES! ANYTHING BUT THAT!
WHO WANTS SUPERFOOD CAKE?
SWEET!
NOT AS SWEET AS YOU.
YUM!

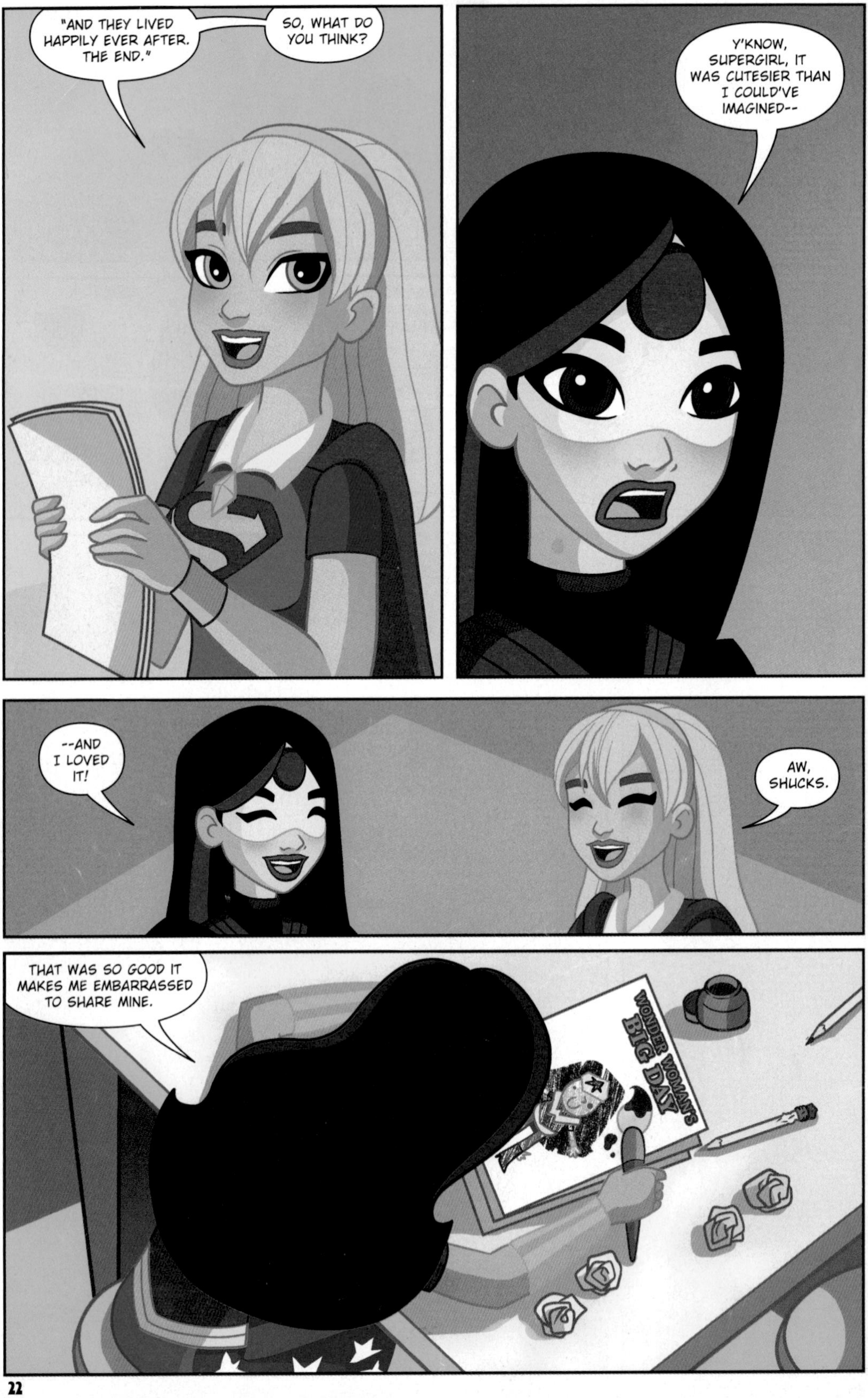
"AND THEY LIVED HAPPILY EVER AFTER. THE END."
SO, WHAT DO YOU THINK?
Y'KNOW, SUPERGIRL, IT WAS CUTESIER THAN I COULD'VE IMAGINED--
--AND I LOVED IT!
AW, SHUCKS.
THAT WAS SO GOOD IT MAKES ME EMBARRASSED TO SHARE MINE.
WONDER WOMAN'S BIG DAY

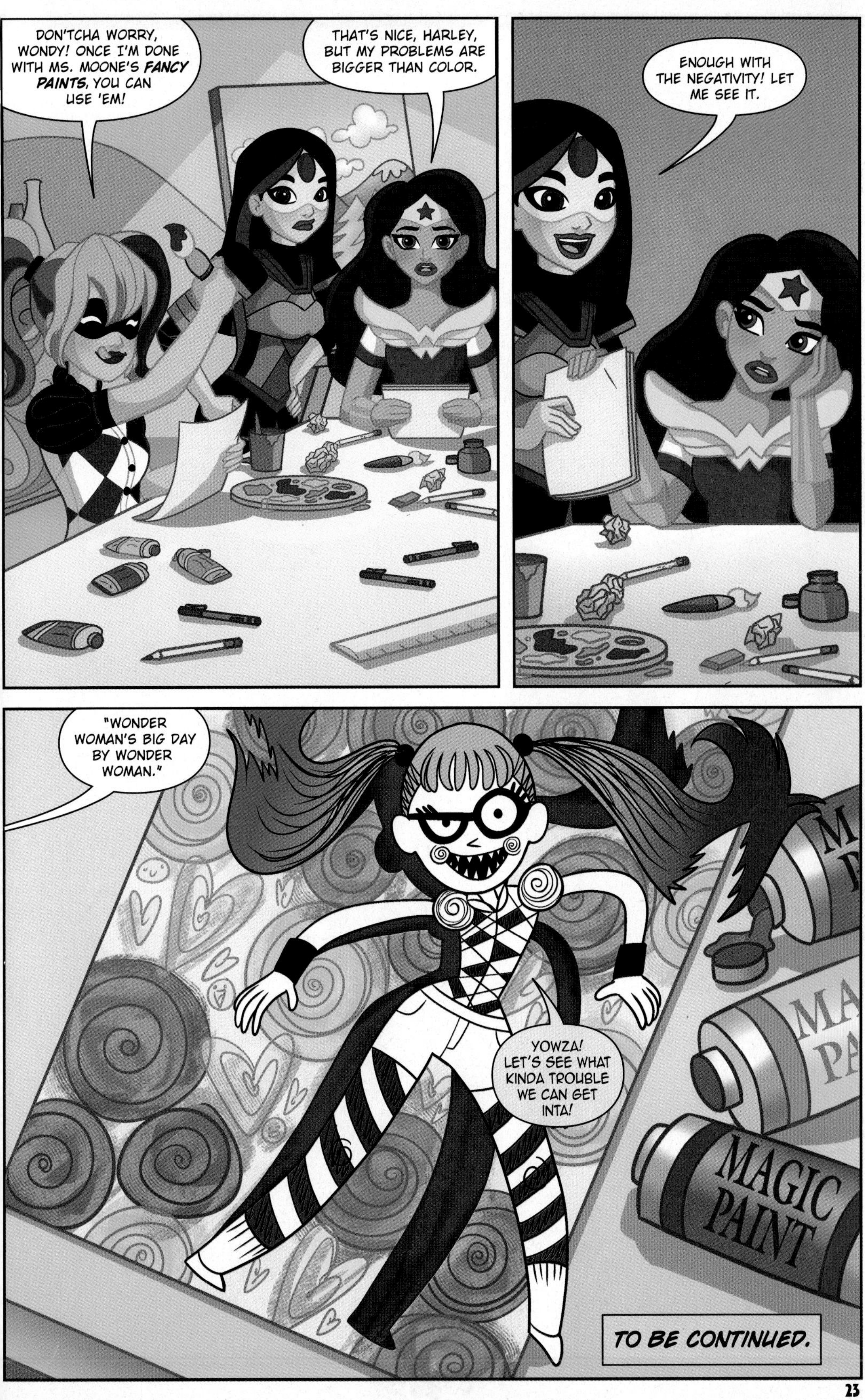
DON'TCHA WORRY, WONDY! ONCE I'M DONE WITH MS. MOONE'S FANCY PAINTS, YOU CAN USE 'EM!
THAT'S NICE, HARLEY, BUT MY PROBLEMS ARE BIGGER THAN COLOR.
ENOUGH WITH THE NEGATIVITY! LET ME SEE IT.
"WONDER WOMAN'S BIG DAY BY WONDER WOMAN."
YOWZA! LET'S SEE WHAT KINDA TROUBLE WE CAN GET INTA!
MAGIC PAINT
TO BE CONTINUED.

CHAPTER TWO

A PUNCH OF COLOR

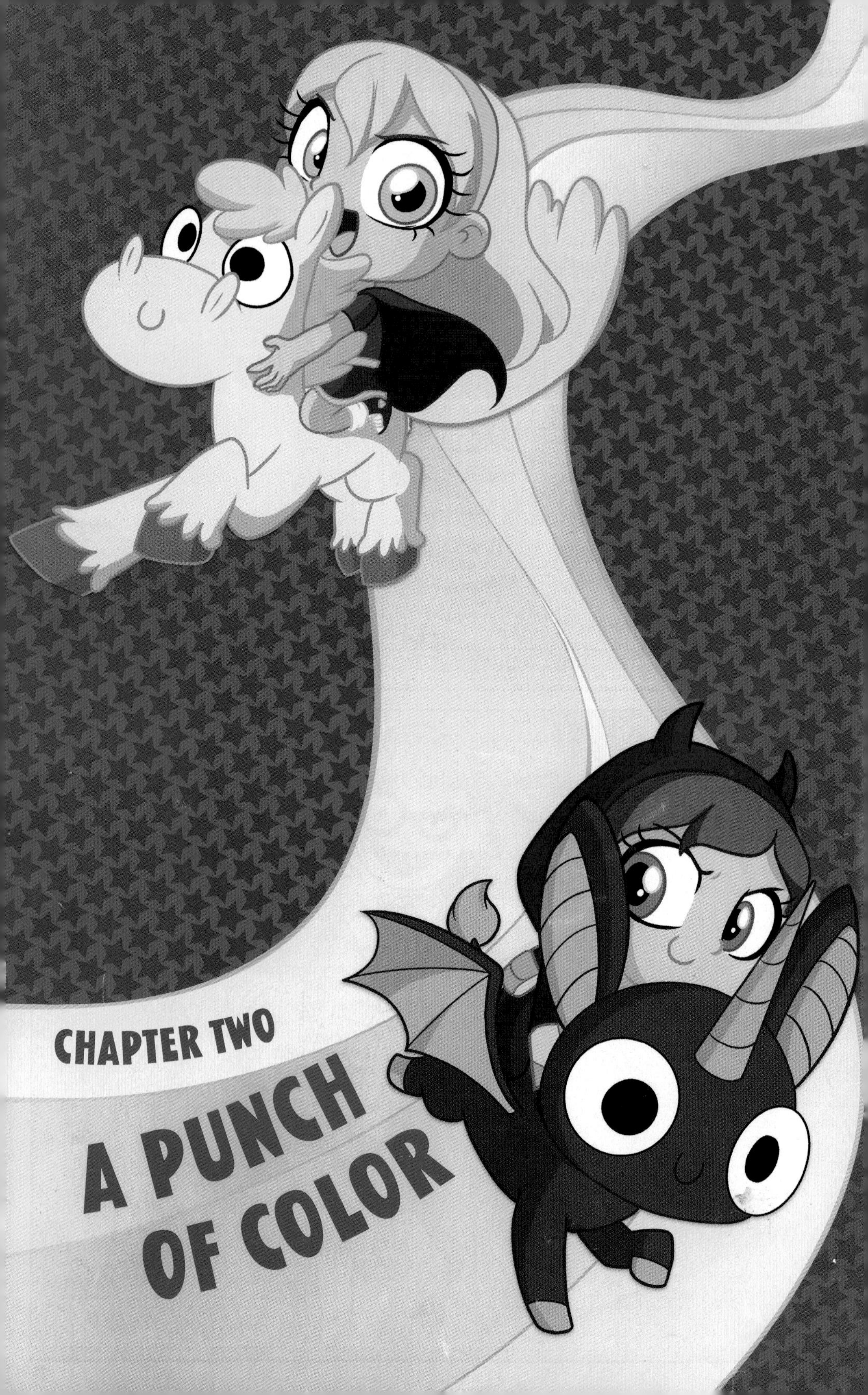

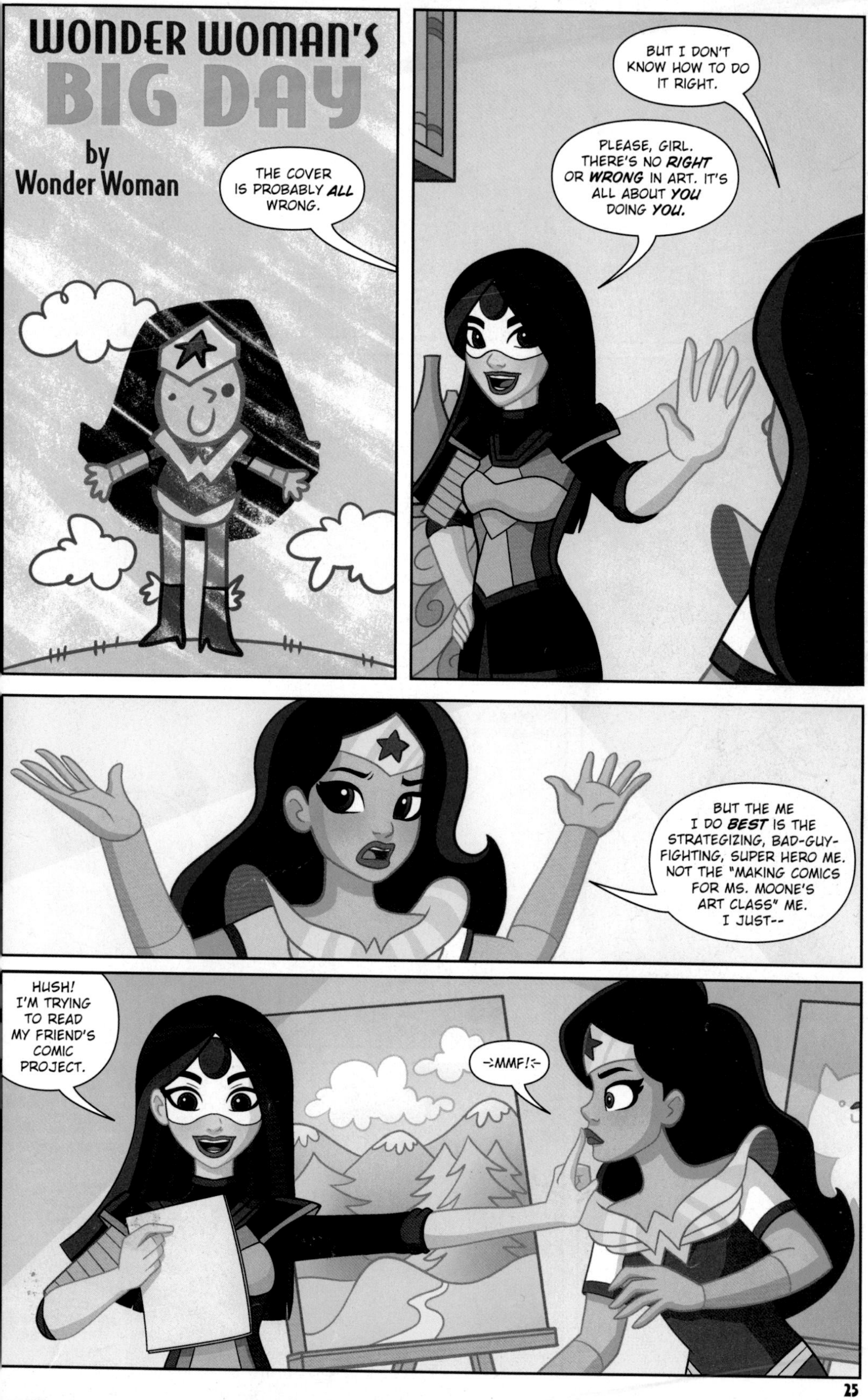
WONDER WOMAN'S
BIG DAY
by
Wonder Woman
THE COVER IS PROBABLY ALL WRONG.
BUT I DON'T KNOW HOW TO DO IT RIGHT.
PLEASE, GIRL. THERE'S NO RIGHT OR WRONG IN ART. IT'S ALL ABOUT YOU DOING YOU.
BUT THE ME I DO BEST IS THE STRATEGIZING, BAD-GUY-FIGHTING, SUPER HERO ME. NOT THE "MAKING COMICS FOR MS. MOONE'S ART CLASS" ME. I JUST--
HUSH! I'M TRYING TO READ MY FRIEND'S COMIC PROJECT.
-MMF!-

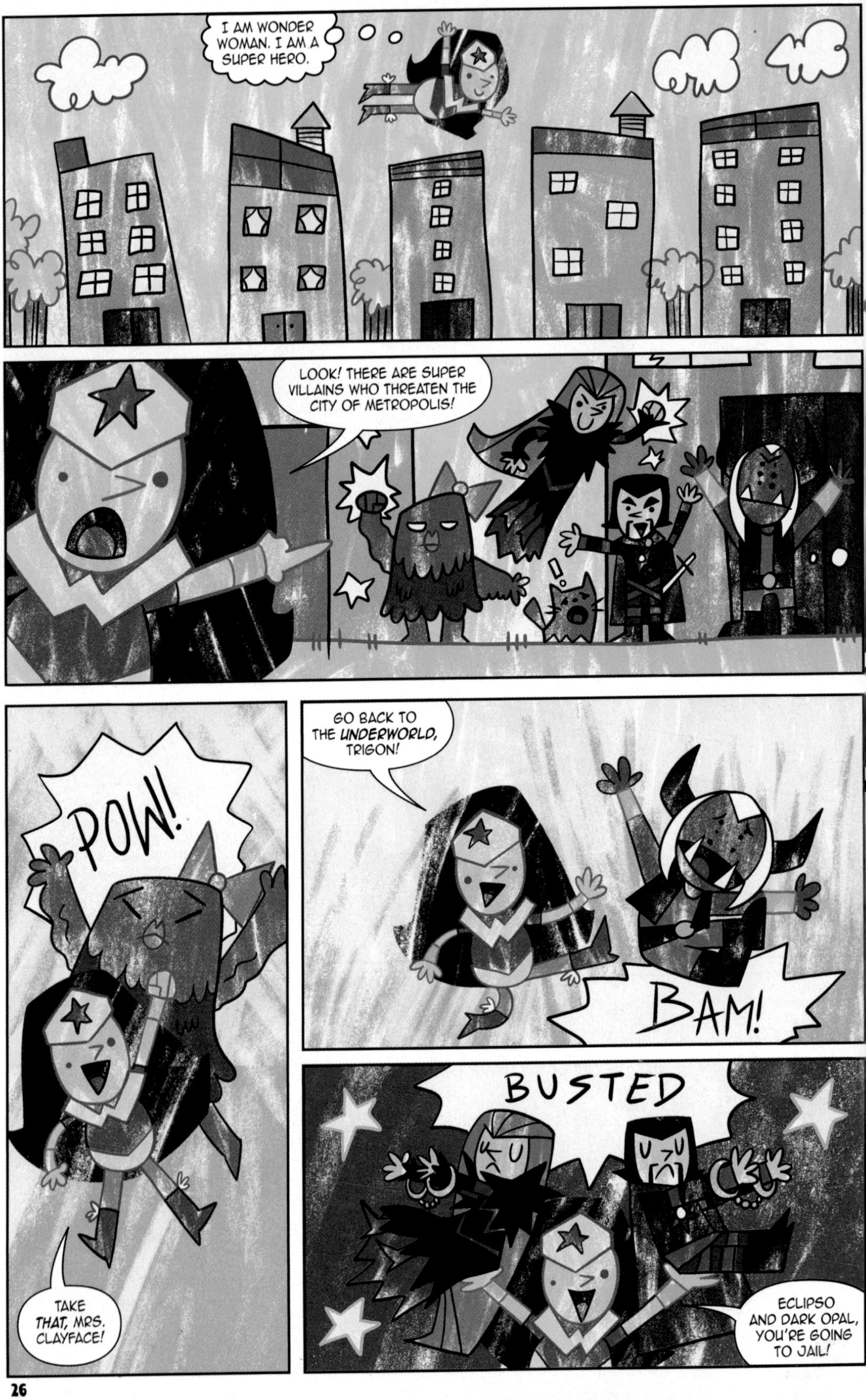
I AM WONDER WOMAN. I AM A SUPER HERO.
LOOK! THERE ARE SUPER VILLAINS WHO THREATEN THE CITY OF METROPOLIS!
!
POW!
TAKE *THAT,* MRS. CLAYFACE!
GO BACK TO THE *UNDERWORLD,* TRIGON!
BAM!
BUSTED
ECLIPSO AND DARK OPAL, YOU'RE GOING TO JAIL!

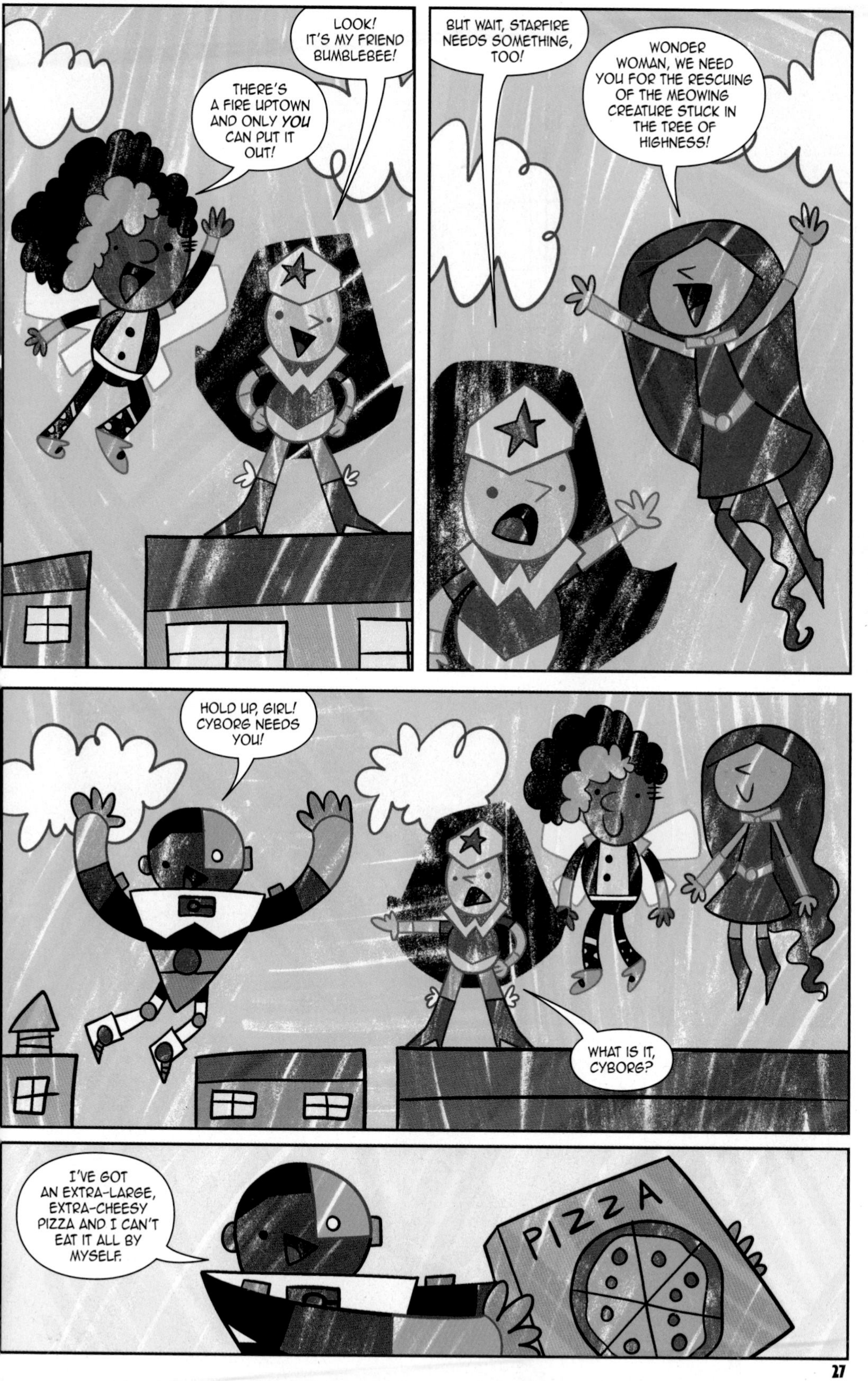
LOOK! IT'S MY FRIEND BUMBLEBEE!
THERE'S A FIRE UPTOWN AND ONLY YOU CAN PUT IT OUT!
BUT WAIT, STARFIRE NEEDS SOMETHING, TOO!
WONDER WOMAN, WE NEED YOU FOR THE RESCUING OF THE MEOWING CREATURE STUCK IN THE TREE OF HIGHNESS!
HOLD UP, GIRL! CYBORG NEEDS YOU!
WHAT IS IT, CYBORG?
I'VE GOT AN EXTRA-LARGE, EXTRA-CHEESY PIZZA AND I CAN'T EAT IT ALL BY MYSELF.
PIZZA

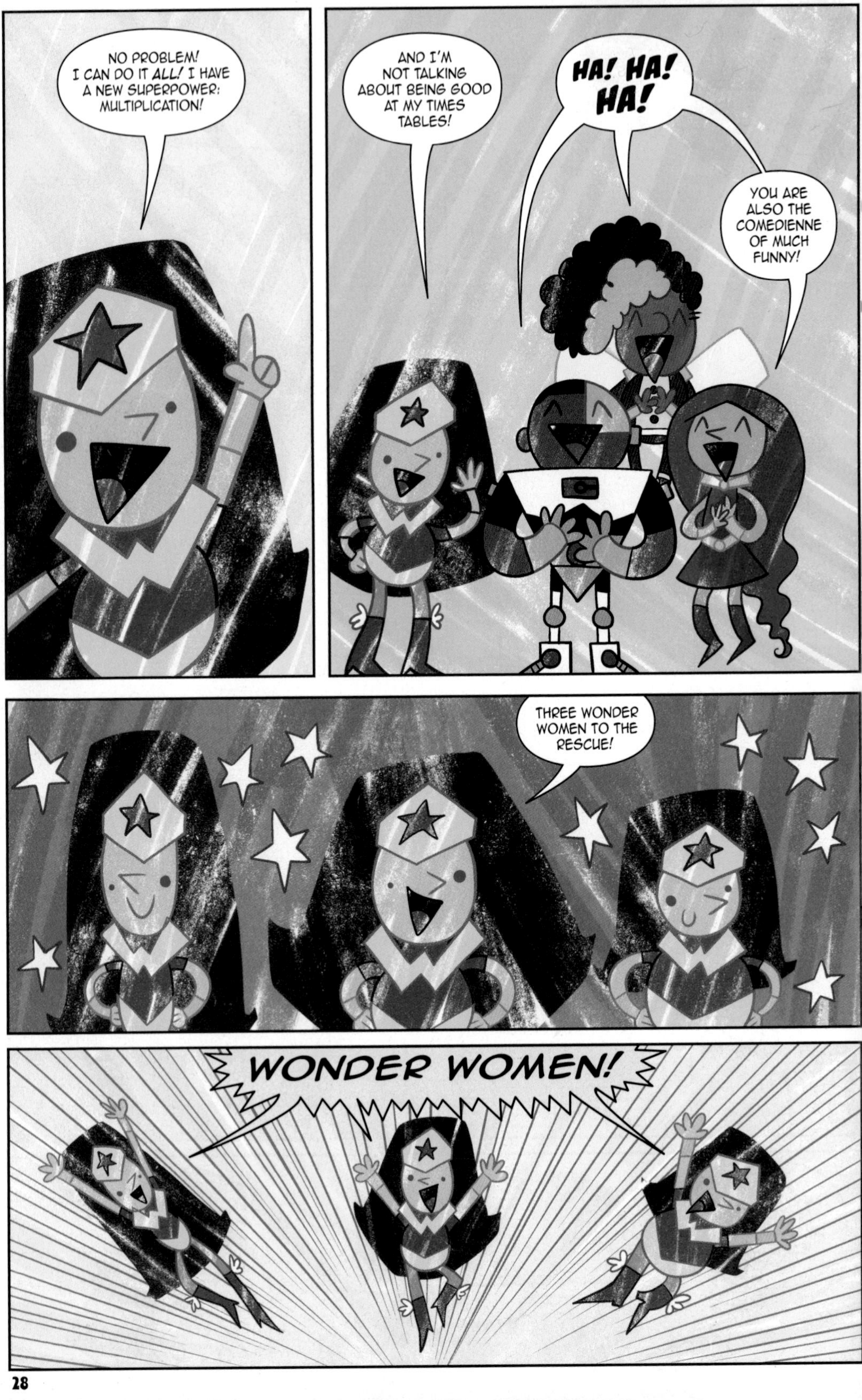
NO PROBLEM! I CAN DO IT ALL! I HAVE A NEW SUPERPOWER: MULTIPLICATION!
AND I'M NOT TALKING ABOUT BEING GOOD AT MY TIMES TABLES!
HA! HA! HA!
YOU ARE ALSO THE COMEDIENNE OF MUCH FUNNY!
THREE WONDER WOMEN TO THE RESCUE!
WONDER WOMEN!

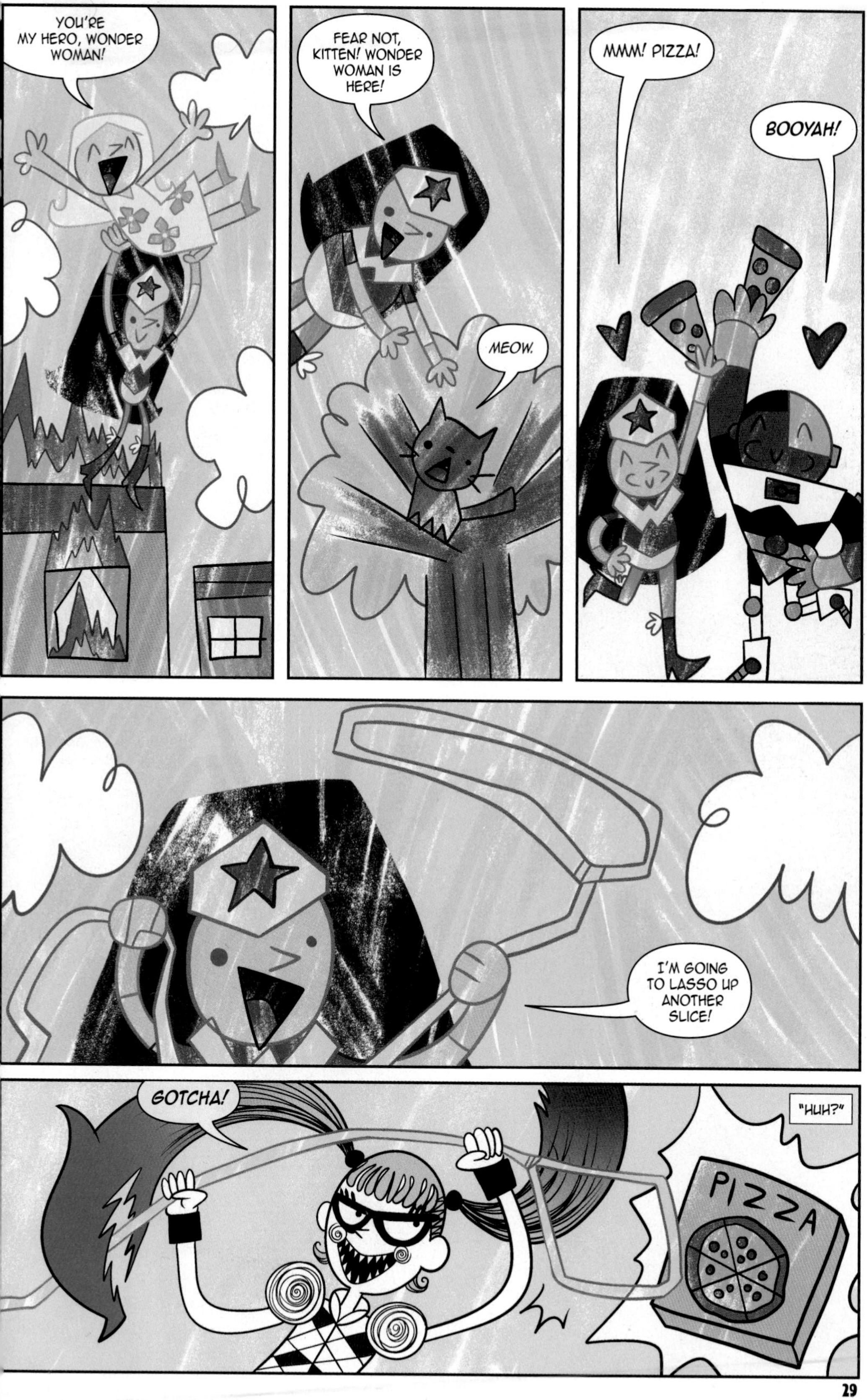
YOU'RE MY HERO, WONDER WOMAN!
FEAR NOT, KITTEN! WONDER WOMAN IS HERE!
MEOW.
MMM! PIZZA!
BOOYAH!
I'M GOING TO LASSO UP ANOTHER SLICE!
GOTCHA!
"HUH?"
PIZZA

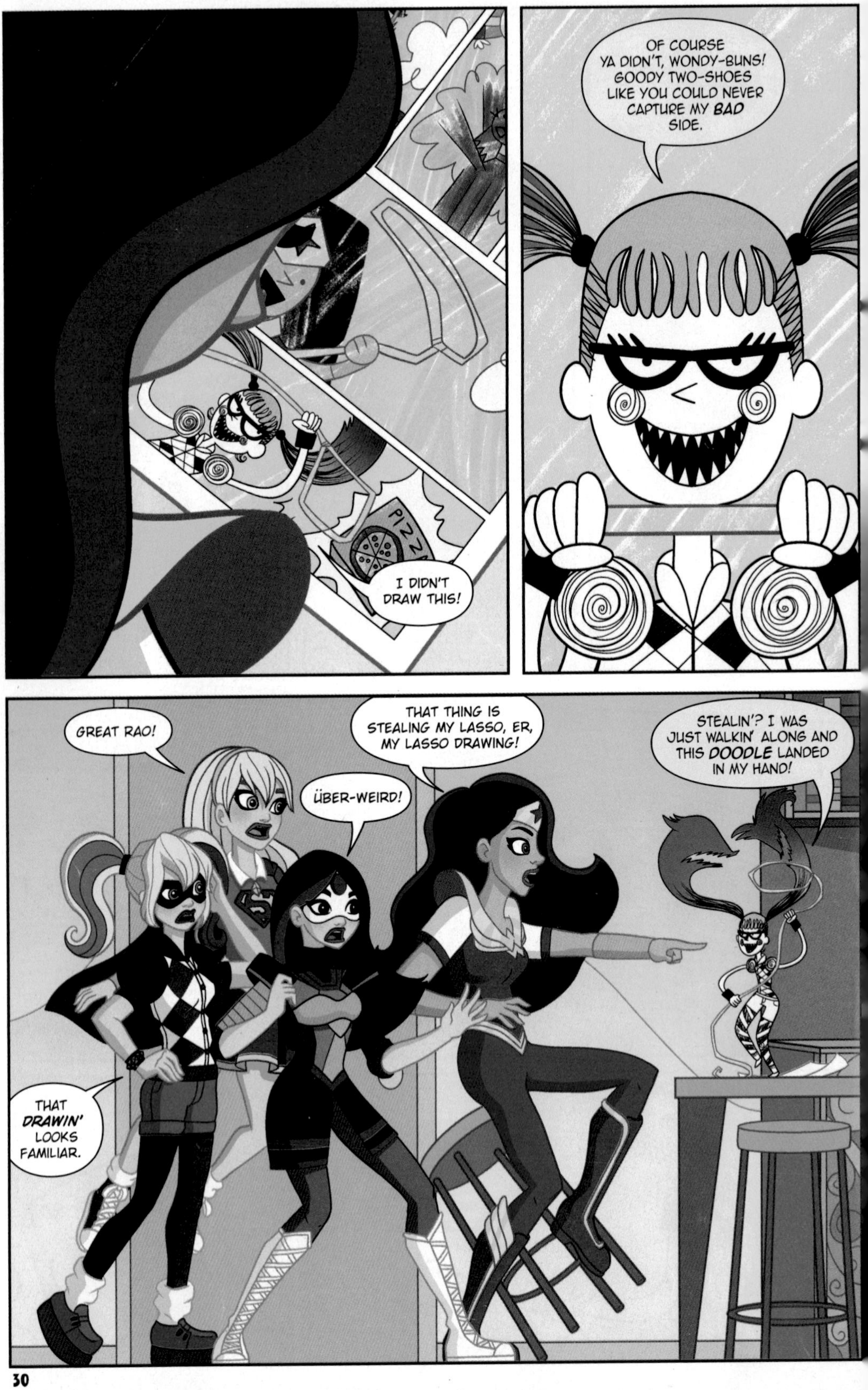

I DIDN'T DRAW THIS!
OF COURSE YA DIDN'T, WONDY-BUNS! GOODY TWO-SHOES LIKE YOU COULD NEVER CAPTURE MY BAD SIDE.
GREAT RAO!
ÜBER-WEIRD!
THAT THING IS STEALING MY LASSO, ER, MY LASSO DRAWING!
STEALIN'? I WAS JUST WALKIN' ALONG AND THIS DOODLE LANDED IN MY HAND!
THAT DRAWIN' LOOKS FAMILIAR.

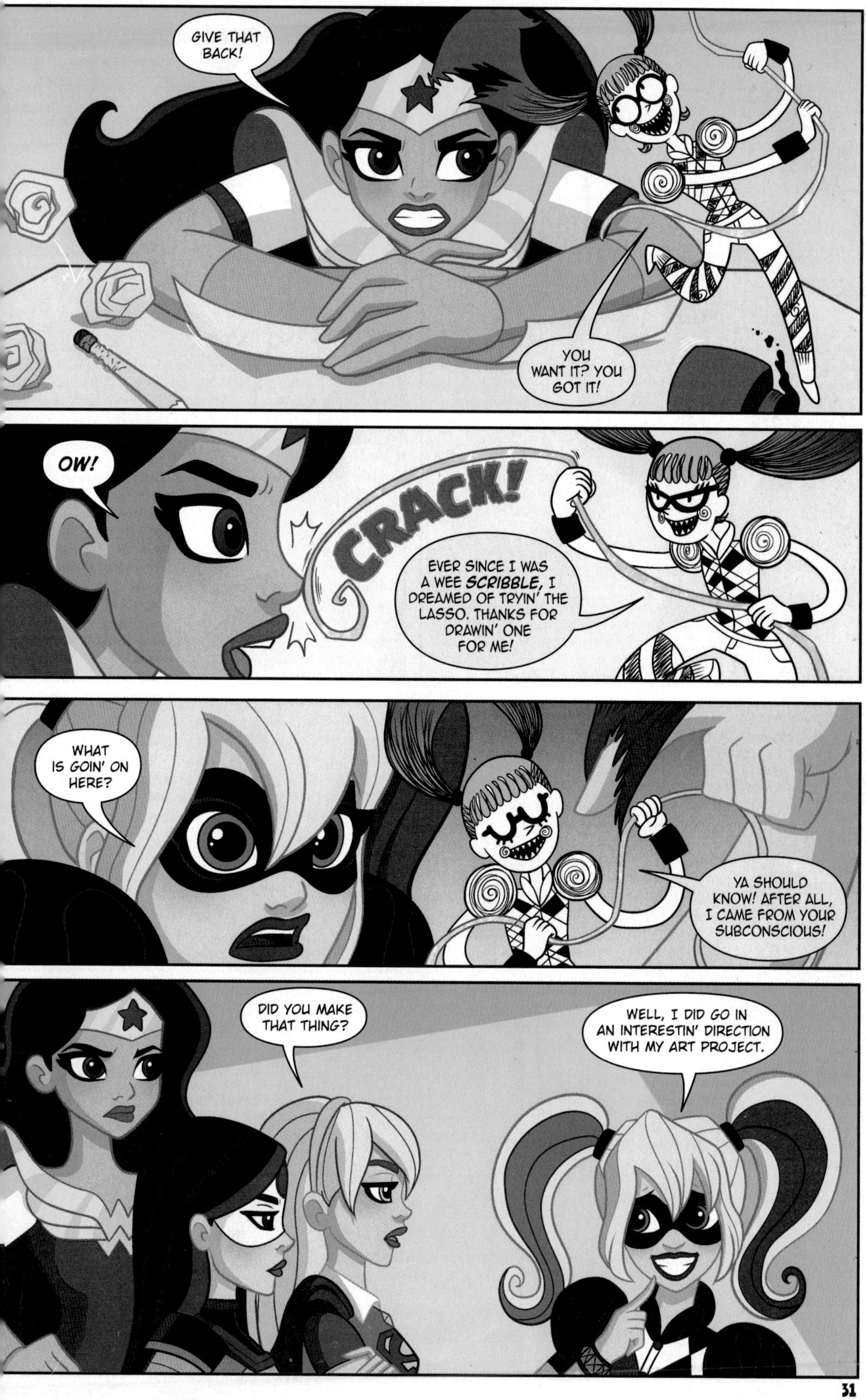
GIVE THAT BACK!
YOU WANT IT? YOU GOT IT!
OW!
CRACK!
EVER SINCE I WAS A WEE SCRIBBLE, I DREAMED OF TRYIN' THE LASSO. THANKS FOR DRAWIN' ONE FOR ME!
WHAT IS GOIN' ON HERE?
YA SHOULD KNOW! AFTER ALL, I CAME FROM YOUR SUBCONSCIOUS!
DID YOU MAKE THAT THING?
WELL, I DID GO IN AN INTERESTIN' DIRECTION WITH MY ART PROJECT.

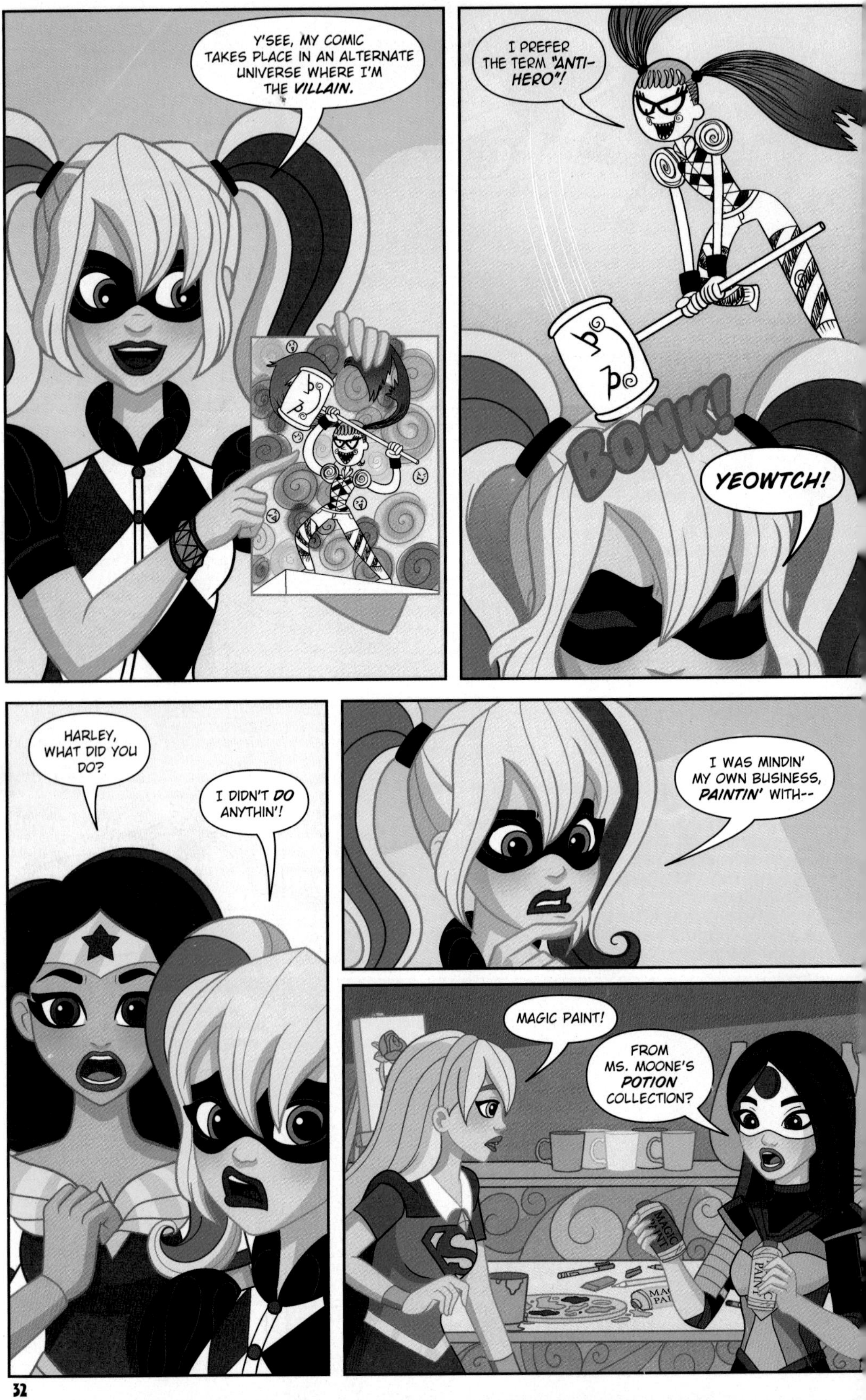
Y'SEE, MY COMIC TAKES PLACE IN AN ALTERNATE UNIVERSE WHERE I'M THE VILLAIN.
I PREFER THE TERM "ANTI-HERO"!
BONK!
YEOWTCH!
HARLEY, WHAT DID YOU DO?
I DIDN'T DO ANYTHIN'!
I WAS MINDIN' MY OWN BUSINESS, PAINTIN' WITH--
MAGIC PAINT!
FROM MS. MOONE'S POTION COLLECTION?
MAGIC PAINT

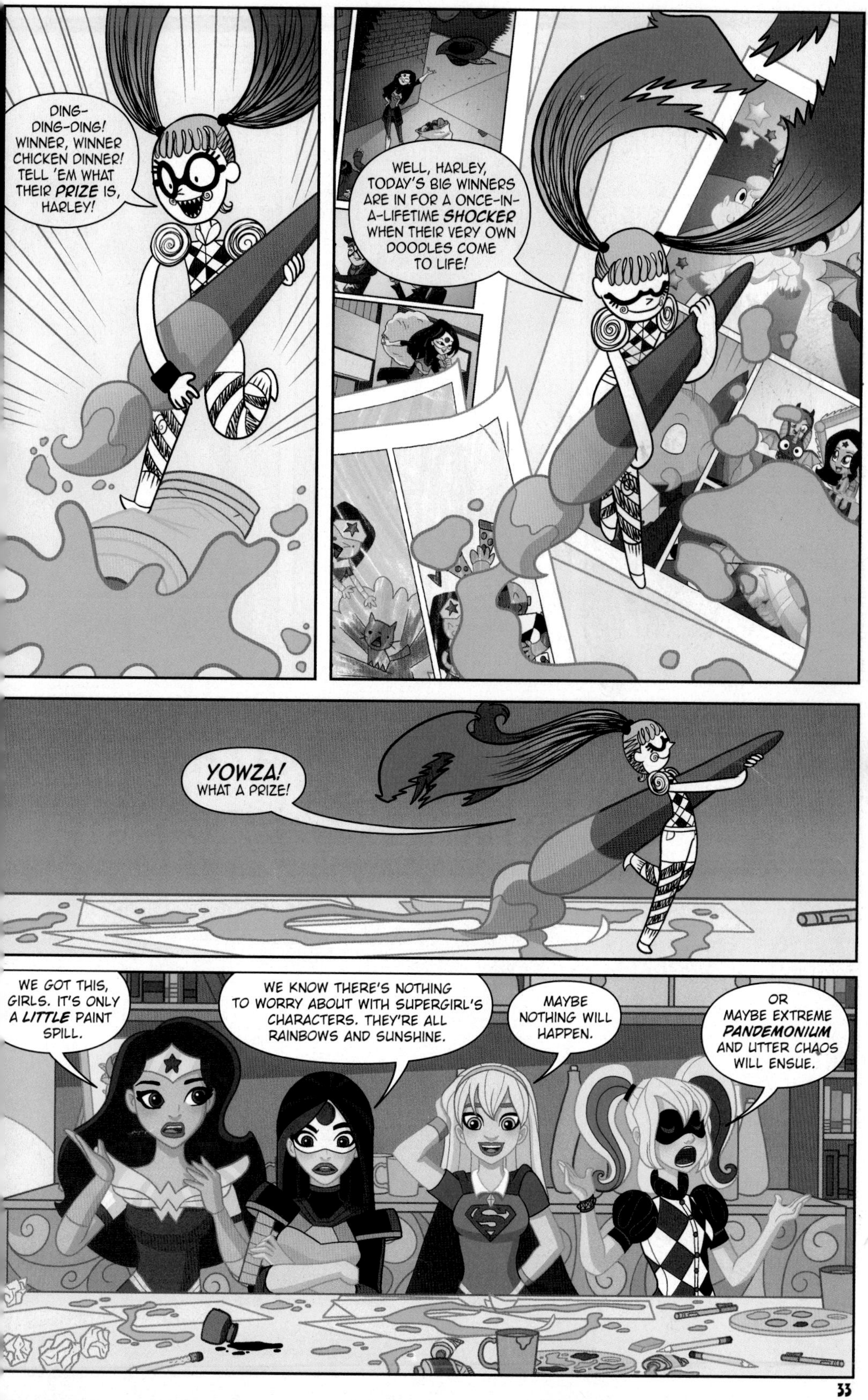
DING-DING-DING! WINNER, WINNER CHICKEN DINNER! TELL 'EM WHAT THEIR PRIZE IS, HARLEY!
WELL, HARLEY, TODAY'S BIG WINNERS ARE IN FOR A ONCE-IN-A-LIFETIME SHOCKER WHEN THEIR VERY OWN DOODLES COME TO LIFE!
YOWZA! WHAT A PRIZE!
WE GOT THIS, GIRLS. IT'S ONLY A LITTLE PAINT SPILL.
WE KNOW THERE'S NOTHING TO WORRY ABOUT WITH SUPERGIRL'S CHARACTERS. THEY'RE ALL RAINBOWS AND SUNSHINE.
MAYBE NOTHING WILL HAPPEN.
OR MAYBE EXTREME PANDEMONIUM AND UTTER CHAOS WILL ENSUE.

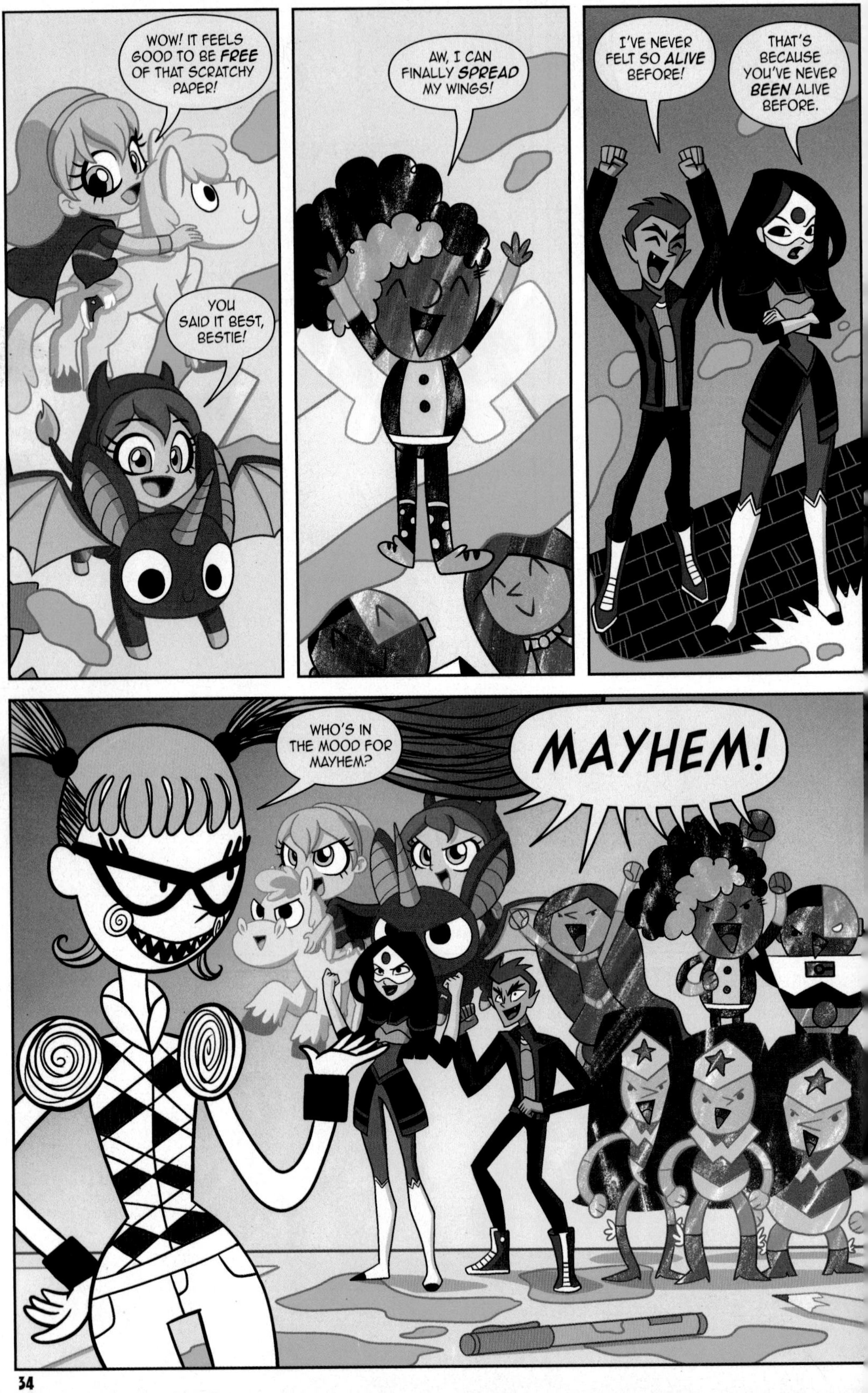
WOW! IT FEELS GOOD TO BE FREE OF THAT SCRATCHY PAPER!
YOU SAID IT BEST, BESTIE!
AW, I CAN FINALLY SPREAD MY WINGS!
I'VE NEVER FELT SO ALIVE BEFORE!
THAT'S BECAUSE YOU'VE NEVER BEEN ALIVE BEFORE.
WHO'S IN THE MOOD FOR MAYHEM?
MAYHEM!

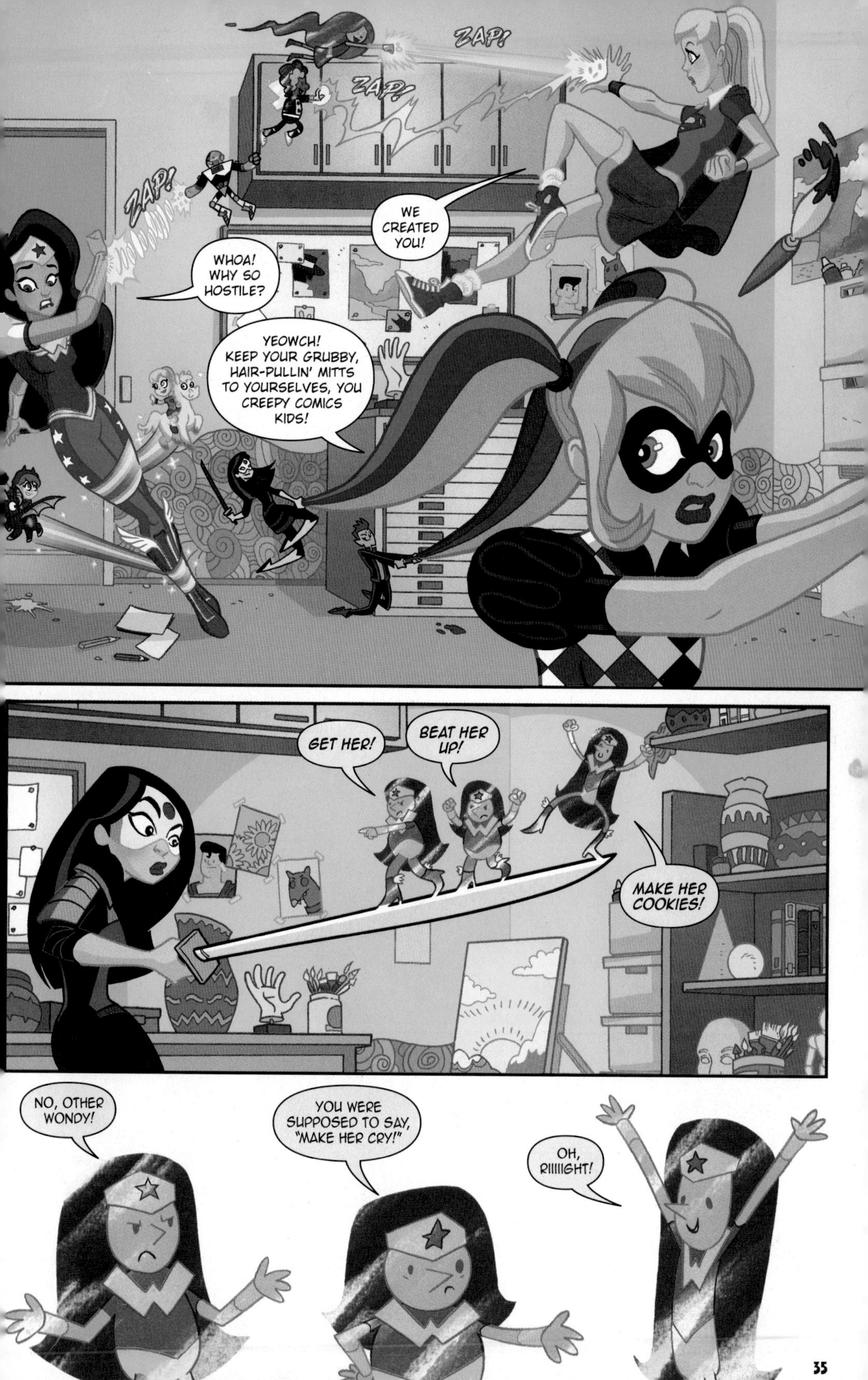

ZAP!
ZAP!
ZAP!
WE CREATED YOU!
WHOA! WHY SO HOSTILE?
YEOWCH! KEEP YOUR GRUBBY, HAIR-PULLIN' MITTS TO YOURSELVES, YOU CREEPY COMICS KIDS!
GET HER!
BEAT HER UP!
MAKE HER COOKIES!
NO, OTHER WONDY!
YOU WERE SUPPOSED TO SAY, "MAKE HER CRY!"
OH, RIIIIGHT!

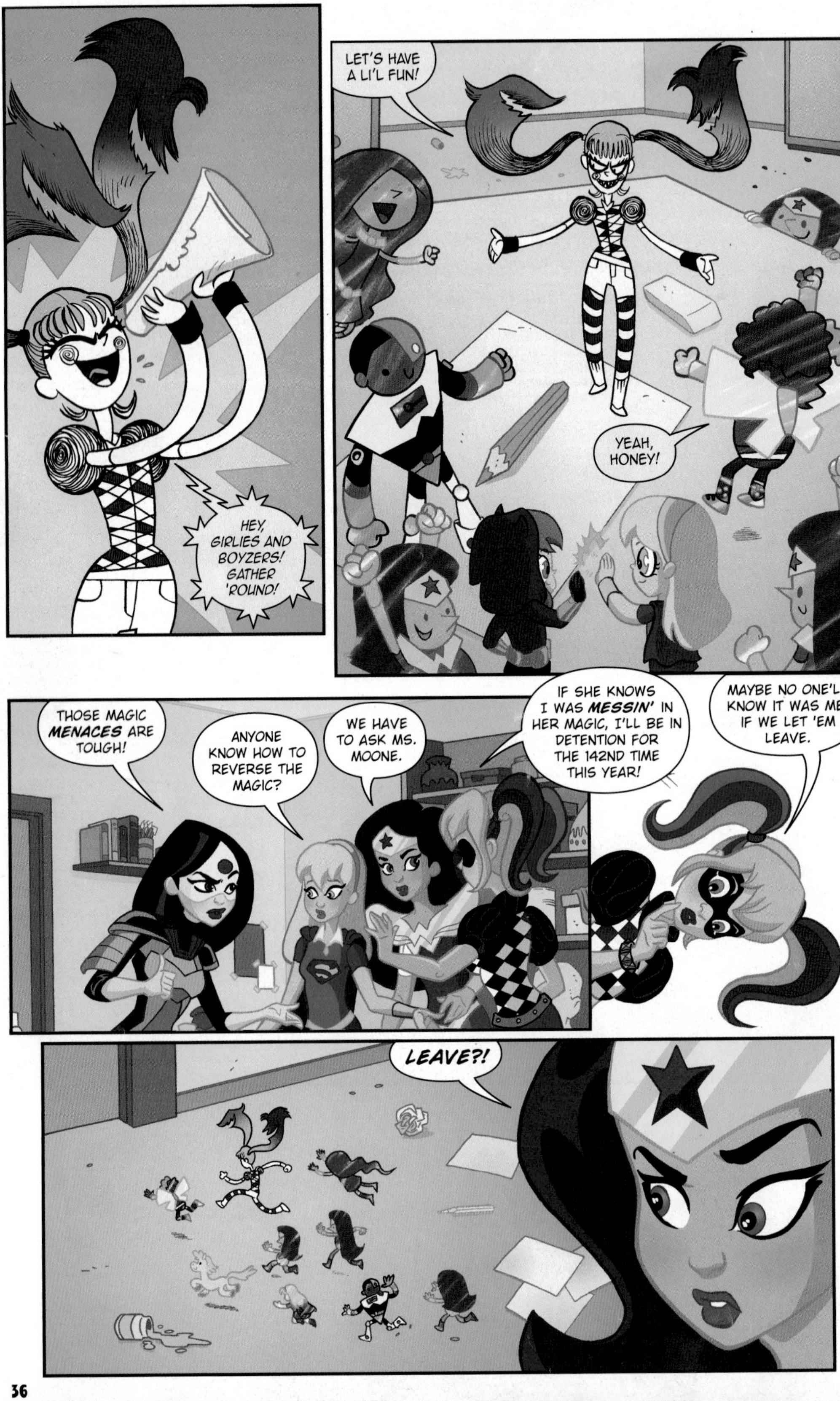
HEY, GIRLIES AND BOYZERS! GATHER 'ROUND!
LET'S HAVE A LI'L FUN!
YEAH, HONEY!
THOSE MAGIC MENACES ARE TOUGH!
ANYONE KNOW HOW TO REVERSE THE MAGIC?
WE HAVE TO ASK MS. MOONE.
IF SHE KNOWS I WAS MESSIN' IN HER MAGIC, I'LL BE IN DETENTION FOR THE 142ND TIME THIS YEAR!
MAYBE NO ONE'LL KNOW IT WAS ME. IF WE LET 'EM LEAVE.
LEAVE?!

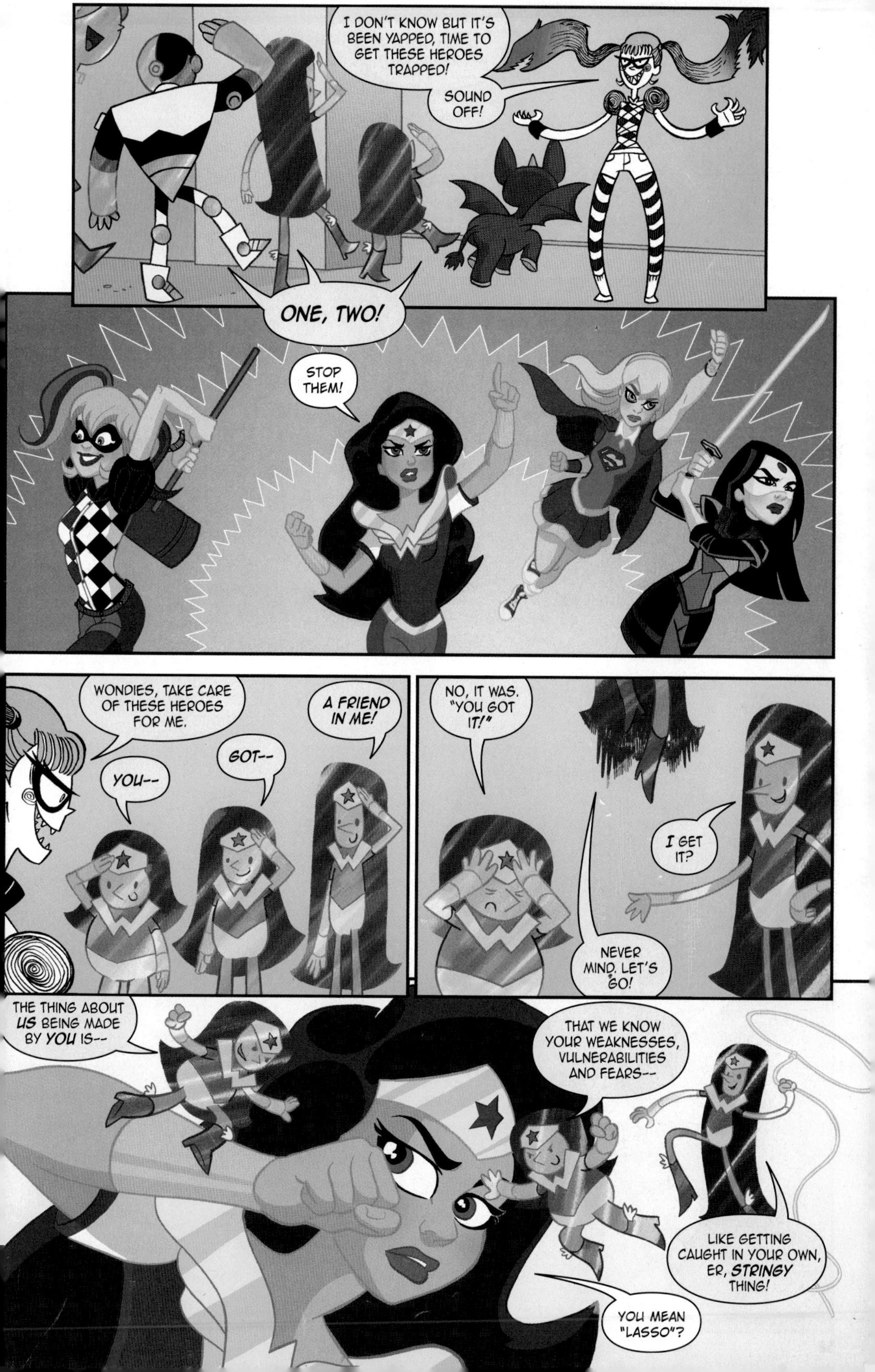
I DON'T KNOW BUT IT'S BEEN YAPPED, TIME TO GET THESE HEROES TRAPPED!
SOUND OFF!
ONE, TWO!
STOP THEM!
WONDIES, TAKE CARE OF THESE HEROES FOR ME.
YOU--
GOT--
A FRIEND IN ME!
NO, IT WAS. "YOU GOT IT!"
I GET IT?
NEVER MIND. LET'S GO!
THE THING ABOUT US BEING MADE BY YOU IS--
THAT WE KNOW YOUR WEAKNESSES, VULNERABILITIES AND FEARS--
LIKE GETTING CAUGHT IN YOUR OWN, ER, STRINGY THING!
YOU MEAN "LASSO"?

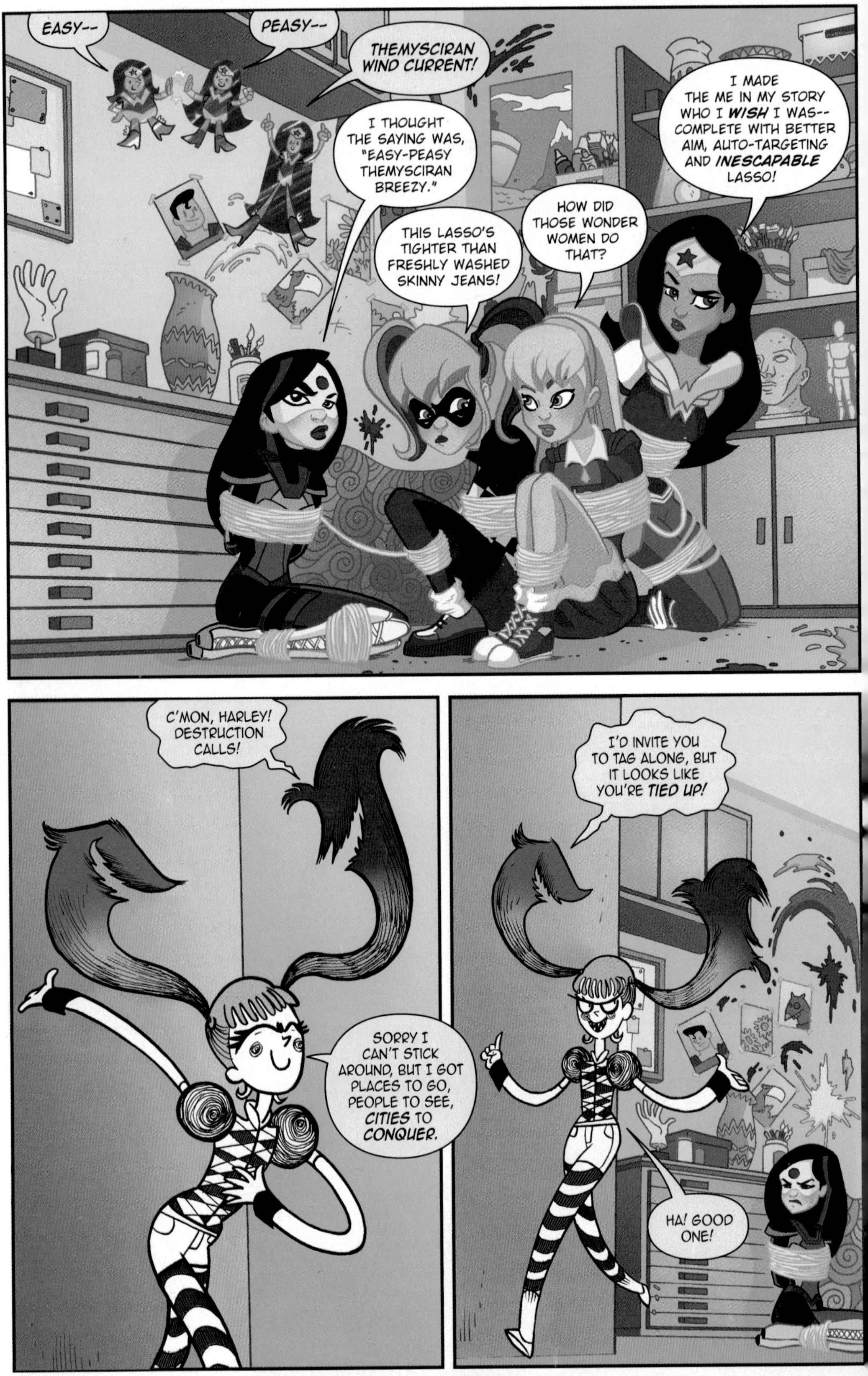
EASY--
PEASY--
THEMYSCIRAN WIND CURRENT!
I THOUGHT THE SAYING WAS, "EASY-PEASY THEMYSCIRAN BREEZY."
THIS LASSO'S TIGHTER THAN FRESHLY WASHED SKINNY JEANS!
HOW DID THOSE WONDER WOMEN DO THAT?
I MADE THE ME IN MY STORY WHO I WISH I WAS--COMPLETE WITH BETTER AIM, AUTO-TARGETING AND INESCAPABLE LASSO!
C'MON, HARLEY! DESTRUCTION CALLS!
SORRY I CAN'T STICK AROUND, BUT I GOT PLACES TO GO, PEOPLE TO SEE, CITIES TO CONQUER.
I'D INVITE YOU TO TAG ALONG, BUT IT LOOKS LIKE YOU'RE TIED UP!
HA! GOOD ONE!

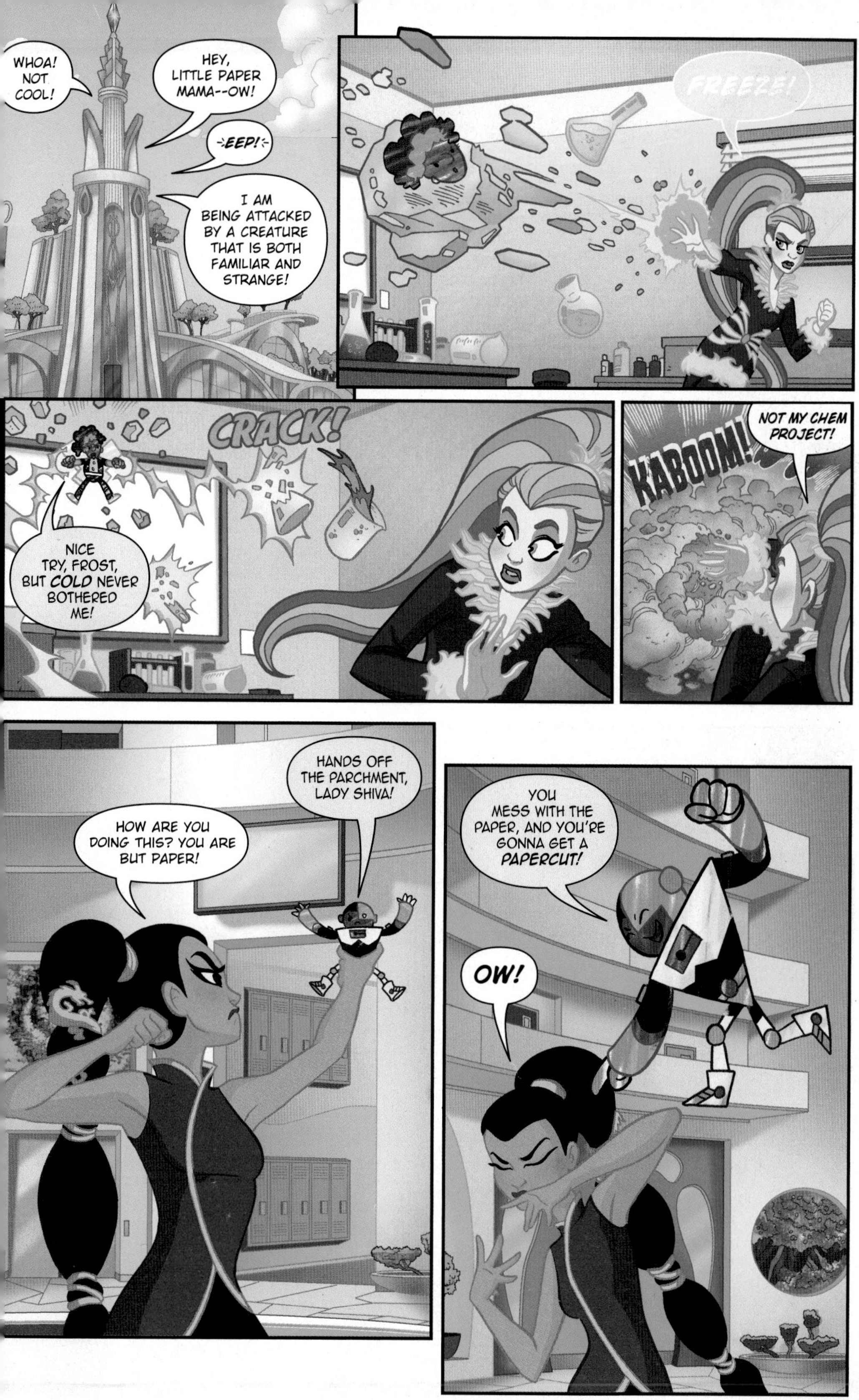
WHOA! NOT COOL!
HEY, LITTLE PAPER MAMA--OW!
EEP!
I AM BEING ATTACKED BY A CREATURE THAT IS BOTH FAMILIAR AND STRANGE!
FREEZE!
CRACK!
NICE TRY, FROST, BUT COLD NEVER BOTHERED ME!
KABOOM!
NOT MY CHEM PROJECT!
HANDS OFF THE PARCHMENT, LADY SHIVA!
HOW ARE YOU DOING THIS? YOU ARE BUT PAPER!
YOU MESS WITH THE PAPER, AND YOU'RE GONNA GET A PAPERCUT!
OW!

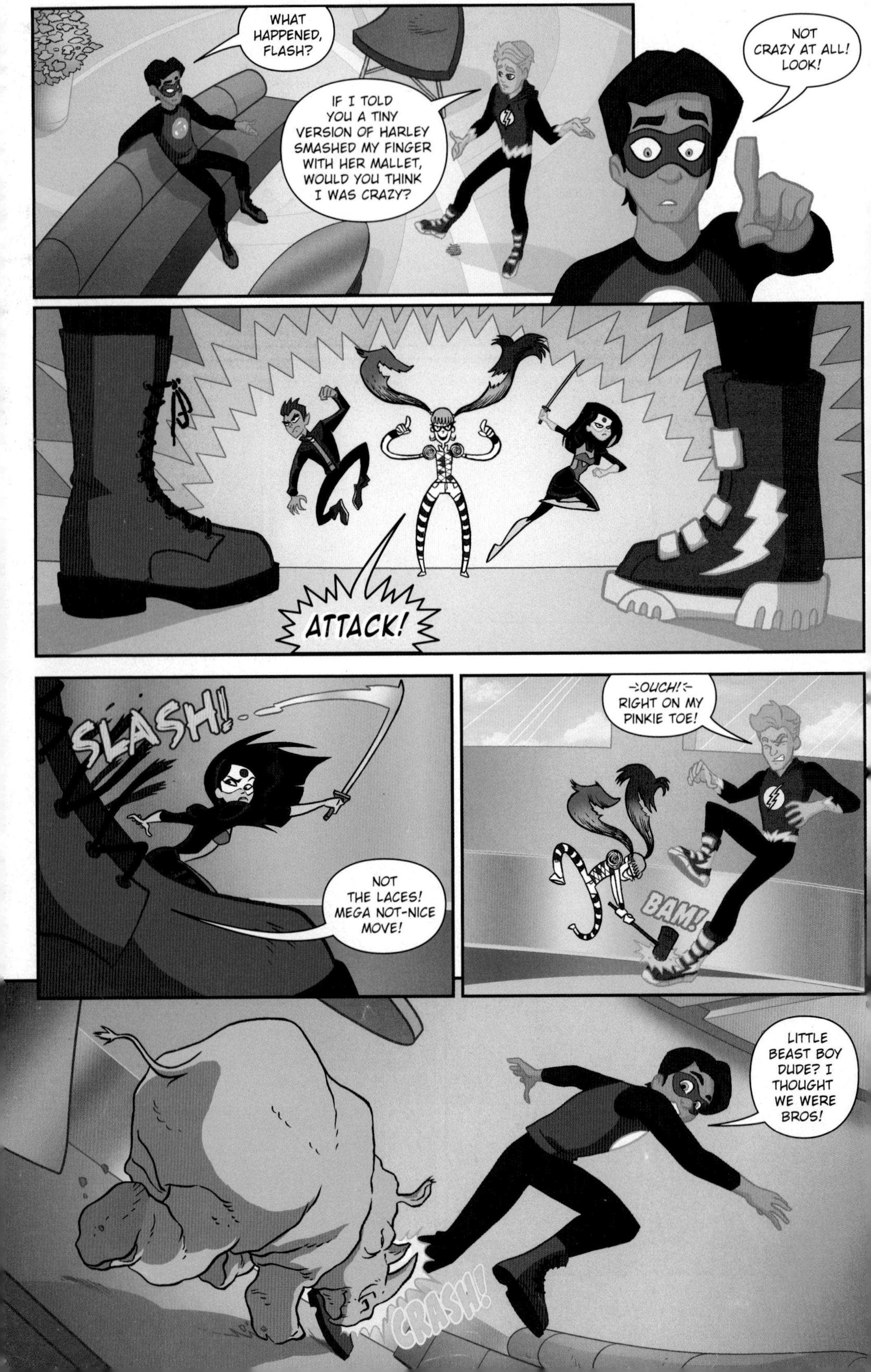
WHAT HAPPENED, FLASH?
IF I TOLD YOU A TINY VERSION OF HARLEY SMASHED MY FINGER WITH HER MALLET, WOULD YOU THINK I WAS CRAZY?
NOT CRAZY AT ALL! LOOK!
ATTACK!
SLASH!
NOT THE LACES! MEGA NOT-NICE MOVE!
OUCH! RIGHT ON MY PINKIE TOE!
BAM!
LITTLE BEAST BOY DUDE? I THOUGHT WE WERE BROS!
CRASH!

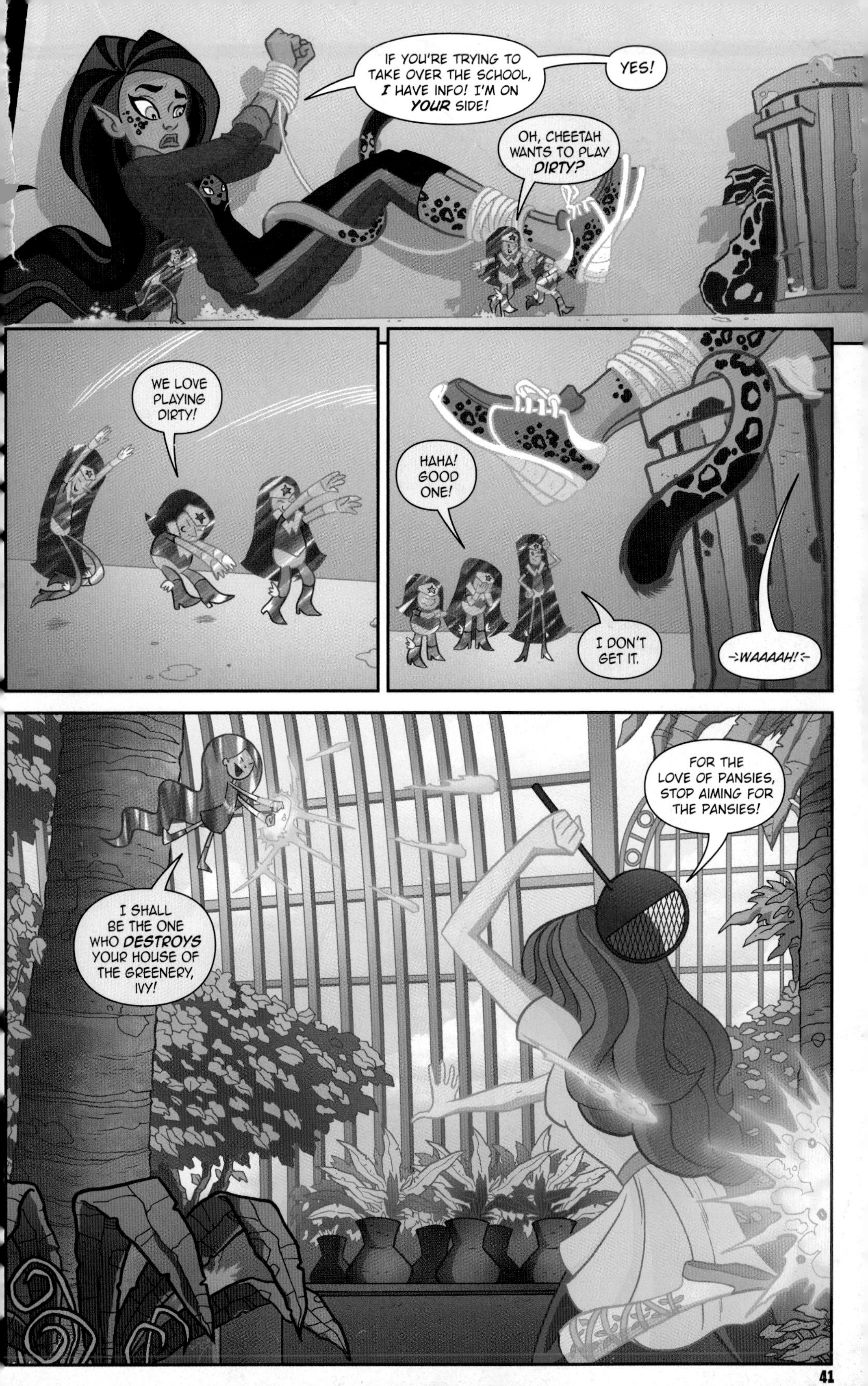
IF YOU'RE TRYING TO TAKE OVER THE SCHOOL, I HAVE INFO! I'M ON YOUR SIDE!
YES!
OH, CHEETAH WANTS TO PLAY DIRTY?
WE LOVE PLAYING DIRTY!
HAHA! GOOD ONE!
I DON'T GET IT.
WAAAAH!
FOR THE LOVE OF PANSIES, STOP AIMING FOR THE PANSIES!
I SHALL BE THE ONE WHO DESTROYS YOUR HOUSE OF THE GREENERY, IVY!

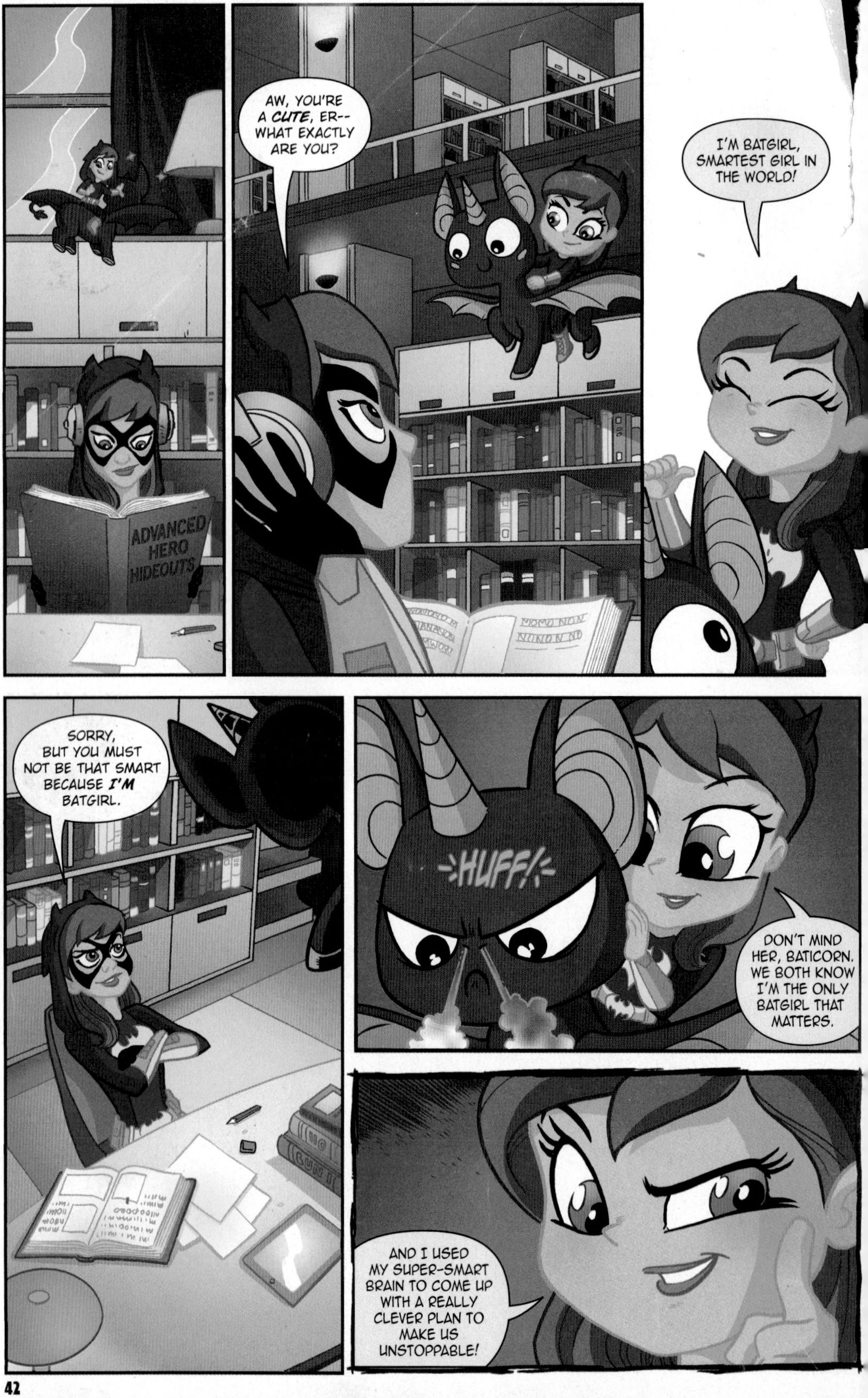
ADVANCED HERO HIDEOUTS
AW, YOU'RE A **CUTE**, ER-- WHAT EXACTLY ARE YOU?
I'M BATGIRL, SMARTEST GIRL IN THE WORLD!
SORRY, BUT YOU MUST NOT BE THAT SMART BECAUSE **I'M** BATGIRL.
HUFF!
DON'T MIND HER, BATICORN. WE BOTH KNOW I'M THE ONLY BATGIRL THAT MATTERS.
AND I USED MY SUPER-SMART BRAIN TO COME UP WITH A REALLY CLEVER PLAN TO MAKE US UNSTOPPABLE!

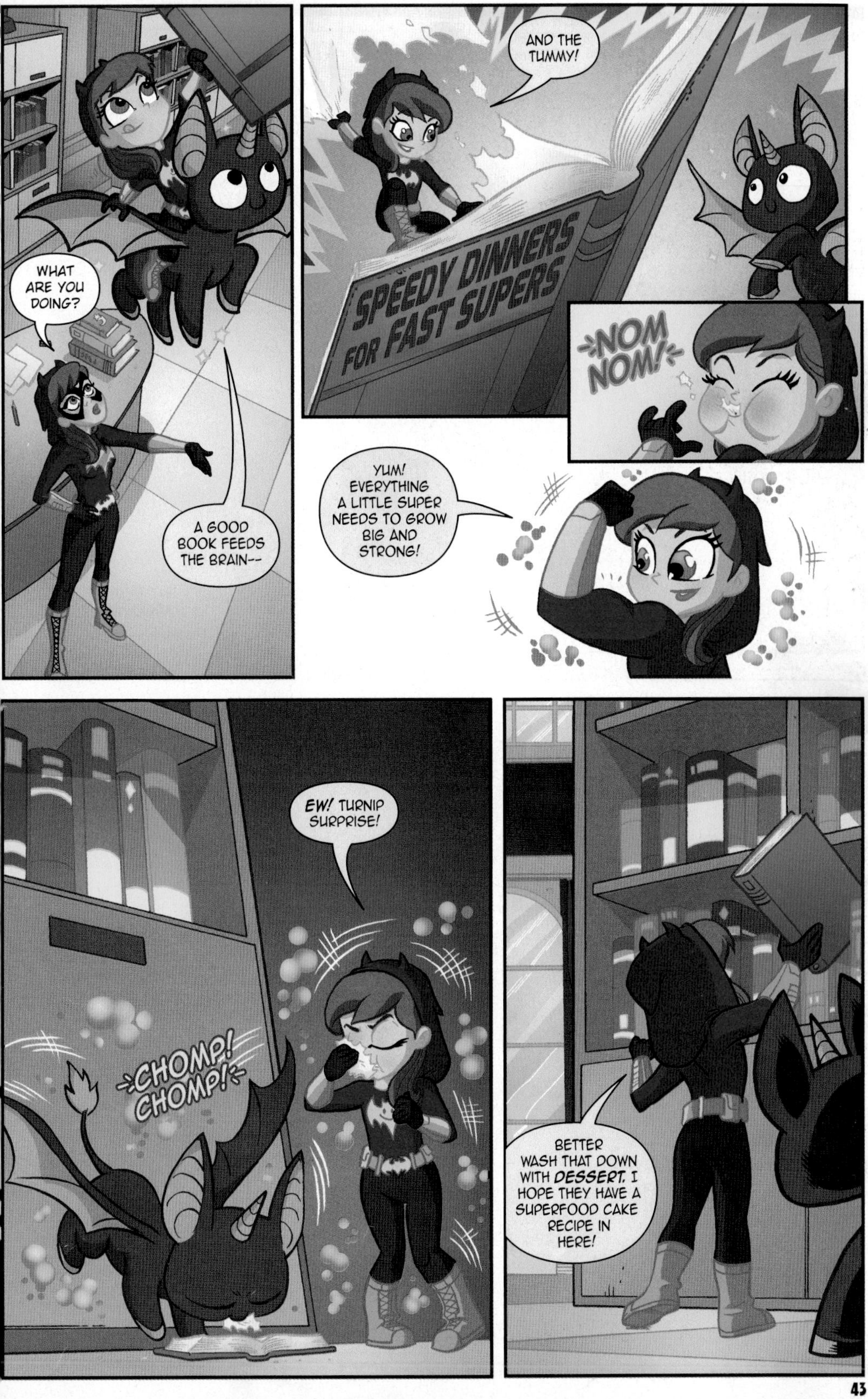
WHAT ARE YOU DOING?
A GOOD BOOK FEEDS THE BRAIN--
AND THE TUMMY!
SPEEDY DINNERS FOR FAST SUPERS
NOM NOM!
YUM! EVERYTHING A LITTLE SUPER NEEDS TO GROW BIG AND STRONG!
EW! TURNIP SURPRISE!
CHOMP! CHOMP!
BETTER WASH THAT DOWN WITH DESSERT. I HOPE THEY HAVE A SUPERFOOD CAKE RECIPE IN HERE!

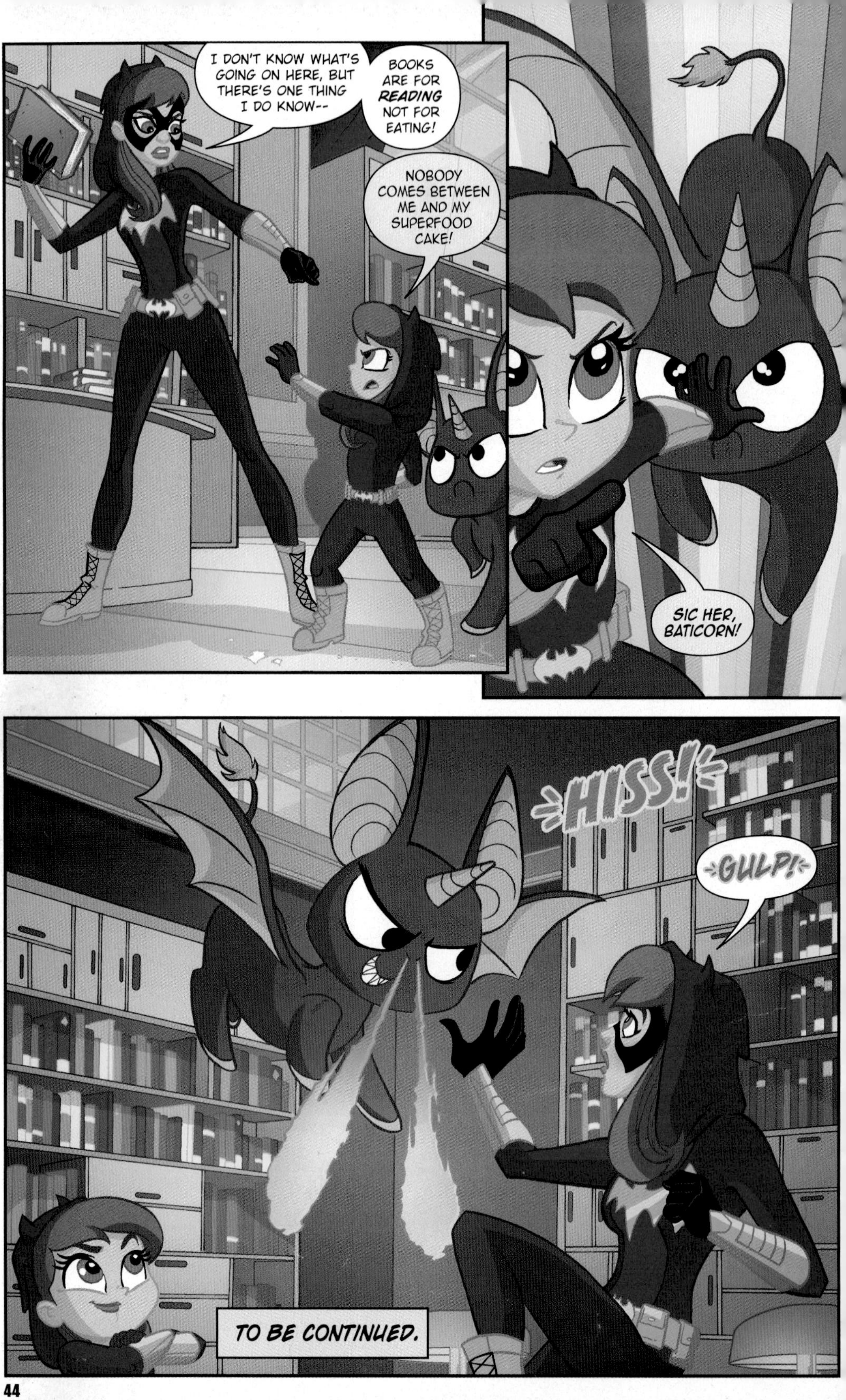
I DON'T KNOW WHAT'S GOING ON HERE, BUT THERE'S ONE THING I DO KNOW--
BOOKS ARE FOR *READING* NOT FOR EATING!
NOBODY COMES BETWEEN ME AND MY SUPERFOOD CAKE!
SIC HER, BATICORN!
HISS!
GULP!
TO BE CONTINUED.

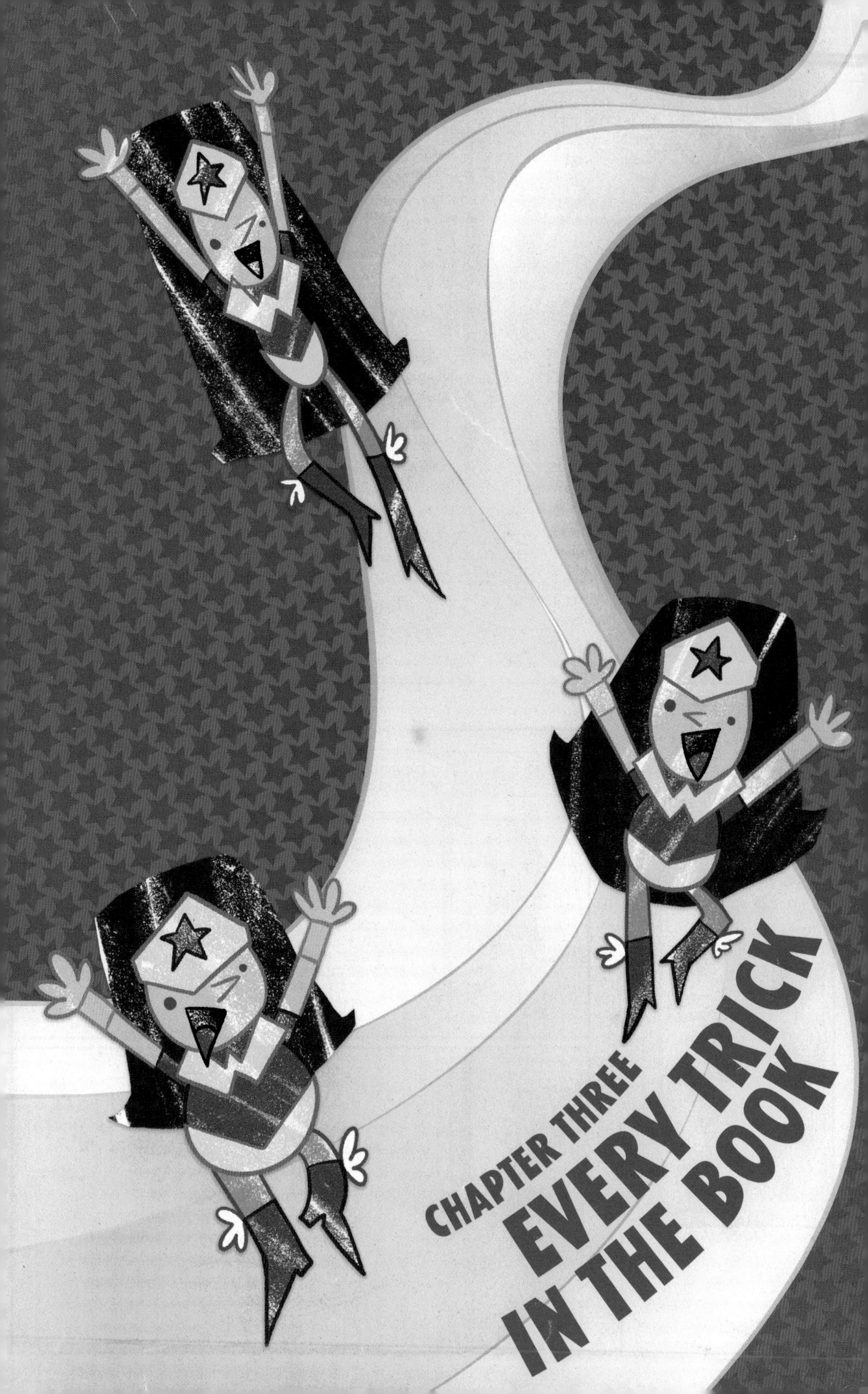

CHAPTER THREE

EVERY TRICK IN THE BOOK

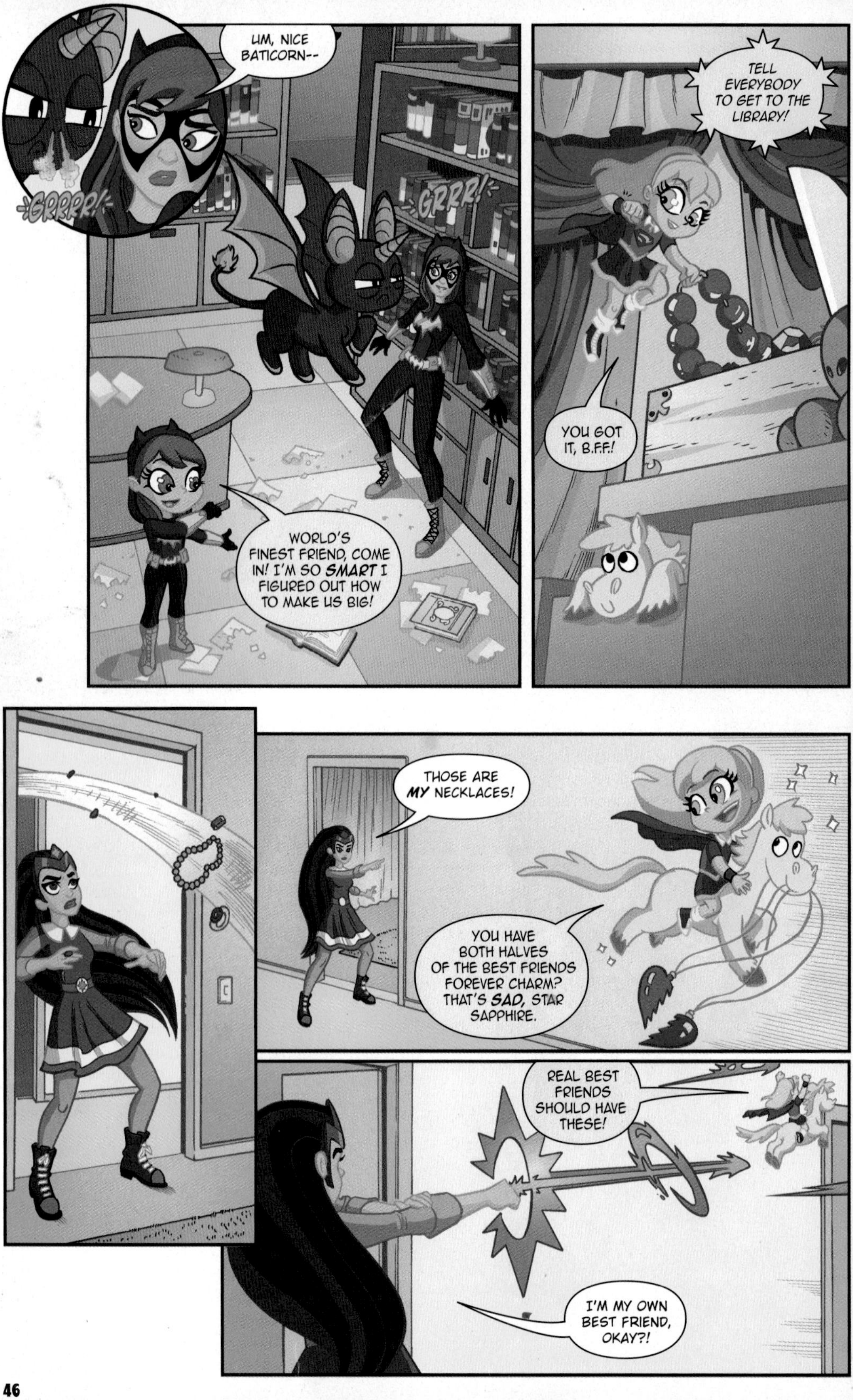
UM, NICE BATICORN--
GRRRR!
GRRR!
WORLD'S FINEST FRIEND, COME IN! I'M SO SMART I FIGURED OUT HOW TO MAKE US BIG!
TELL EVERYBODY TO GET TO THE LIBRARY!
YOU GOT IT, B.F.F.!
THOSE ARE MY NECKLACES!
YOU HAVE BOTH HALVES OF THE BEST FRIENDS FOREVER CHARM? THAT'S SAD, STAR SAPPHIRE.
REAL BEST FRIENDS SHOULD HAVE THESE!
I'M MY OWN BEST FRIEND, OKAY?!

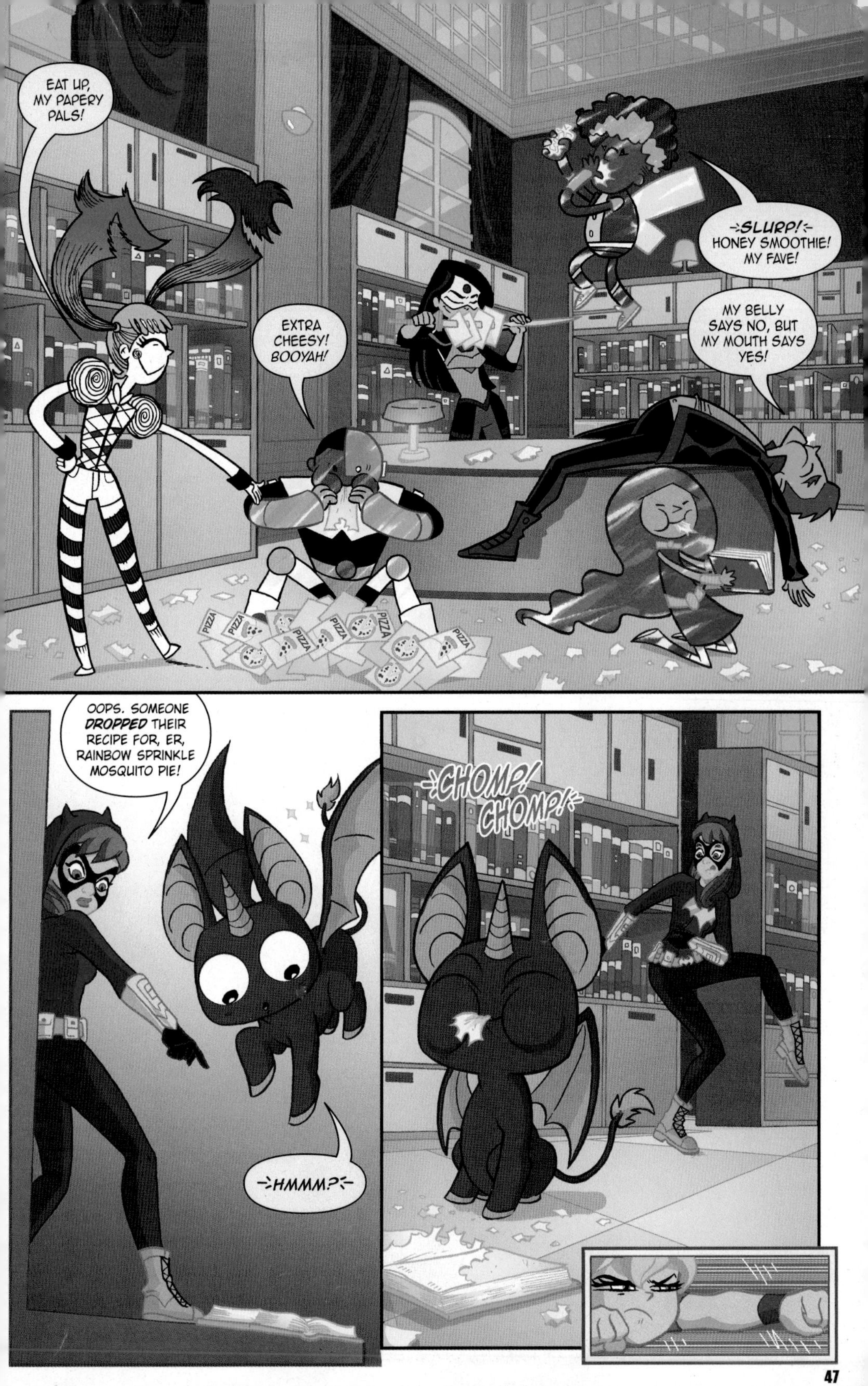

EAT UP, MY PAPERY PALS!
EXTRA CHEESY! BOOYAH!
-SLURP!- HONEY SMOOTHIE! MY FAVE!
MY BELLY SAYS NO, BUT MY MOUTH SAYS YES!
PIZZA
OOPS. SOMEONE DROPPED THEIR RECIPE FOR, ER, RAINBOW SPRINKLE MOSQUITO PIE!
-HMMM?-
-CHOMP! CHOMP!-

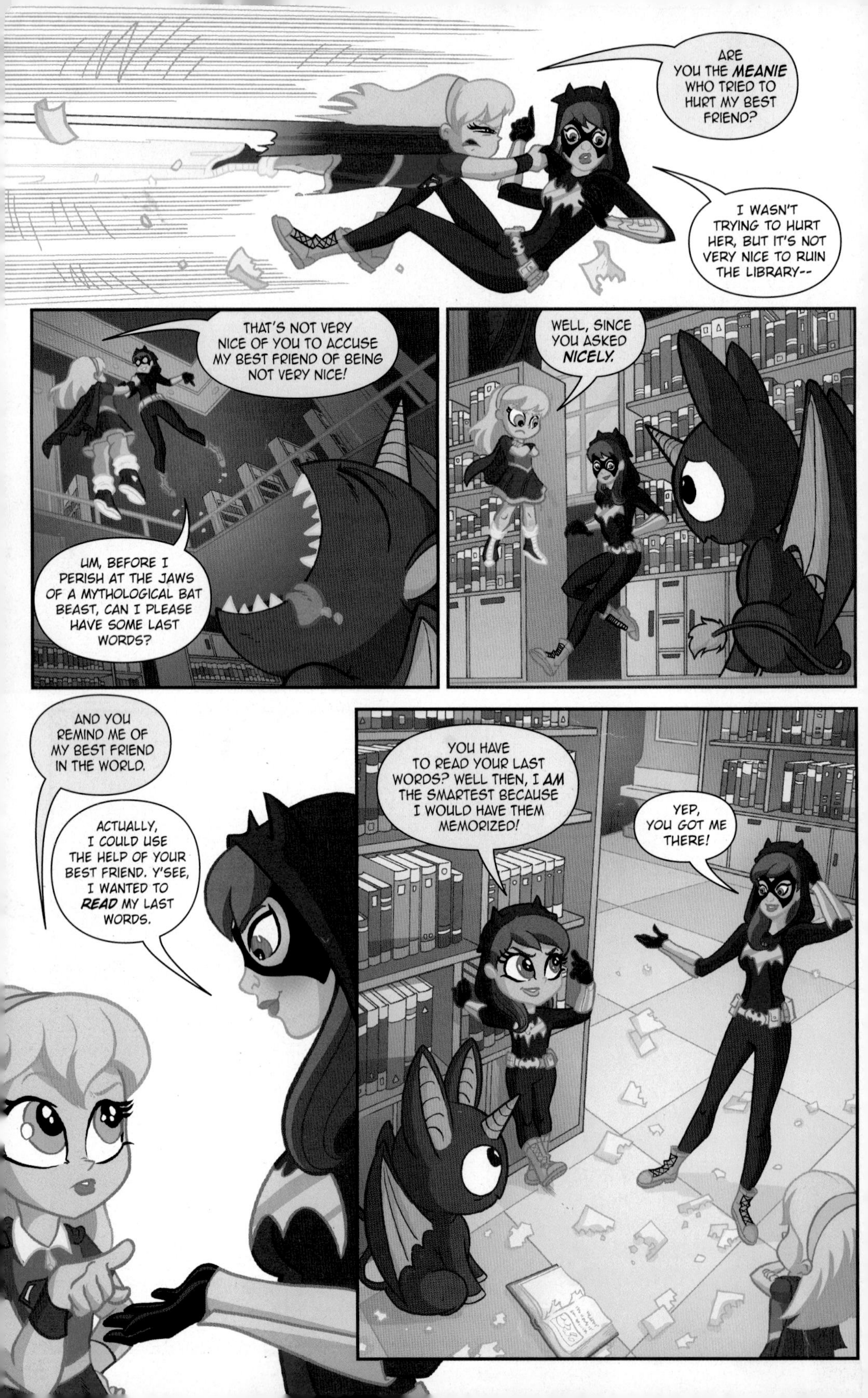

ARE YOU THE MEANIE WHO TRIED TO HURT MY BEST FRIEND?
I WASN'T TRYING TO HURT HER, BUT IT'S NOT VERY NICE TO RUIN THE LIBRARY--
THAT'S NOT VERY NICE OF YOU TO ACCUSE MY BEST FRIEND OF BEING NOT VERY NICE!
UM, BEFORE I PERISH AT THE JAWS OF A MYTHOLOGICAL BAT BEAST, CAN I PLEASE HAVE SOME LAST WORDS?
WELL, SINCE YOU ASKED NICELY.
AND YOU REMIND ME OF MY BEST FRIEND IN THE WORLD.
ACTUALLY, I COULD USE THE HELP OF YOUR BEST FRIEND. Y'SEE, I WANTED TO READ MY LAST WORDS.
YOU HAVE TO READ YOUR LAST WORDS? WELL THEN, I AM THE SMARTEST BECAUSE I WOULD HAVE THEM MEMORIZED!
YEP, YOU GOT ME THERE!

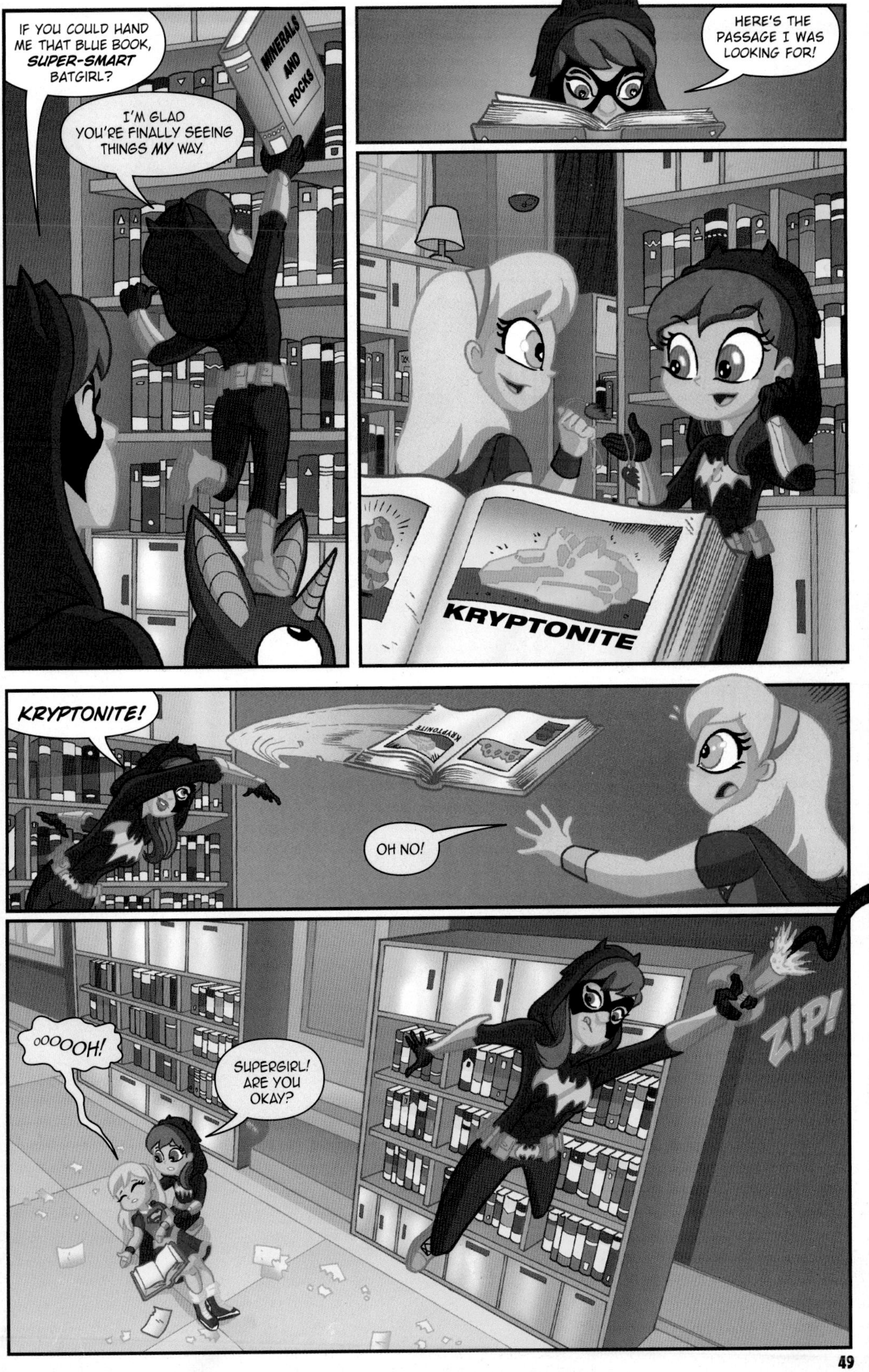
IF YOU COULD HAND ME THAT BLUE BOOK, SUPER-SMART BATGIRL?
MINERALS AND ROCKS
I'M GLAD YOU'RE FINALLY SEEING THINGS MY WAY.
HERE'S THE PASSAGE I WAS LOOKING FOR!
KRYPTONITE
KRYPTONITE!
KRYPTONITE
OH NO!
ZIP!
OOOOOH!
SUPERGIRL! ARE YOU OKAY?

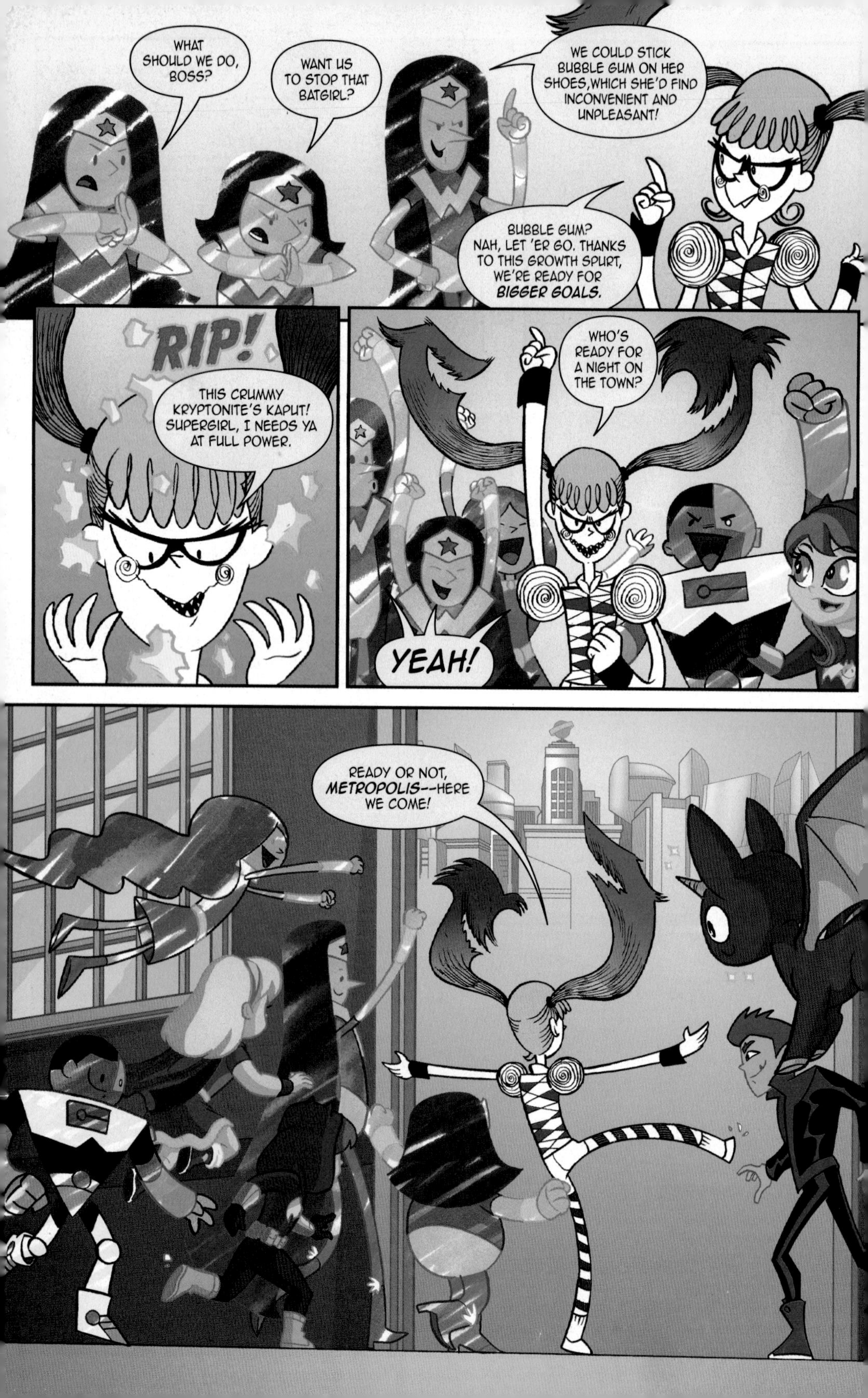
WHAT SHOULD WE DO, BOSS?
WANT US TO STOP THAT BATGIRL?
WE COULD STICK BUBBLE GUM ON HER SHOES, WHICH SHE'D FIND INCONVENIENT AND UNPLEASANT!
BUBBLE GUM? NAH, LET 'ER GO. THANKS TO THIS GROWTH SPURT, WE'RE READY FOR BIGGER GOALS.
RIP!
THIS CRUMMY KRYPTONITE'S KAPUT! SUPERGIRL, I NEEDS YA AT FULL POWER.
WHO'S READY FOR A NIGHT ON THE TOWN?
YEAH!
READY OR NOT, METROPOLIS--HERE WE COME!

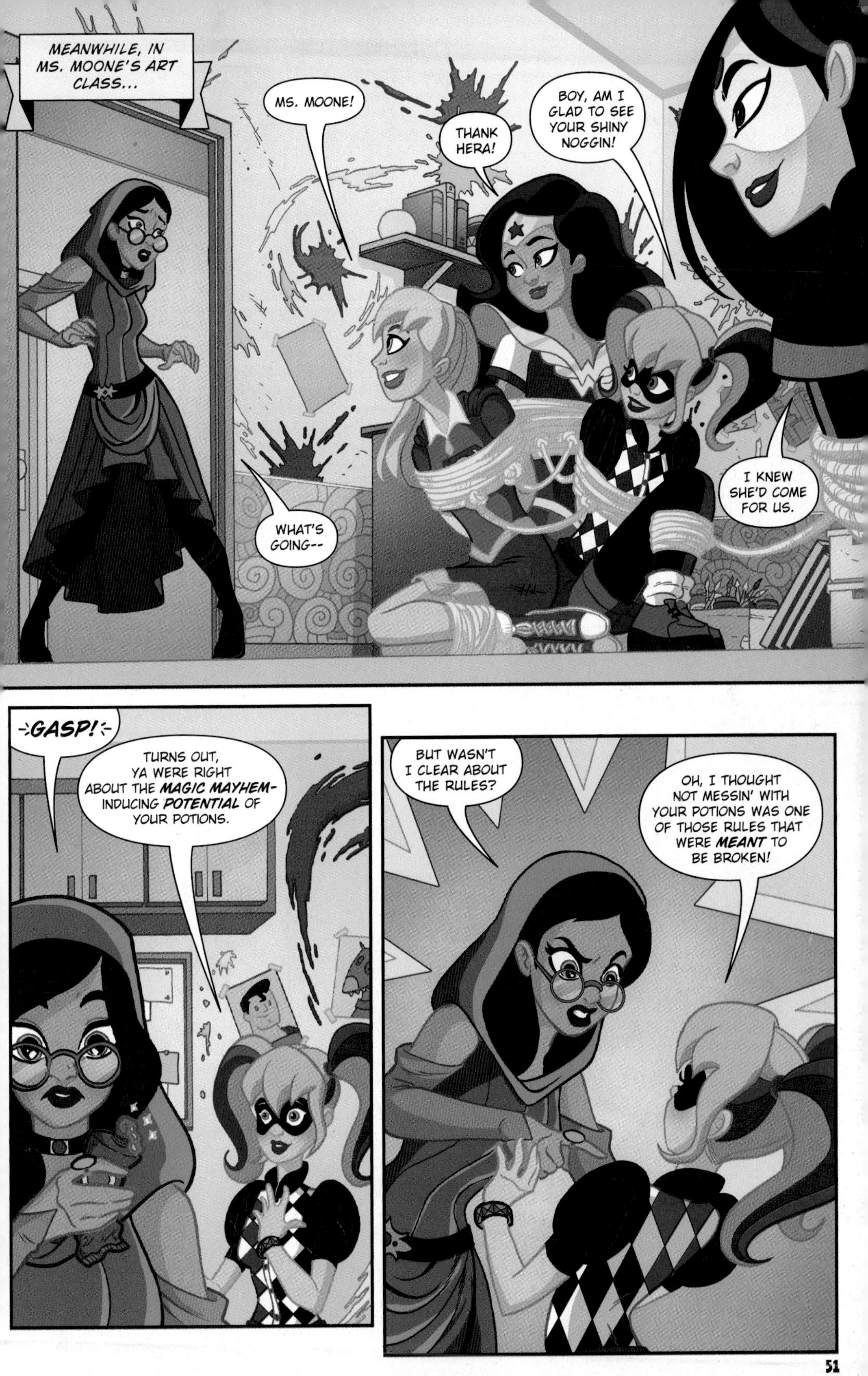
MEANWHILE, IN MS. MOONE'S ART CLASS...
MS. MOONE!
THANK HERA!
BOY, AM I GLAD TO SEE YOUR SHINY NOGGIN!
WHAT'S GOING--
I KNEW SHE'D COME FOR US.
-GASP!-
TURNS OUT, YA WERE RIGHT ABOUT THE MAGIC MAYHEM-INDUCING POTENTIAL OF YOUR POTIONS.
BUT WASN'T I CLEAR ABOUT THE RULES?
OH, I THOUGHT NOT MESSIN' WITH YOUR POTIONS WAS ONE OF THOSE RULES THAT WERE MEANT TO BE BROKEN!

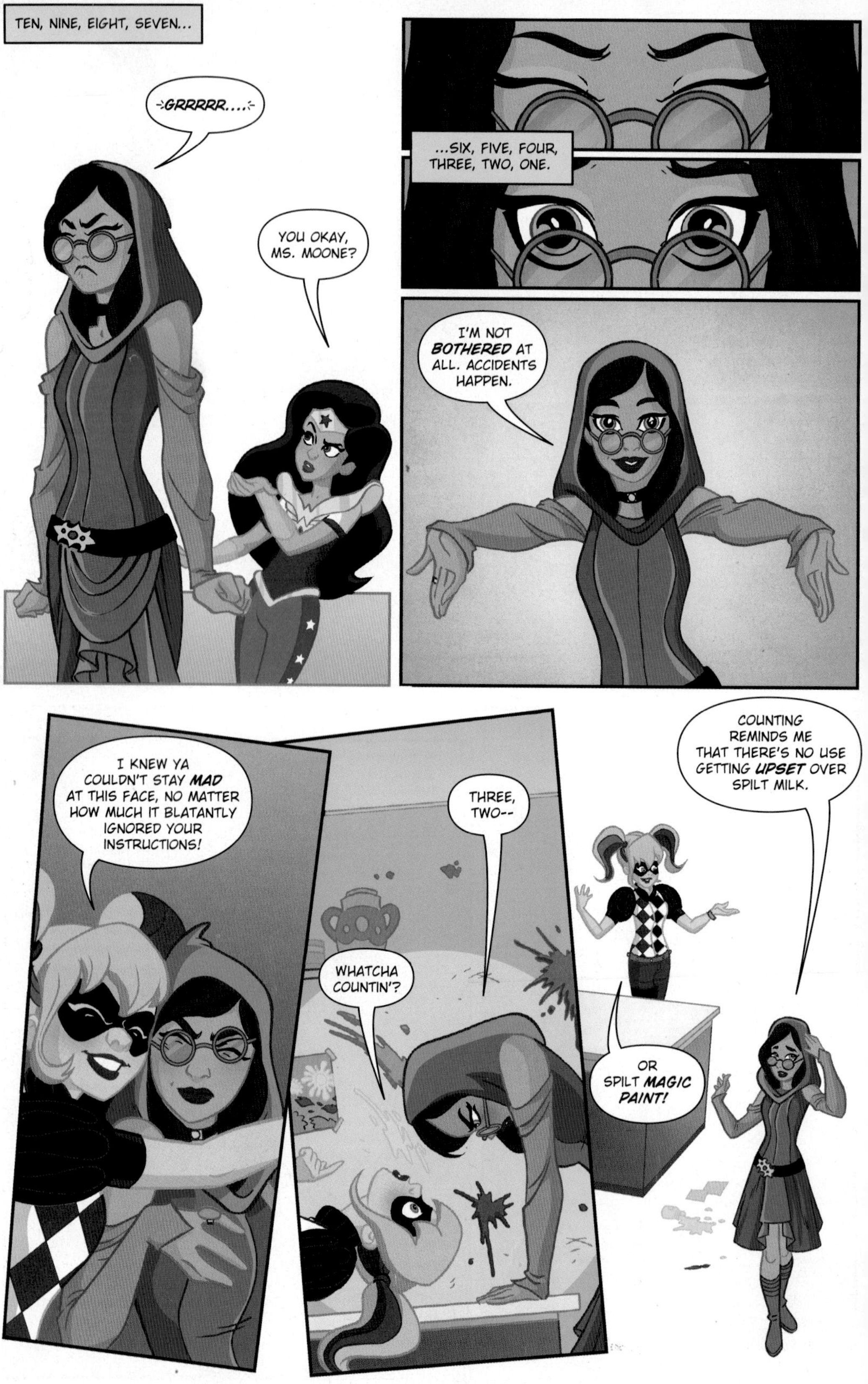
TEN, NINE, EIGHT, SEVEN...
GRRRRR....
YOU OKAY, MS. MOONE?
...SIX, FIVE, FOUR, THREE, TWO, ONE.
I'M NOT BOTHERED AT ALL. ACCIDENTS HAPPEN.
I KNEW YA COULDN'T STAY MAD AT THIS FACE, NO MATTER HOW MUCH IT BLATANTLY IGNORED YOUR INSTRUCTIONS!
THREE, TWO--
WHATCHA COUNTIN'?
COUNTING REMINDS ME THAT THERE'S NO USE GETTING UPSET OVER SPILT MILK.
OR SPILT MAGIC PAINT!

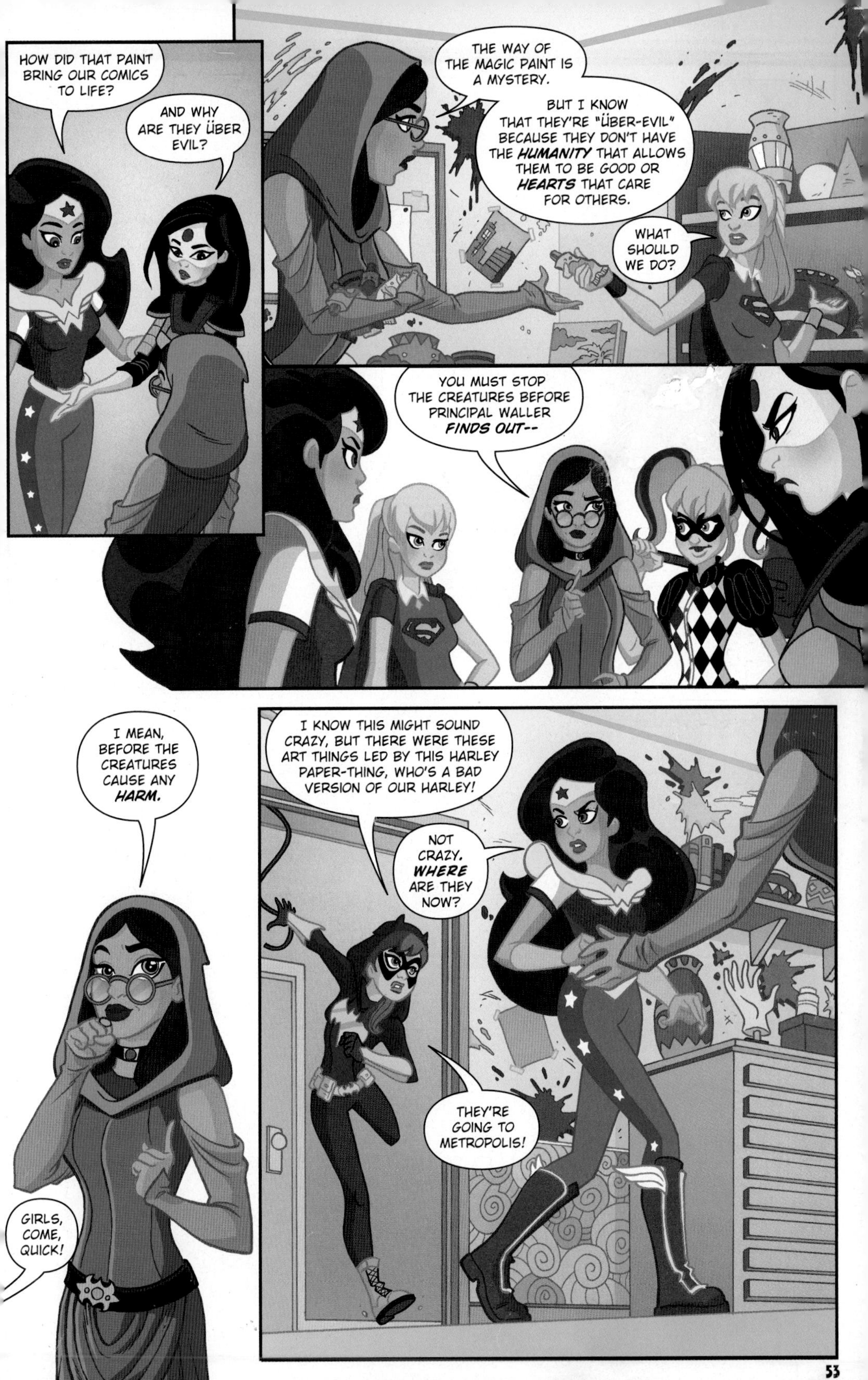
HOW DID THAT PAINT BRING OUR COMICS TO LIFE?
AND WHY ARE THEY ÜBER EVIL?
THE WAY OF THE MAGIC PAINT IS A MYSTERY.
BUT I KNOW THAT THEY'RE "ÜBER-EVIL" BECAUSE THEY DON'T HAVE THE HUMANITY THAT ALLOWS THEM TO BE GOOD OR HEARTS THAT CARE FOR OTHERS.
WHAT SHOULD WE DO?
YOU MUST STOP THE CREATURES BEFORE PRINCIPAL WALLER FINDS OUT--
I MEAN, BEFORE THE CREATURES CAUSE ANY HARM.
GIRLS, COME, QUICK!
I KNOW THIS MIGHT SOUND CRAZY, BUT THERE WERE THESE ART THINGS LED BY THIS HARLEY PAPER-THING, WHO'S A BAD VERSION OF OUR HARLEY!
NOT CRAZY. WHERE ARE THEY NOW?
THEY'RE GOING TO METROPOLIS!

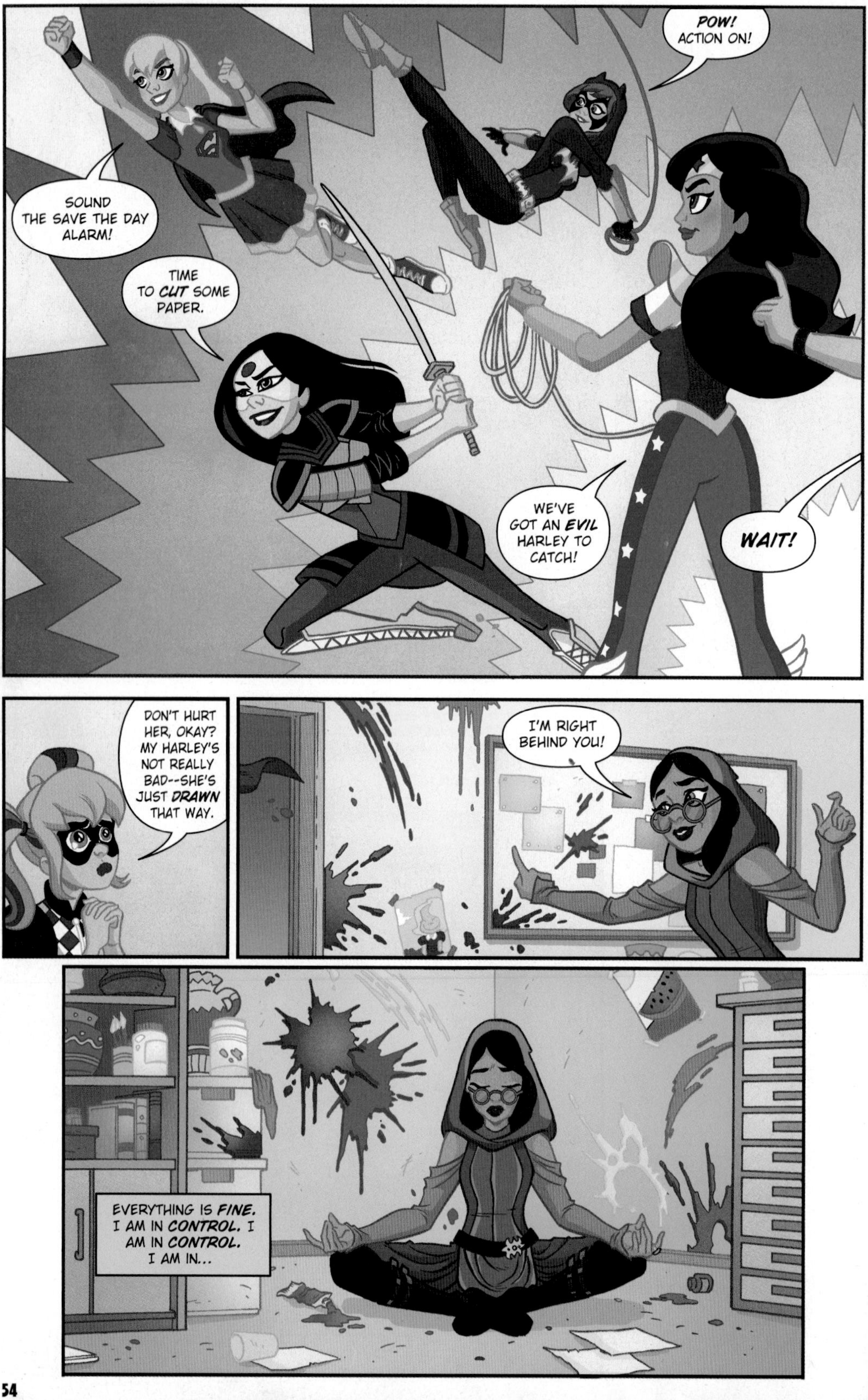
POW! ACTION ON!
SOUND THE SAVE THE DAY ALARM!
TIME TO CUT SOME PAPER.
WE'VE GOT AN EVIL HARLEY TO CATCH!
WAIT!
DON'T HURT HER, OKAY? MY HARLEY'S NOT REALLY BAD--SHE'S JUST DRAWN THAT WAY.
I'M RIGHT BEHIND YOU!
EVERYTHING IS FINE. I AM IN CONTROL. I AM IN CONTROL. I AM IN...

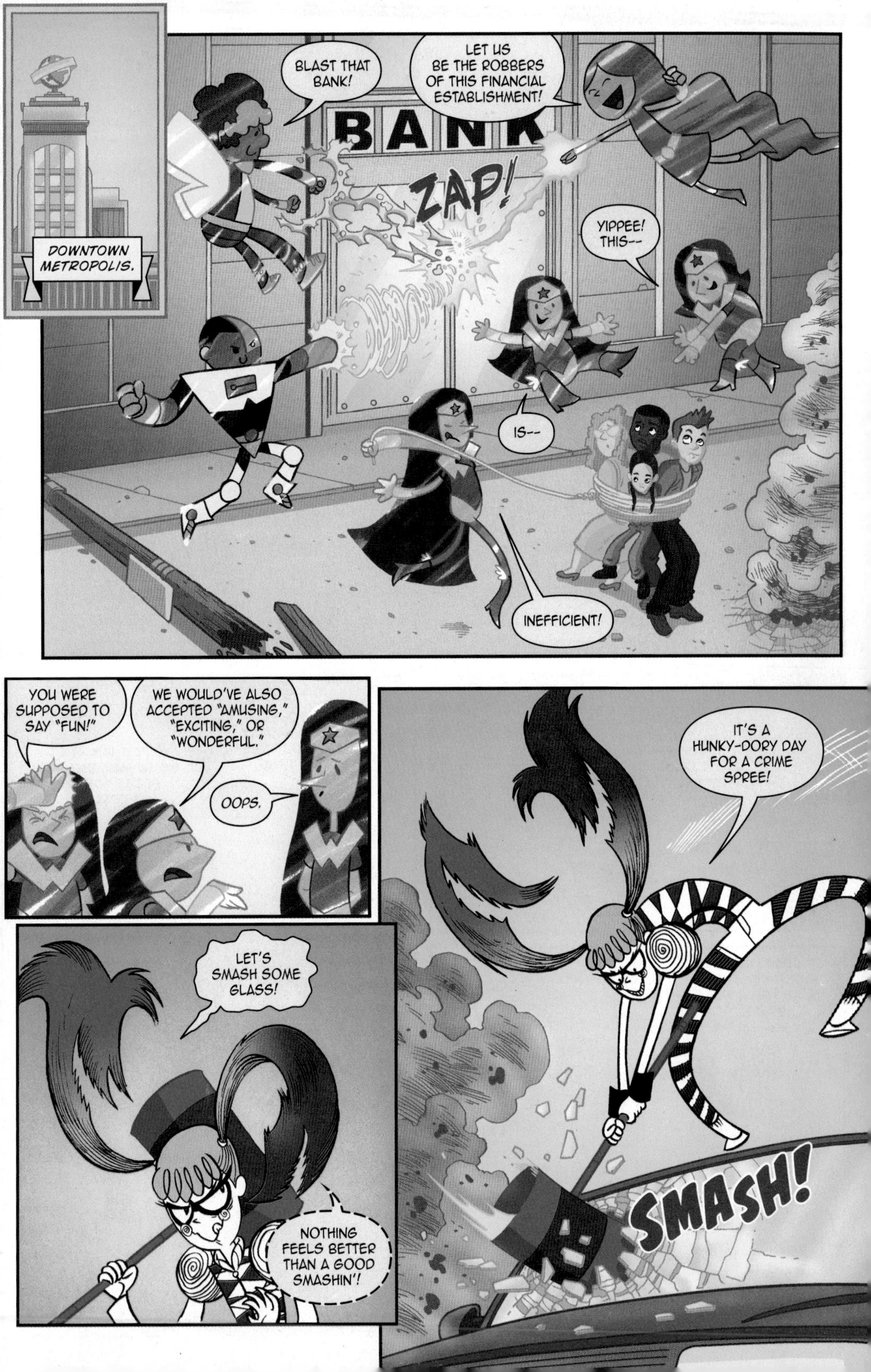
DOWNTOWN METROPOLIS.
BLAST THAT BANK!
LET US BE THE ROBBERS OF THIS FINANCIAL ESTABLISHMENT!
BANK
ZAP!
YIPPEE! THIS--
IS--
INEFFICIENT!
YOU WERE SUPPOSED TO SAY "FUN!"
WE WOULD'VE ALSO ACCEPTED "AMUSING," "EXCITING," OR "WONDERFUL."
OOPS.
IT'S A HUNKY-DORY DAY FOR A CRIME SPREE!
LET'S SMASH SOME GLASS!
NOTHING FEELS BETTER THAN A GOOD SMASHIN'!
SMASH!

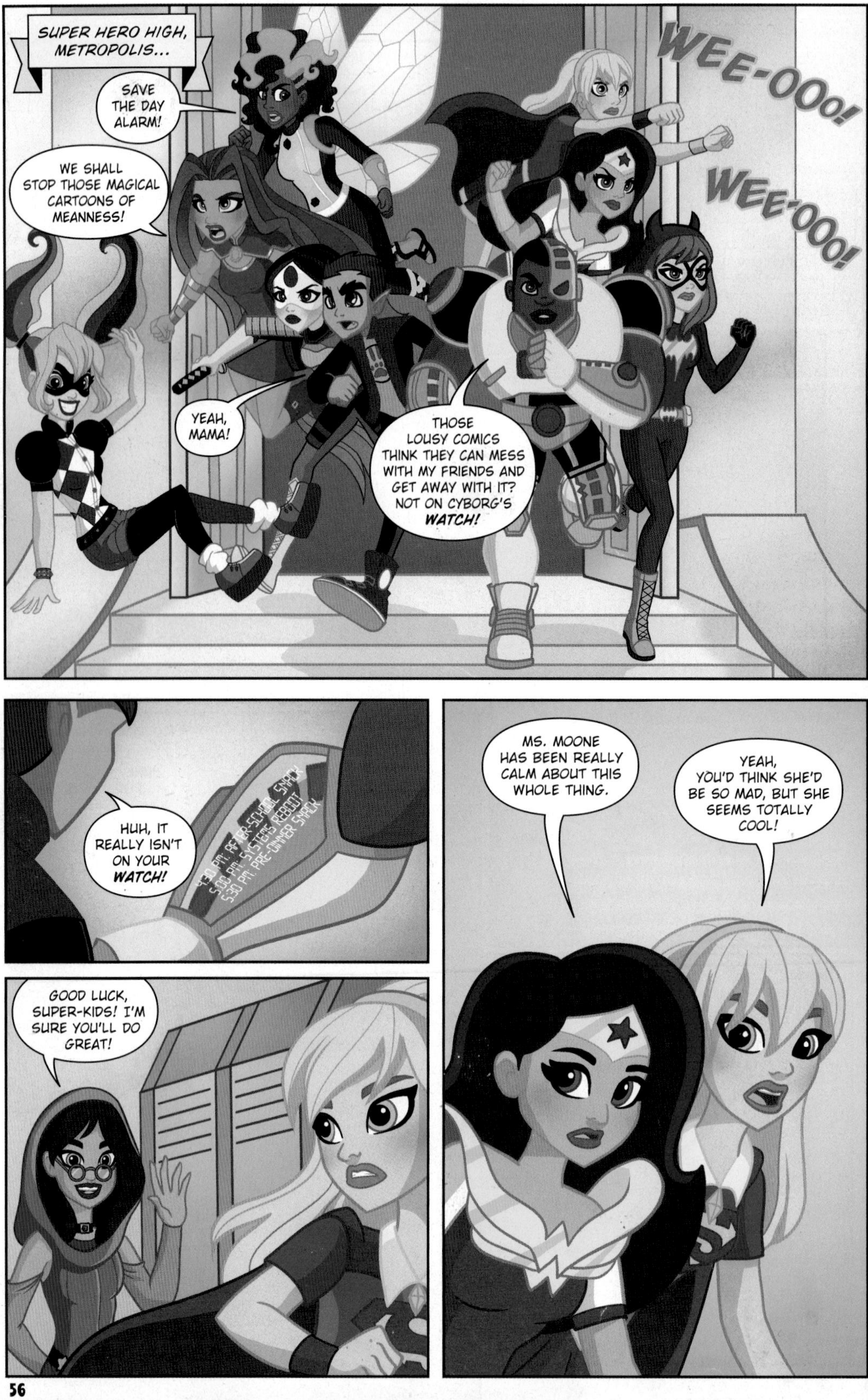
SUPER HERO HIGH, METROPOLIS...
SAVE THE DAY ALARM!
WEE-OOO!
WE SHALL STOP THOSE MAGICAL CARTOONS OF MEANNESS!
WEE-OOO!
YEAH, MAMA!
THOSE LOUSY COMICS THINK THEY CAN MESS WITH MY FRIENDS AND GET AWAY WITH IT? NOT ON CYBORG'S **WATCH!**
HUH, IT REALLY ISN'T ON YOUR **WATCH!**
4:30 PM: AFTER-SCHOOL SNACK
5:00 PM: SYSTEMS REBOOT
5:30 PM: PRE-DINNER SNACK
MS. MOONE HAS BEEN REALLY CALM ABOUT THIS WHOLE THING.
YEAH, YOU'D THINK SHE'D BE SO MAD, BUT SHE SEEMS TOTALLY COOL!
GOOD LUCK, SUPER-KIDS! I'M SURE YOU'LL DO GREAT!

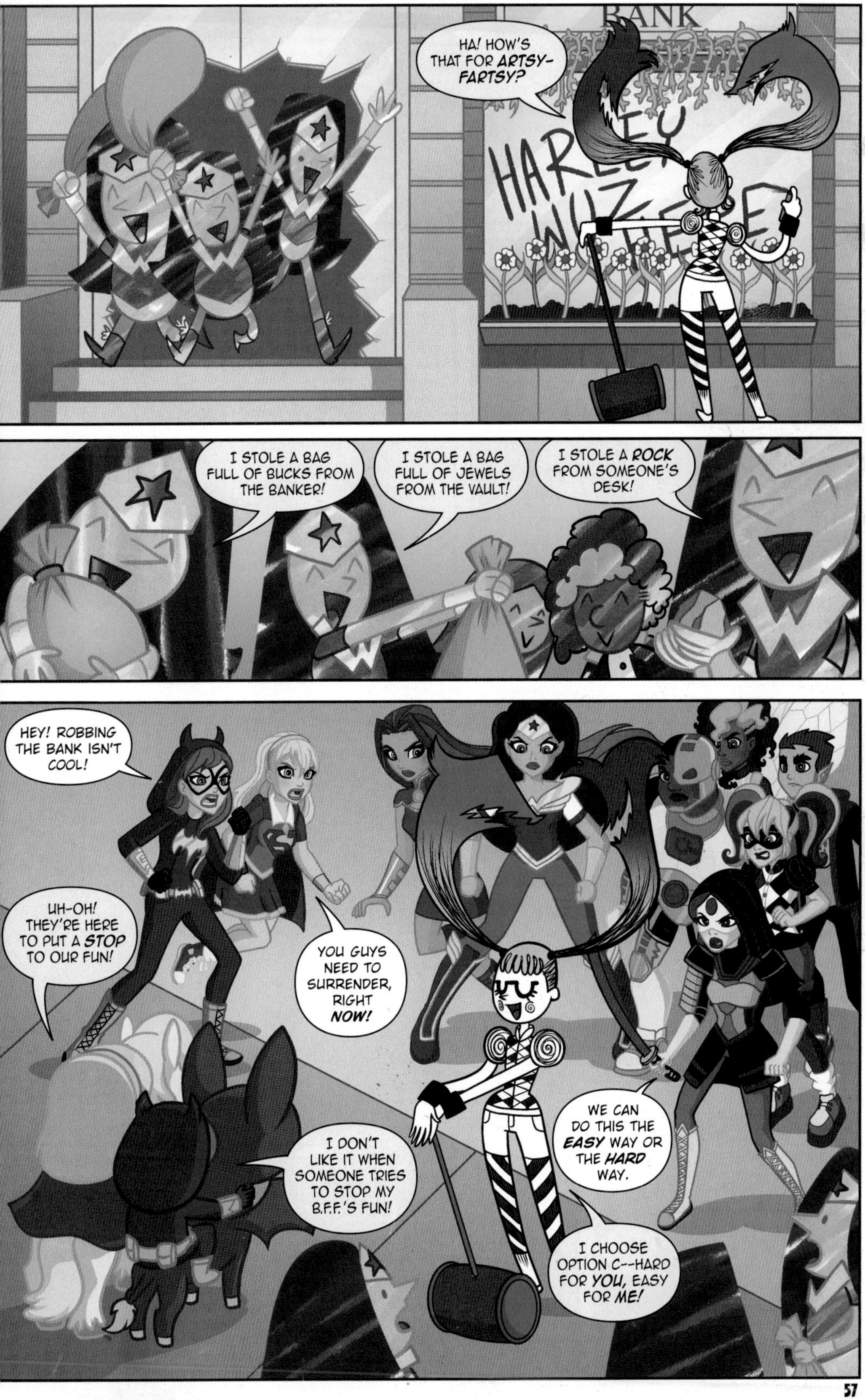
BANK
HA! HOW'S THAT FOR ARTSY-FARTSY?
I STOLE A BAG FULL OF BUCKS FROM THE BANKER!
I STOLE A BAG FULL OF JEWELS FROM THE VAULT!
I STOLE A ROCK FROM SOMEONE'S DESK!
HEY! ROBBING THE BANK ISN'T COOL!
UH-OH! THEY'RE HERE TO PUT A STOP TO OUR FUN!
YOU GUYS NEED TO SURRENDER, RIGHT NOW!
I DON'T LIKE IT WHEN SOMEONE TRIES TO STOP MY B.F.F.'S FUN!
WE CAN DO THIS THE EASY WAY OR THE HARD WAY.
I CHOOSE OPTION C--HARD FOR YOU, EASY FOR ME!

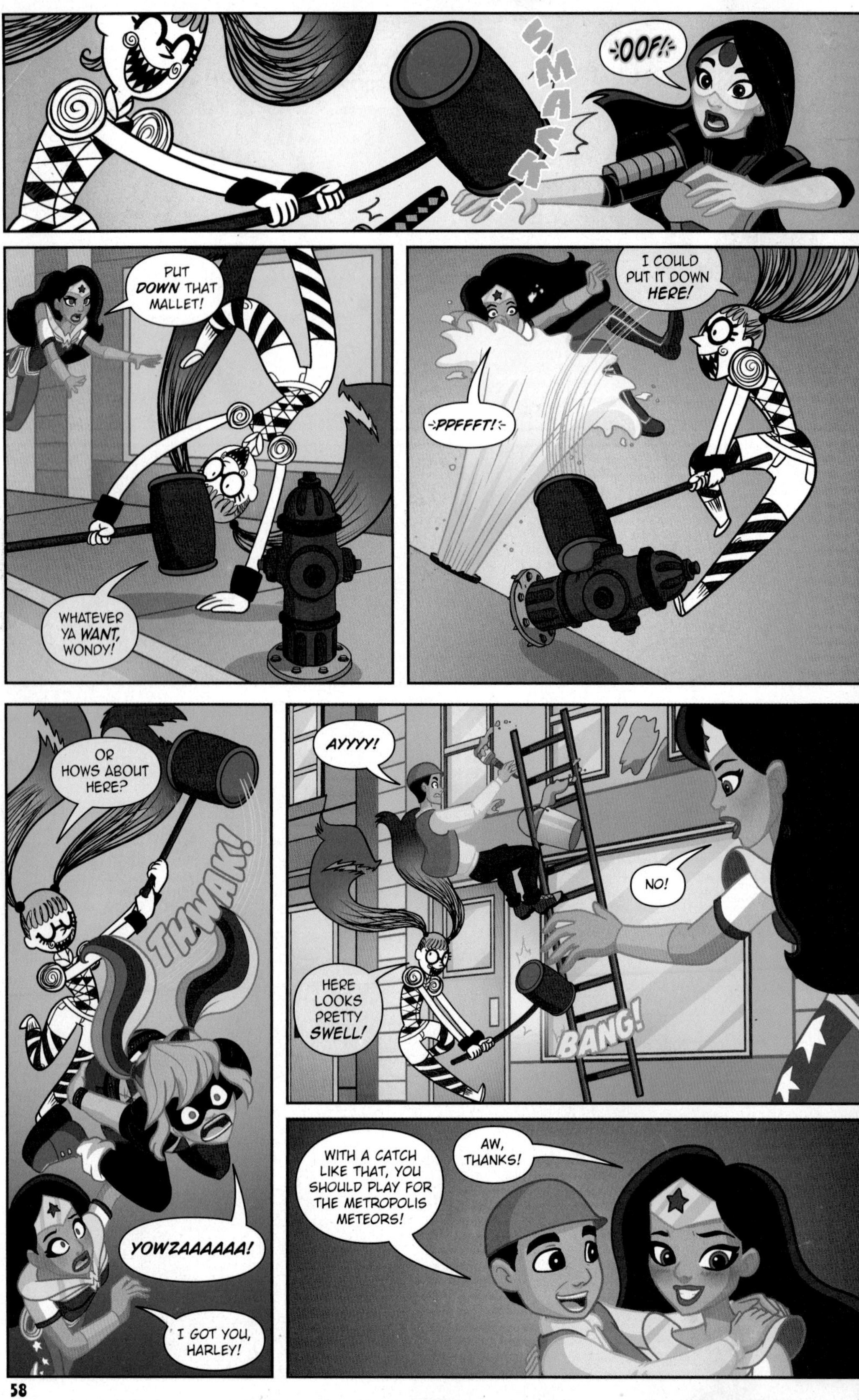
SMACK!!
OOF!
PUT DOWN THAT MALLET!
WHATEVER YA WANT, WONDY!
I COULD PUT IT DOWN HERE!
PPFFFT!
OR HOWS ABOUT HERE?
THWAK!
YOWZAAAAAA!
I GOT YOU, HARLEY!
AYYYY!
NO!
HERE LOOKS PRETTY SWELL!
BANG!
WITH A CATCH LIKE THAT, YOU SHOULD PLAY FOR THE METROPOLIS METEORS!
AW, THANKS!

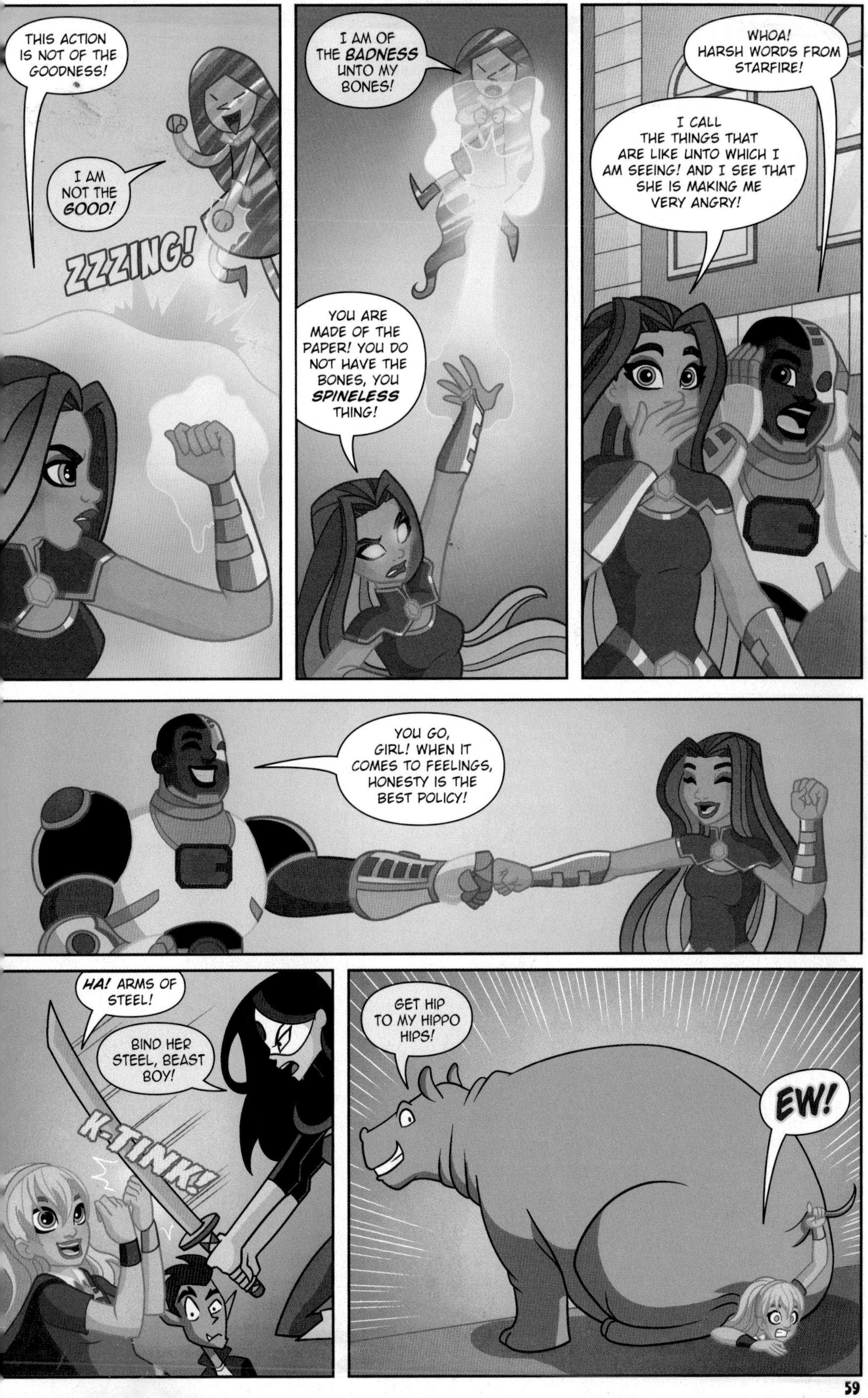
THIS ACTION IS NOT OF THE GOODNESS!
I AM NOT THE GOOD!
ZZZING!
I AM OF THE BADNESS UNTO MY BONES!
YOU ARE MADE OF THE PAPER! YOU DO NOT HAVE THE BONES, YOU SPINELESS THING!
WHOA! HARSH WORDS FROM STARFIRE!
I CALL THE THINGS THAT ARE LIKE UNTO WHICH I AM SEEING! AND I SEE THAT SHE IS MAKING ME VERY ANGRY!
YOU GO, GIRL! WHEN IT COMES TO FEELINGS, HONESTY IS THE BEST POLICY!
HA! ARMS OF STEEL!
BIND HER STEEL, BEAST BOY!
K-TINK!
GET HIP TO MY HIPPO HIPS!
EW!

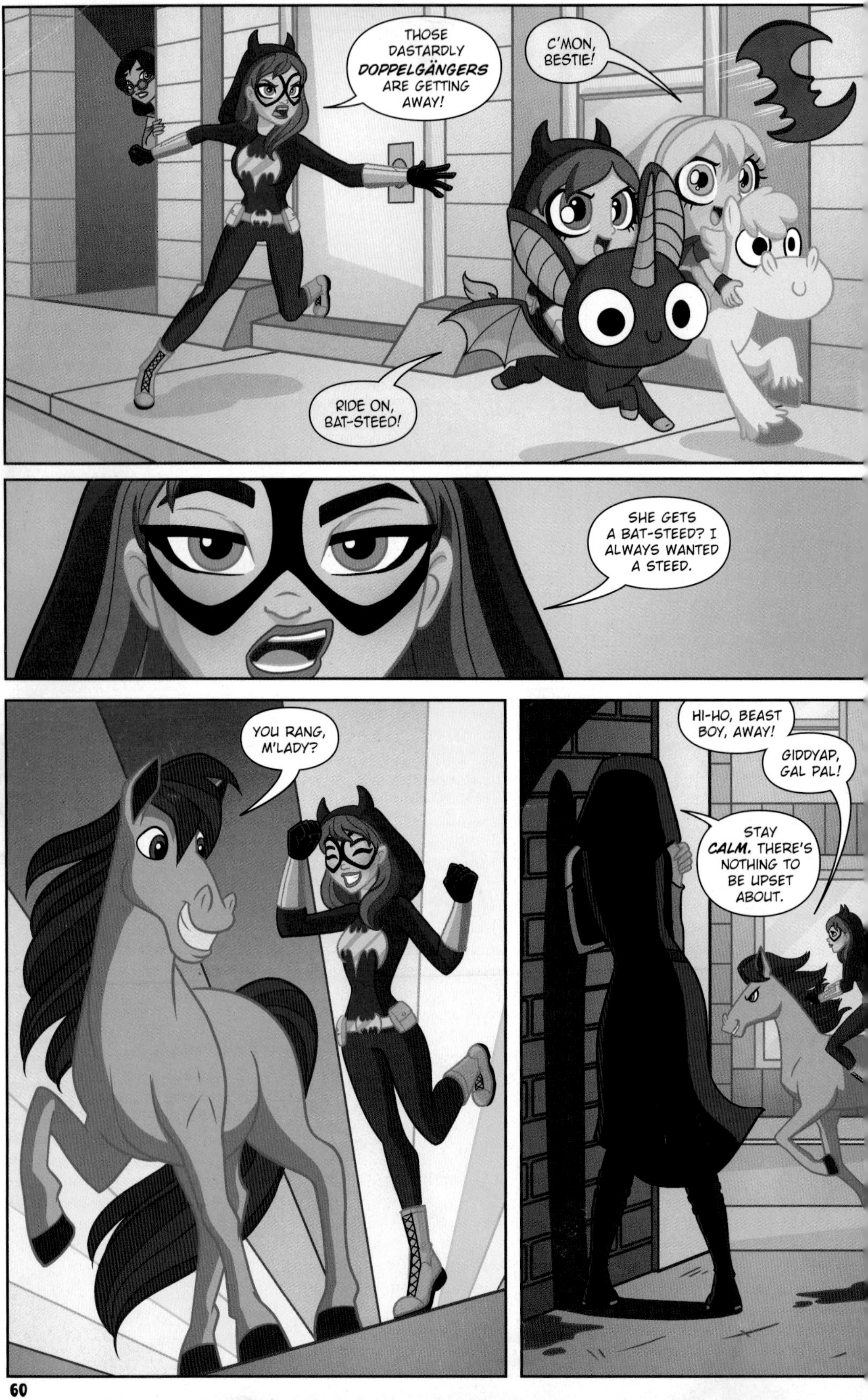
THOSE DASTARDLY *DOPPELGÄNGERS* ARE GETTING AWAY!
C'MON, BESTIE!
RIDE ON, BAT-STEED!
SHE GETS A BAT-STEED? I ALWAYS WANTED A STEED.
YOU RANG, M'LADY?
HI-HO, BEAST BOY, AWAY!
GIDDYAP, GAL PAL!
STAY *CALM.* THERE'S NOTHING TO BE UPSET ABOUT.

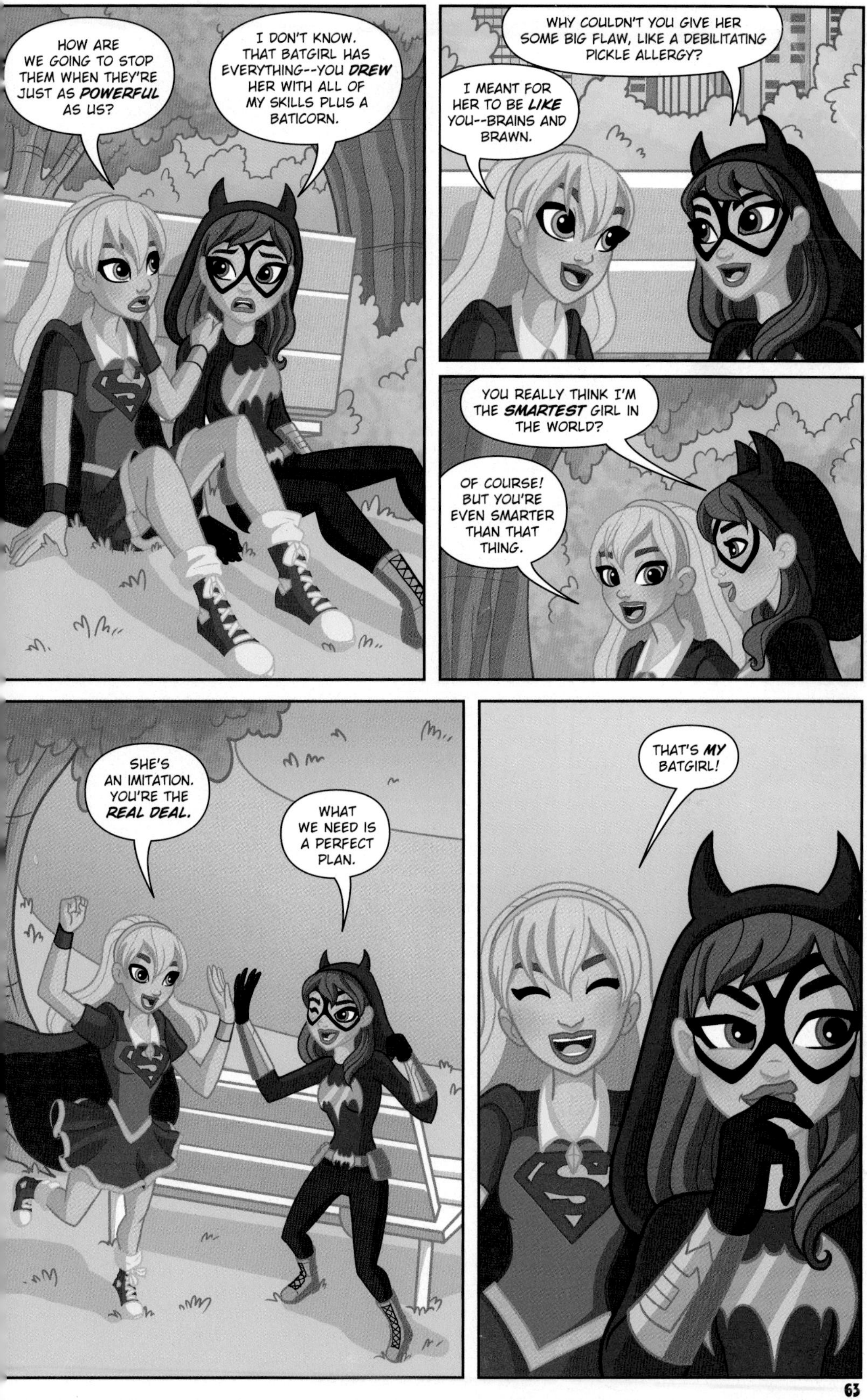
HOW ARE WE GOING TO STOP THEM WHEN THEY'RE JUST AS *POWERFUL* AS US?
I DON'T KNOW. THAT BATGIRL HAS EVERYTHING--YOU *DREW* HER WITH ALL OF MY SKILLS PLUS A BATICORN.
WHY COULDN'T YOU GIVE HER SOME BIG FLAW, LIKE A DEBILITATING PICKLE ALLERGY?
I MEANT FOR HER TO BE *LIKE* YOU--BRAINS AND BRAWN.
YOU REALLY THINK I'M THE *SMARTEST* GIRL IN THE WORLD?
OF COURSE! BUT YOU'RE EVEN SMARTER THAN THAT THING.
SHE'S AN IMITATION. YOU'RE THE *REAL DEAL.*
WHAT WE NEED IS A PERFECT PLAN.
THAT'S *MY* BATGIRL!

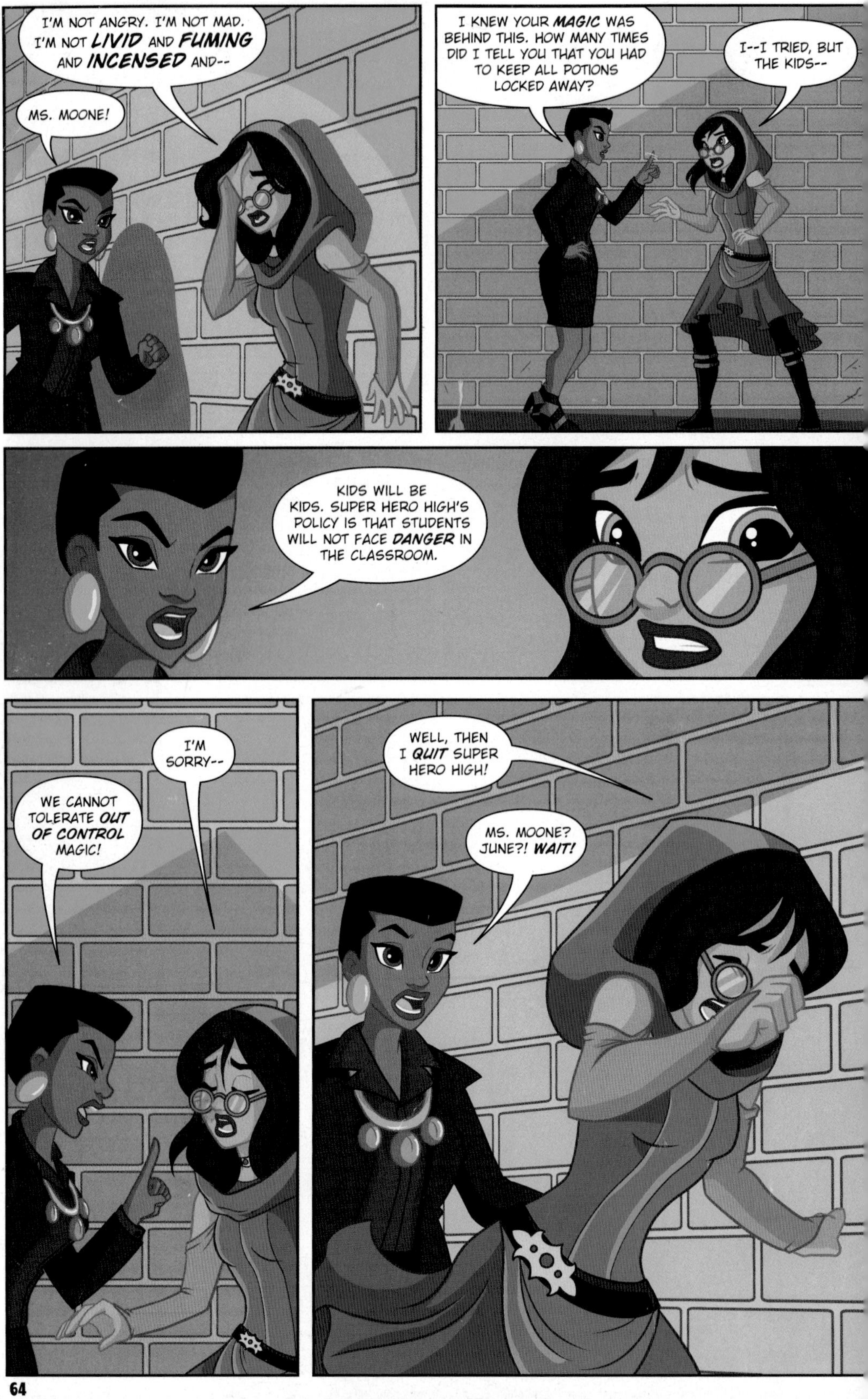
I'M NOT ANGRY. I'M NOT MAD. I'M NOT LIVID AND FUMING AND INCENSED AND--
MS. MOONE!
I KNEW YOUR MAGIC WAS BEHIND THIS. HOW MANY TIMES DID I TELL YOU THAT YOU HAD TO KEEP ALL POTIONS LOCKED AWAY?
I--I TRIED, BUT THE KIDS--
KIDS WILL BE KIDS. SUPER HERO HIGH'S POLICY IS THAT STUDENTS WILL NOT FACE DANGER IN THE CLASSROOM.
I'M SORRY--
WE CANNOT TOLERATE OUT OF CONTROL MAGIC!
WELL, THEN I QUIT SUPER HERO HIGH!
MS. MOONE? JUNE?! WAIT!

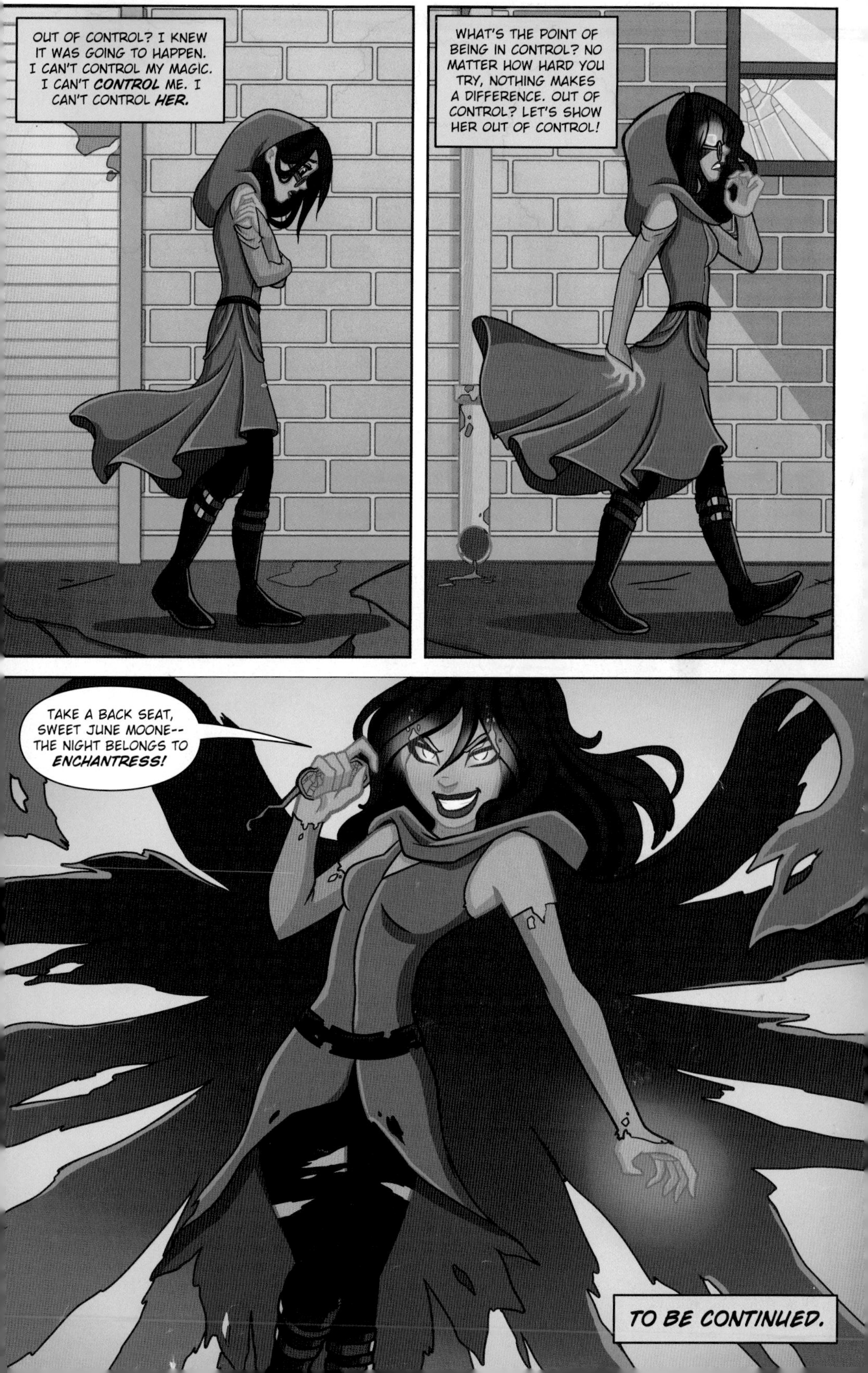
OUT OF CONTROL? I KNEW IT WAS GOING TO HAPPEN. I CAN'T CONTROL MY MAGIC. I CAN'T CONTROL ME. I CAN'T CONTROL HER.
WHAT'S THE POINT OF BEING IN CONTROL? NO MATTER HOW HARD YOU TRY, NOTHING MAKES A DIFFERENCE. OUT OF CONTROL? LET'S SHOW HER OUT OF CONTROL!
TAKE A BACK SEAT, SWEET JUNE MOONE-- THE NIGHT BELONGS TO ENCHANTRESS!
TO BE CONTINUED.

CHAPTER FOUR
THE WRITE STUFF

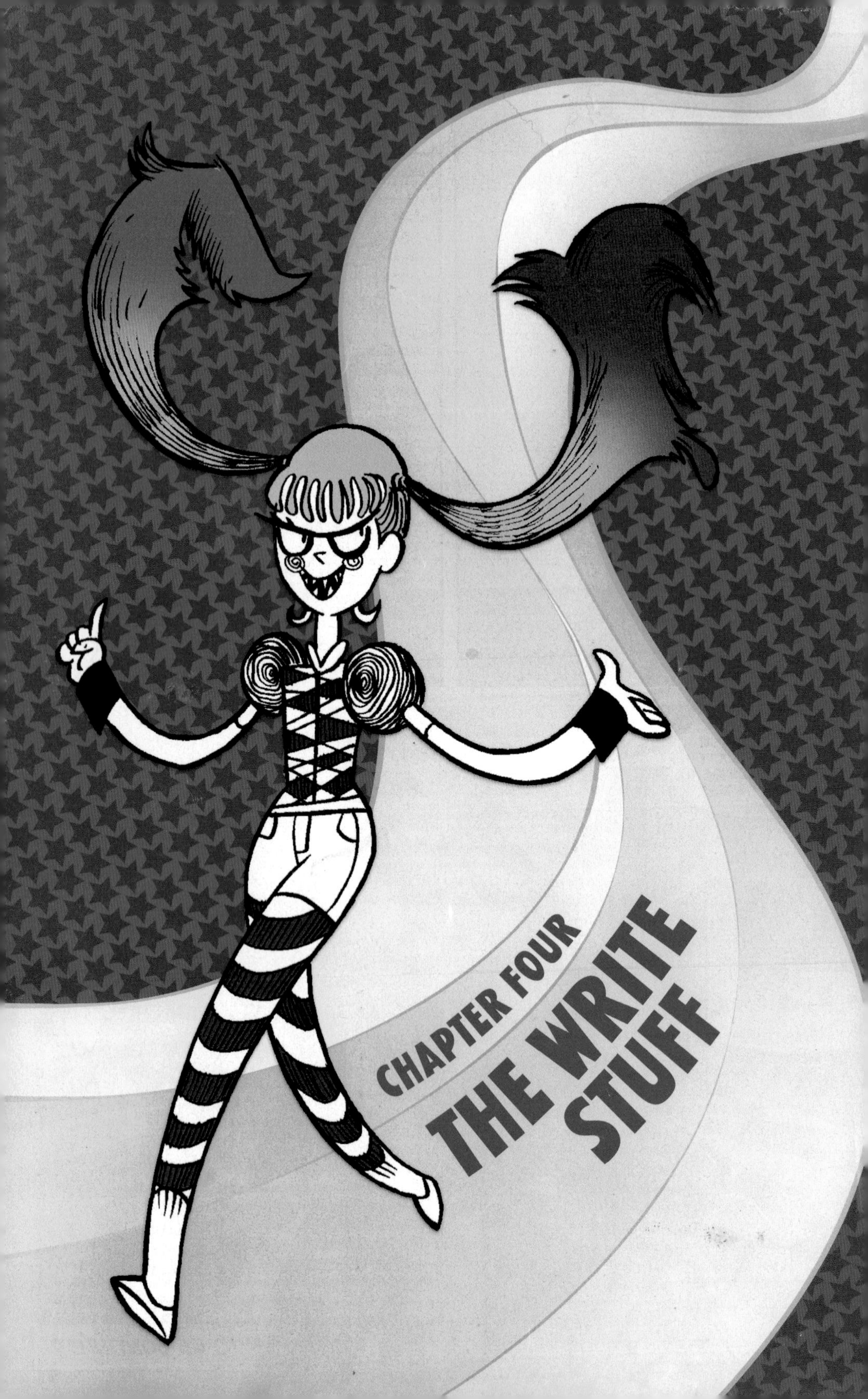

68

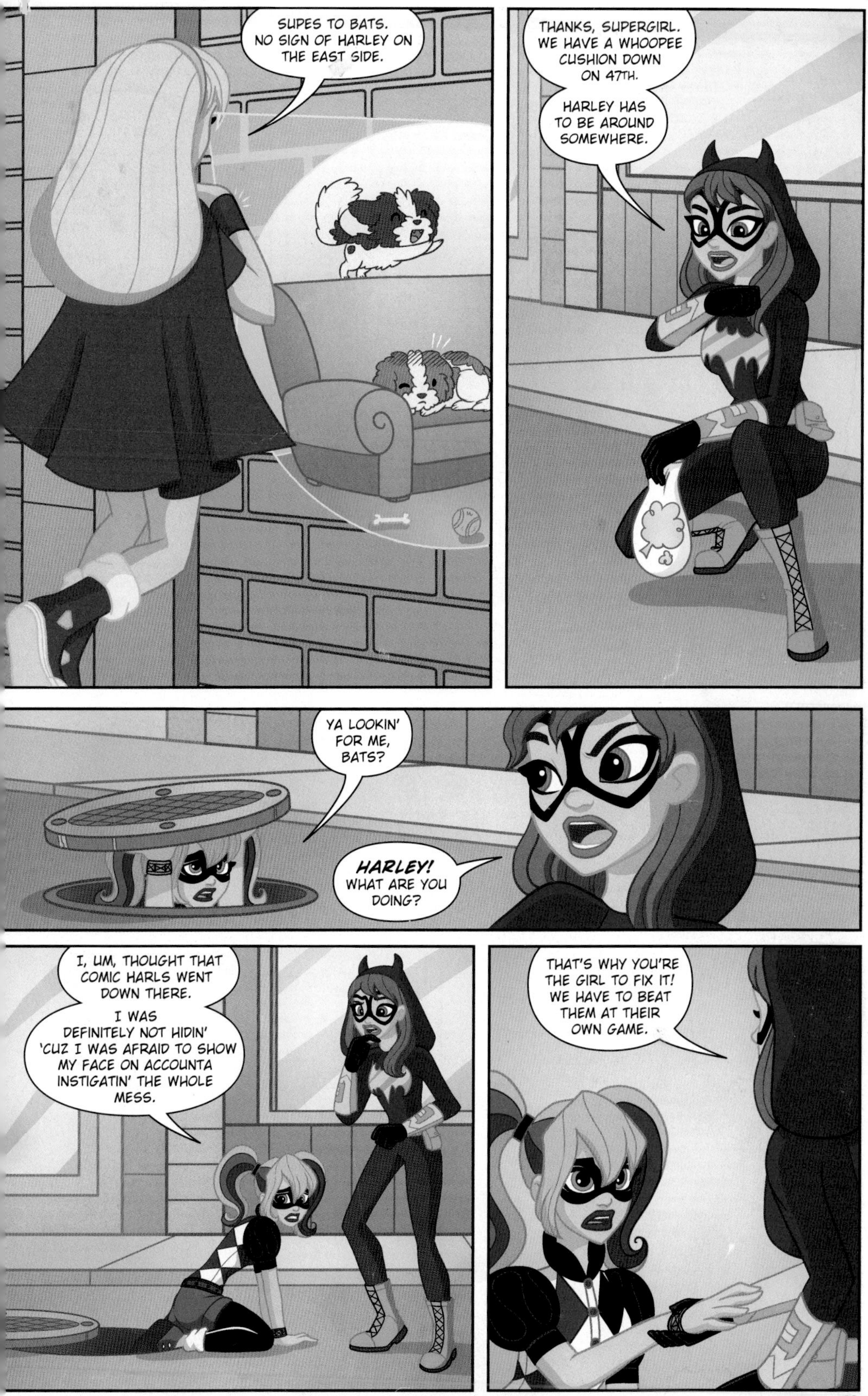
SUPES TO BATS. NO SIGN OF HARLEY ON THE EAST SIDE.
THANKS, SUPERGIRL. WE HAVE A WHOOPEE CUSHION DOWN ON 47TH.
HARLEY HAS TO BE AROUND SOMEWHERE.
YA LOOKIN' FOR ME, BATS?
HARLEY! WHAT ARE YOU DOING?
I, UM, THOUGHT THAT COMIC HARLS WENT DOWN THERE.
I WAS DEFINITELY NOT HIDIN' 'CUZ I WAS AFRAID TO SHOW MY FACE ON ACCOUNTA INSTIGATIN' THE WHOLE MESS.
THAT'S WHY YOU'RE THE GIRL TO FIX IT! WE HAVE TO BEAT THEM AT THEIR OWN GAME.

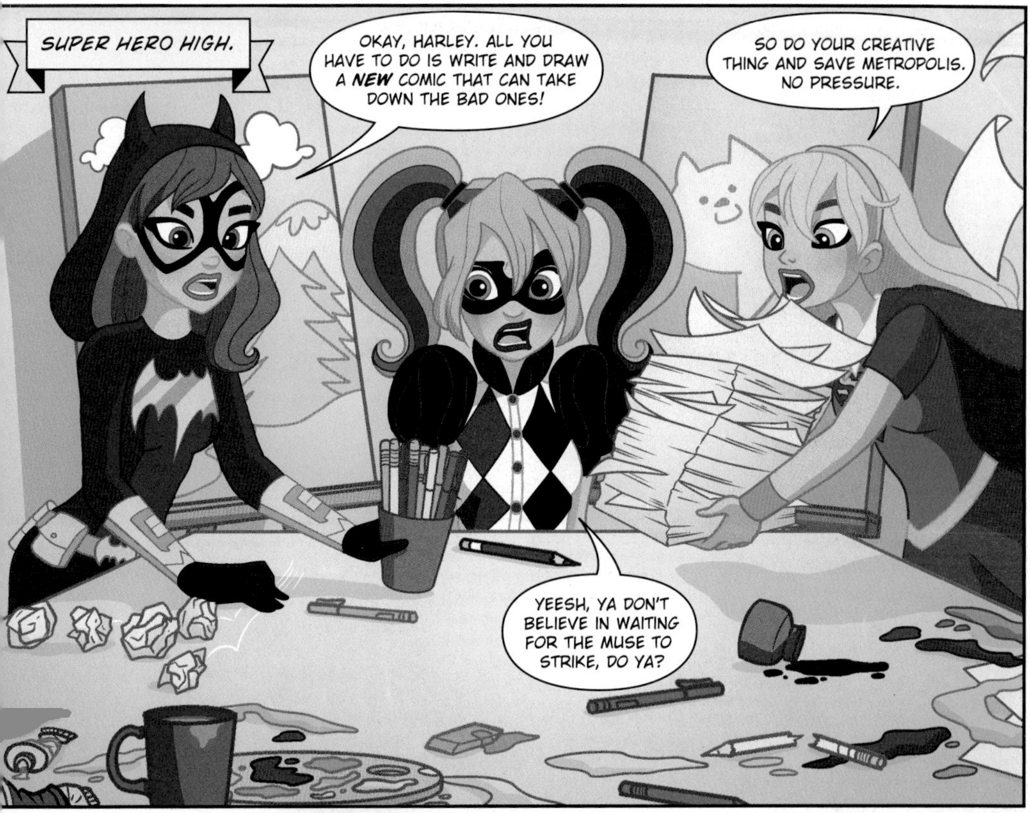
SUPER HERO HIGH.
OKAY, HARLEY. ALL YOU HAVE TO DO IS WRITE AND DRAW A NEW COMIC THAT CAN TAKE DOWN THE BAD ONES!
SO DO YOUR CREATIVE THING AND SAVE METROPOLIS. NO PRESSURE.
YEESH, YA DON'T BELIEVE IN WAITING FOR THE MUSE TO STRIKE, DO YA?

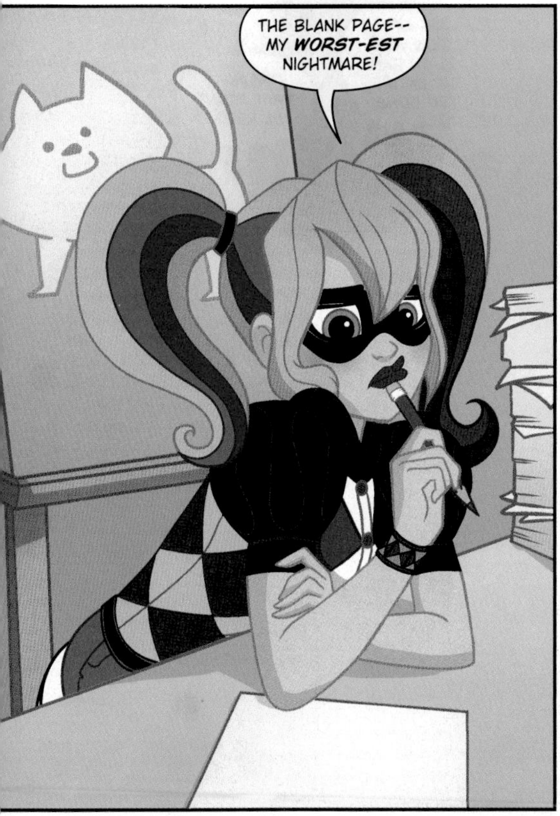
THE BLANK PAGE-- MY WORST-EST NIGHTMARE!

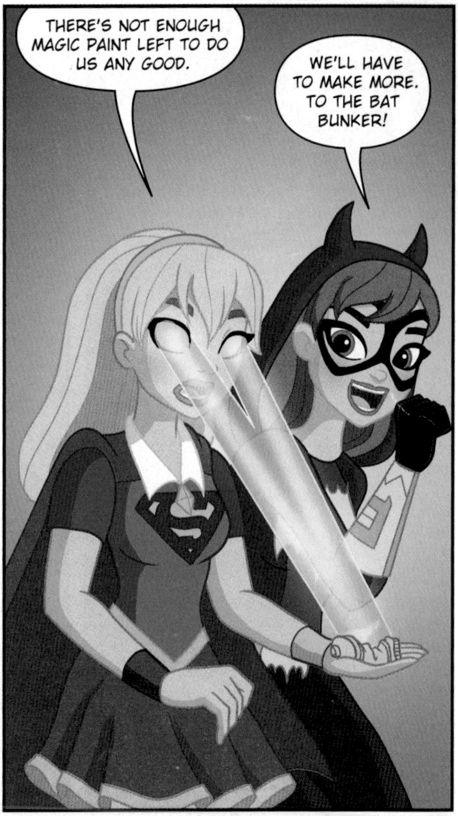
THERE'S NOT ENOUGH MAGIC PAINT LEFT TO DO US ANY GOOD.
WE'LL HAVE TO MAKE MORE. TO THE BAT BUNKER!

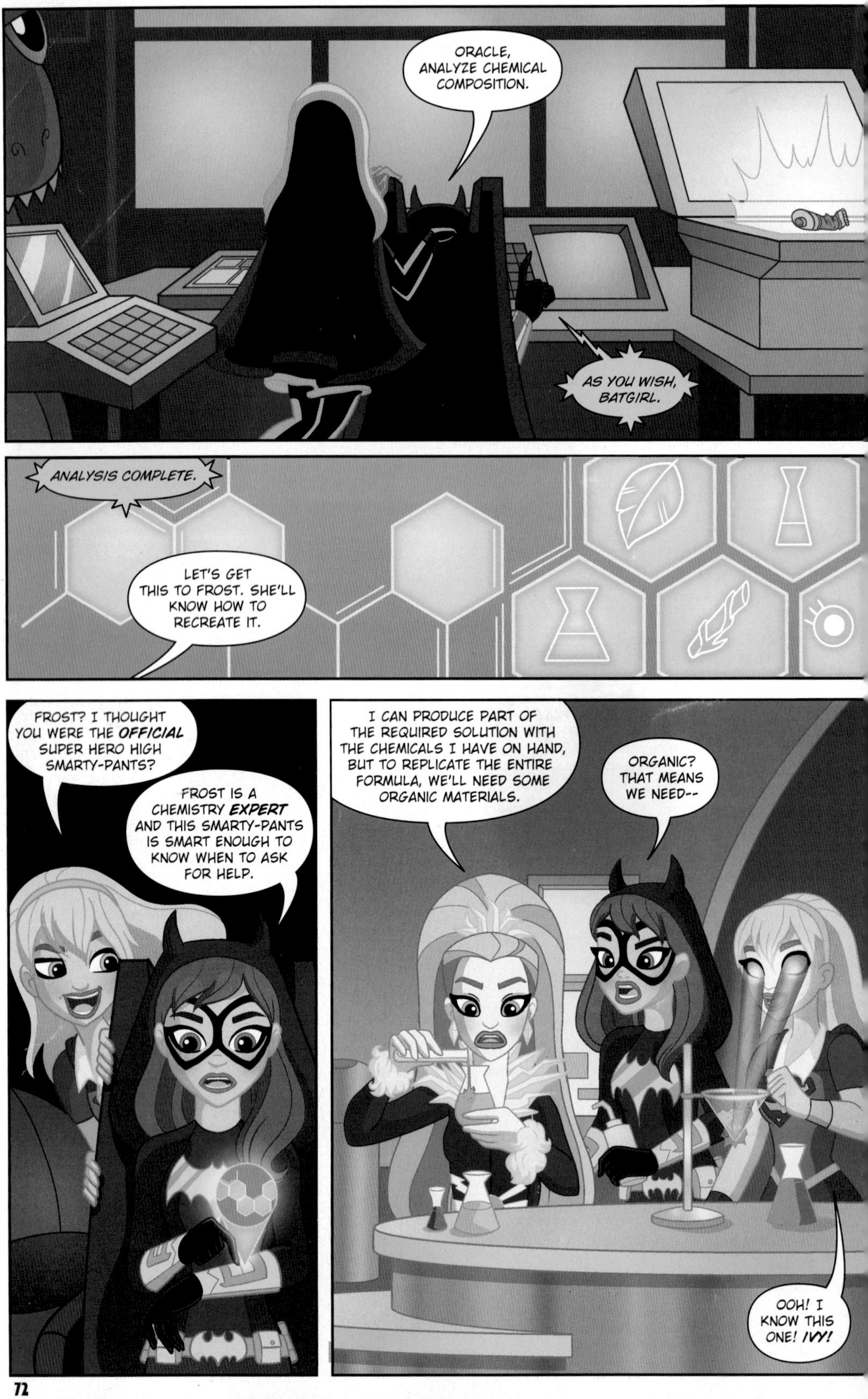
ORACLE, ANALYZE CHEMICAL COMPOSITION.
AS YOU WISH, BATGIRL.
ANALYSIS COMPLETE.
LET'S GET THIS TO FROST. SHE'LL KNOW HOW TO RECREATE IT.
FROST? I THOUGHT YOU WERE THE OFFICIAL SUPER HERO HIGH SMARTY-PANTS?
FROST IS A CHEMISTRY EXPERT AND THIS SMARTY-PANTS IS SMART ENOUGH TO KNOW WHEN TO ASK FOR HELP.
I CAN PRODUCE PART OF THE REQUIRED SOLUTION WITH THE CHEMICALS I HAVE ON HAND, BUT TO REPLICATE THE ENTIRE FORMULA, WE'LL NEED SOME ORGANIC MATERIALS.
ORGANIC? THAT MEANS WE NEED--
OOH! I KNOW THIS ONE! IVY!

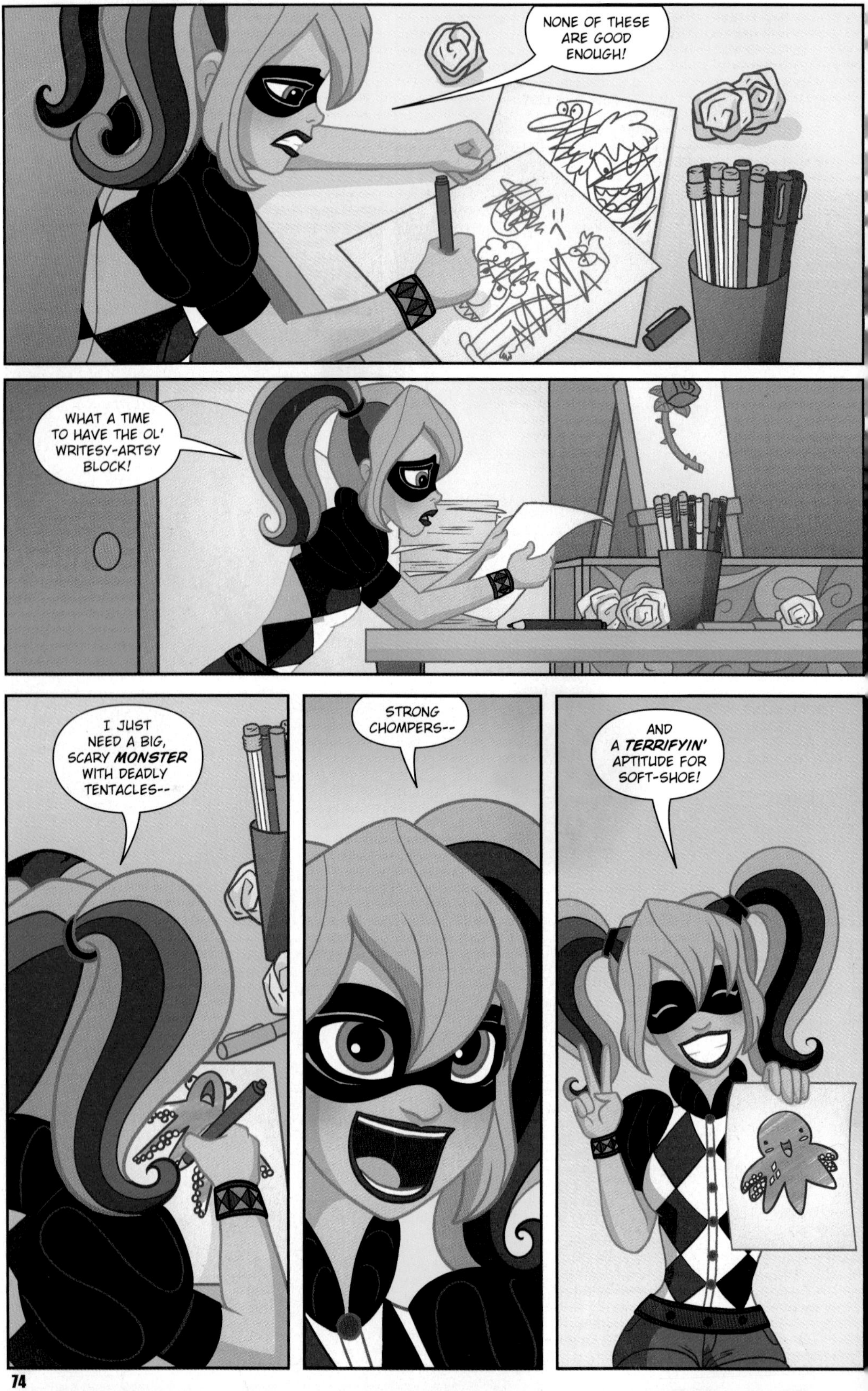
NONE OF THESE ARE GOOD ENOUGH!
WHAT A TIME TO HAVE THE OL' WRITESY-ARTSY BLOCK!
I JUST NEED A BIG, SCARY **MONSTER** WITH DEADLY TENTACLES--
STRONG CHOMPERS--
AND A **TERRIFYIN'** APTITUDE FOR SOFT-SHOE!

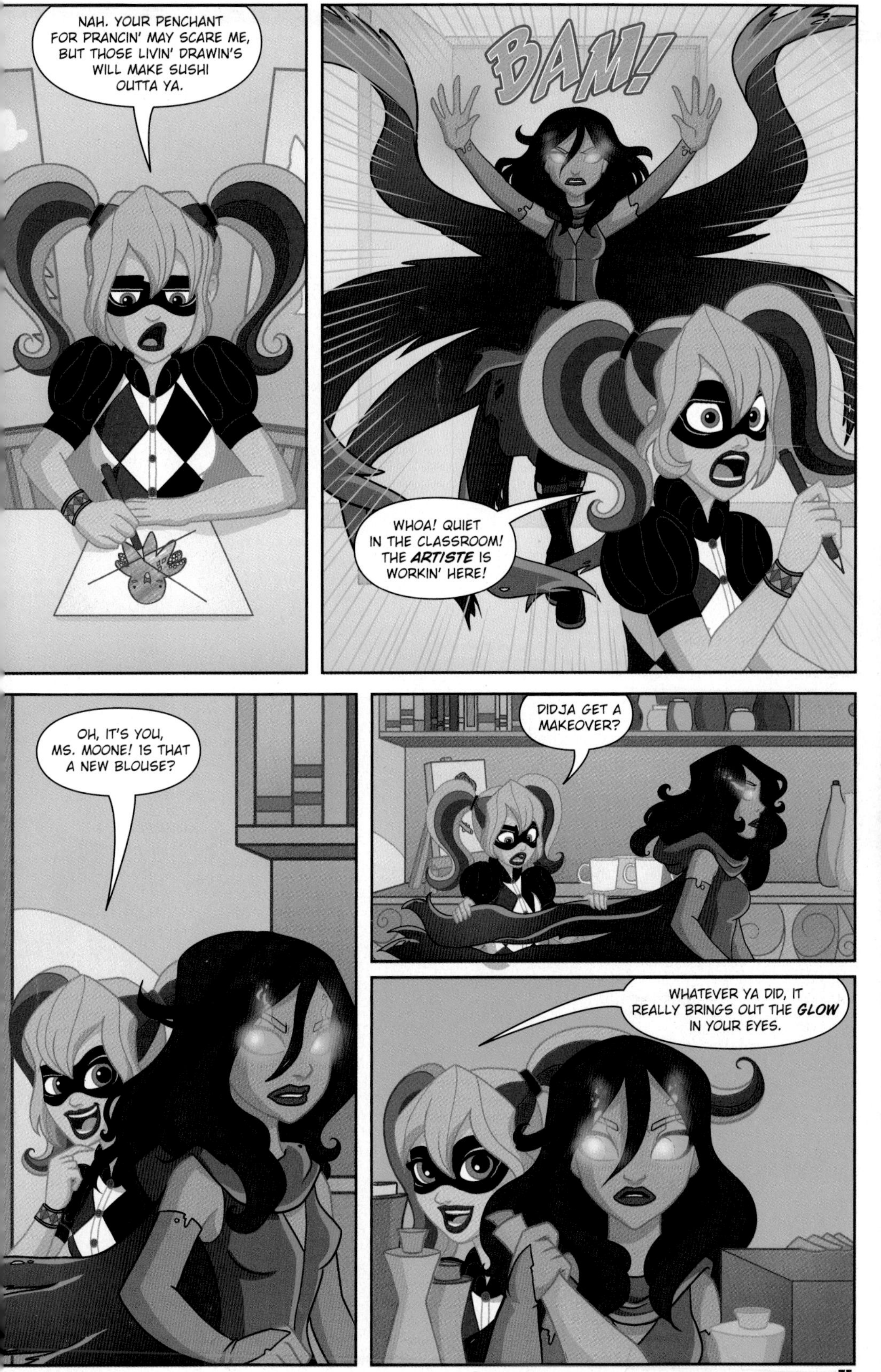
NAH. YOUR PENCHANT FOR PRANCIN' MAY SCARE ME, BUT THOSE LIVIN' DRAWIN'S WILL MAKE SUSHI OUTTA YA.
BAM!
WHOA! QUIET IN THE CLASSROOM! THE *ARTISTE* IS WORKIN' HERE!
OH, IT'S YOU, MS. MOONE! IS THAT A NEW BLOUSE?
DIDJA GET A MAKEOVER?
WHATEVER YA DID, IT REALLY BRINGS OUT THE *GLOW* IN YOUR EYES.

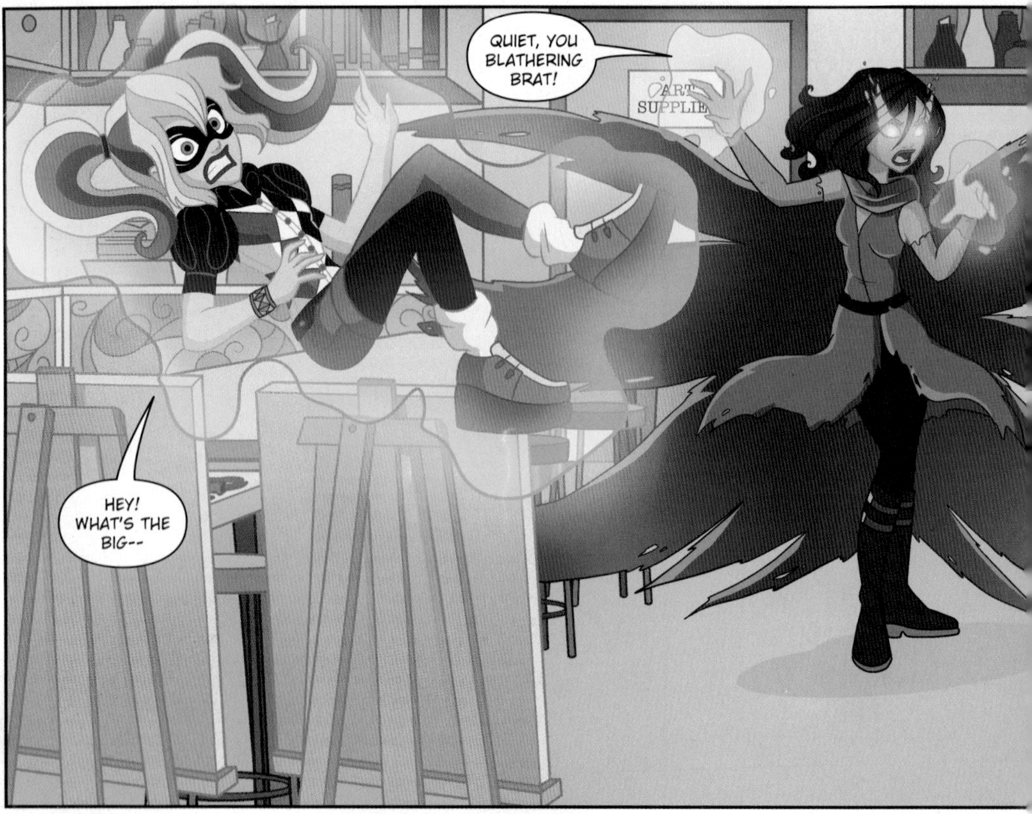
HEY! WHAT'S THE BIG--
QUIET, YOU BLATHERING BRAT!
ART SUPPLIE

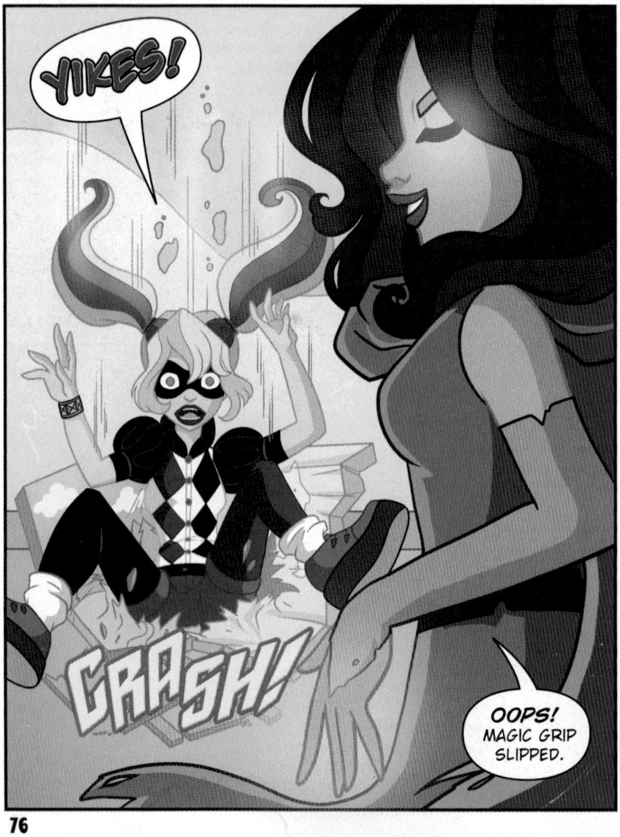
YIKES!
CRASH!
OOPS! MAGIC GRIP SLIPPED.

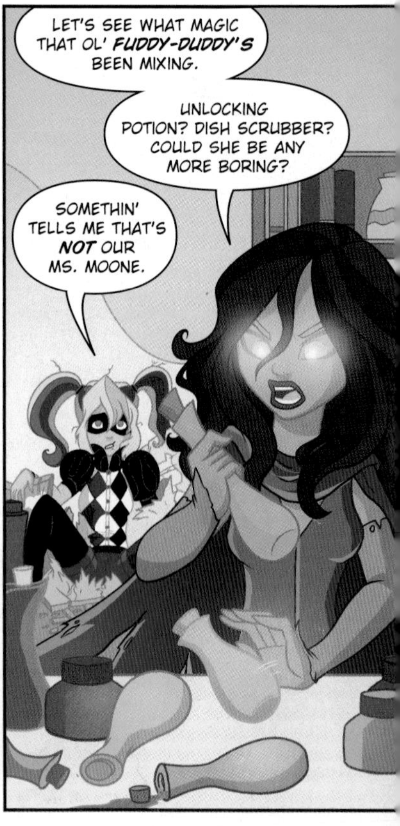
LET'S SEE WHAT MAGIC THAT OL' FUDDY-DUDDY'S BEEN MIXING.
UNLOCKING POTION? DISH SCRUBBER? COULD SHE BE ANY MORE BORING?
SOMETHIN' TELLS ME THAT'S NOT OUR MS. MOONE.

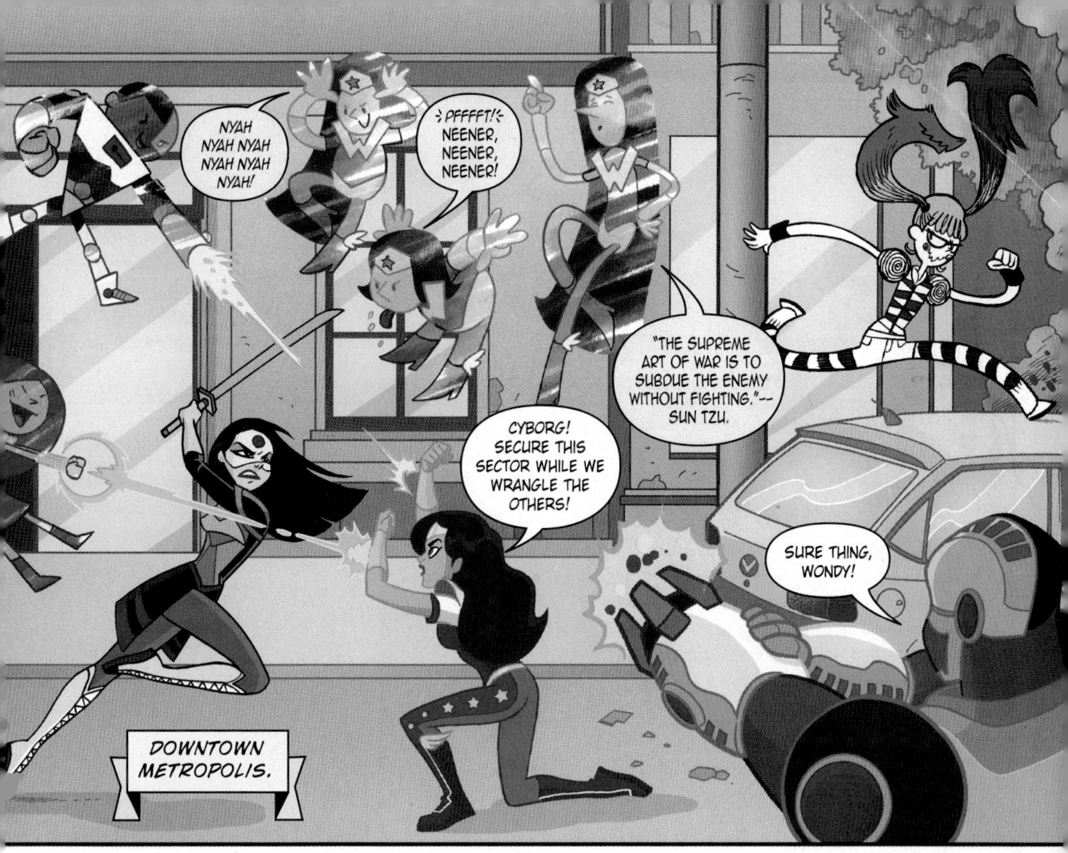
NYAH NYAH NYAH NYAH NYAH NYAH!
PFFFFT! NEENER, NEENER, NEENER!
"THE SUPREME ART OF WAR IS TO SUBDUE THE ENEMY WITHOUT FIGHTING."-- SUN TZU.
CYBORG! SECURE THIS SECTOR WHILE WE WRANGLE THE OTHERS!
SURE THING, WONDY!
DOWNTOWN METROPOLIS.

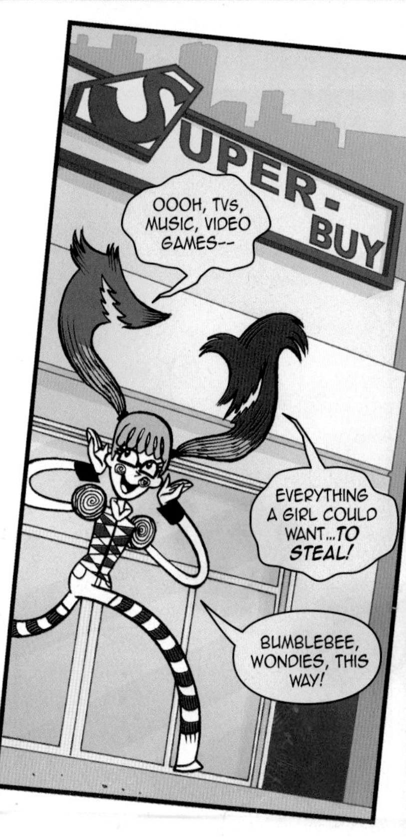
SUPER-BUY
OOOH, TVS, MUSIC, VIDEO GAMES--
EVERYTHING A GIRL COULD WANT...TO STEAL!
BUMBLEBEE, WONDIES, THIS WAY!

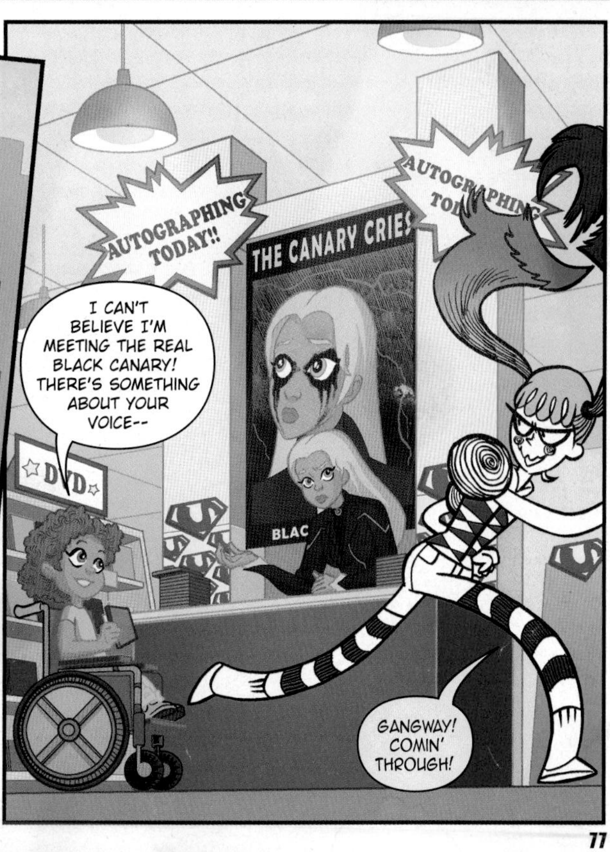
AUTOGRAPHING TODAY!!
THE CANARY CRIES
I CAN'T BELIEVE I'M MEETING THE REAL BLACK CANARY! THERE'S SOMETHING ABOUT YOUR VOICE--
DVD
GANGWAY! COMIN' THROUGH!

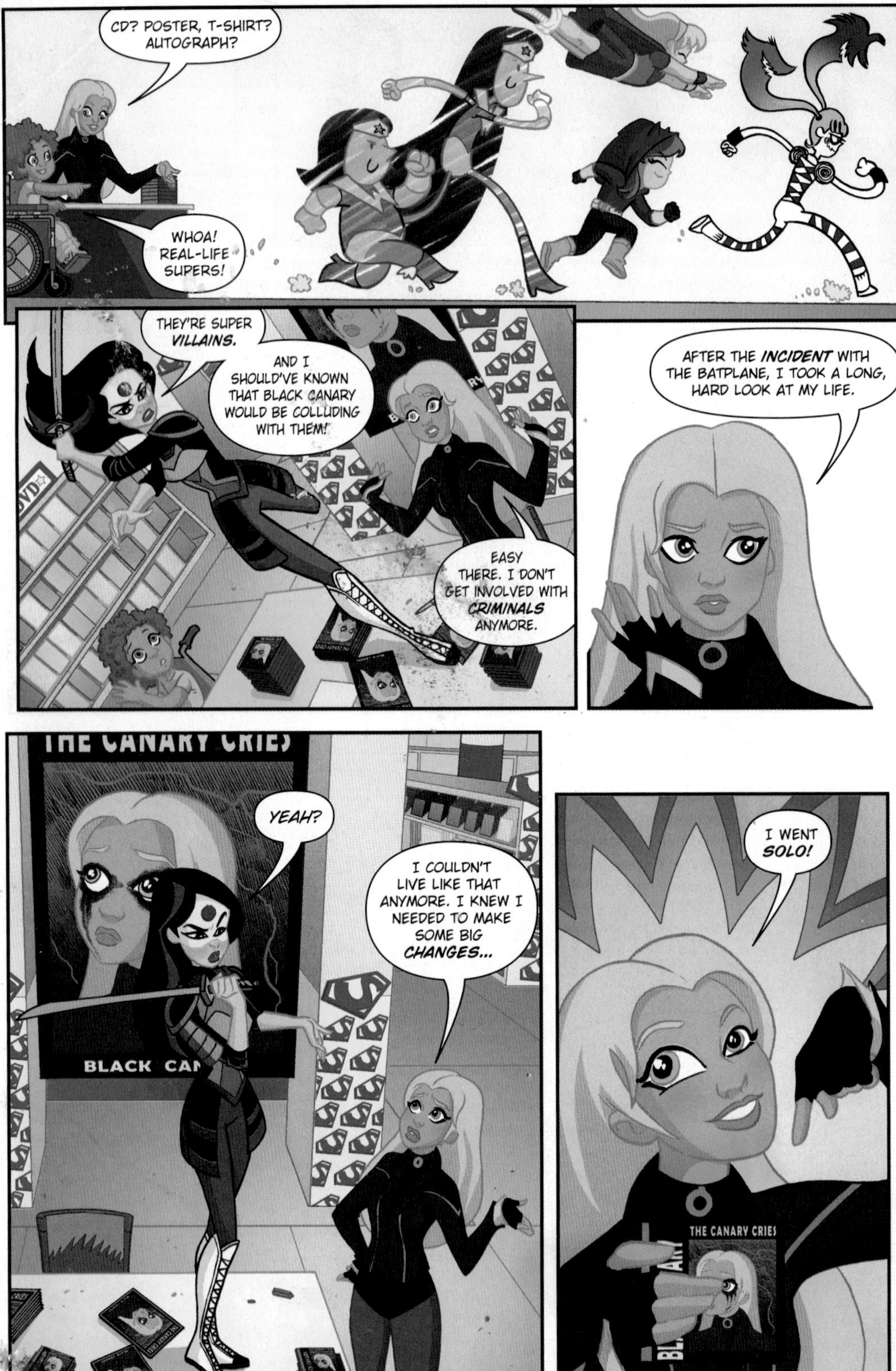

CD? POSTER, T-SHIRT? AUTOGRAPH?
WHOA! REAL-LIFE SUPERS!
THEY'RE SUPER *VILLAINS.*
AND I SHOULD'VE KNOWN THAT BLACK CANARY WOULD BE COLLUDING WITH THEM!
EASY THERE. I DON'T GET INVOLVED WITH *CRIMINALS* ANYMORE.
AFTER THE *INCIDENT* WITH THE BATPLANE, I TOOK A LONG, HARD LOOK AT MY LIFE.
THE CANARY CRIES
BLACK CAN
YEAH?
I COULDN'T LIVE LIKE THAT ANYMORE. I KNEW I NEEDED TO MAKE SOME BIG *CHANGES...*
I WENT *SOLO!*
THE CANARY CRIES

79

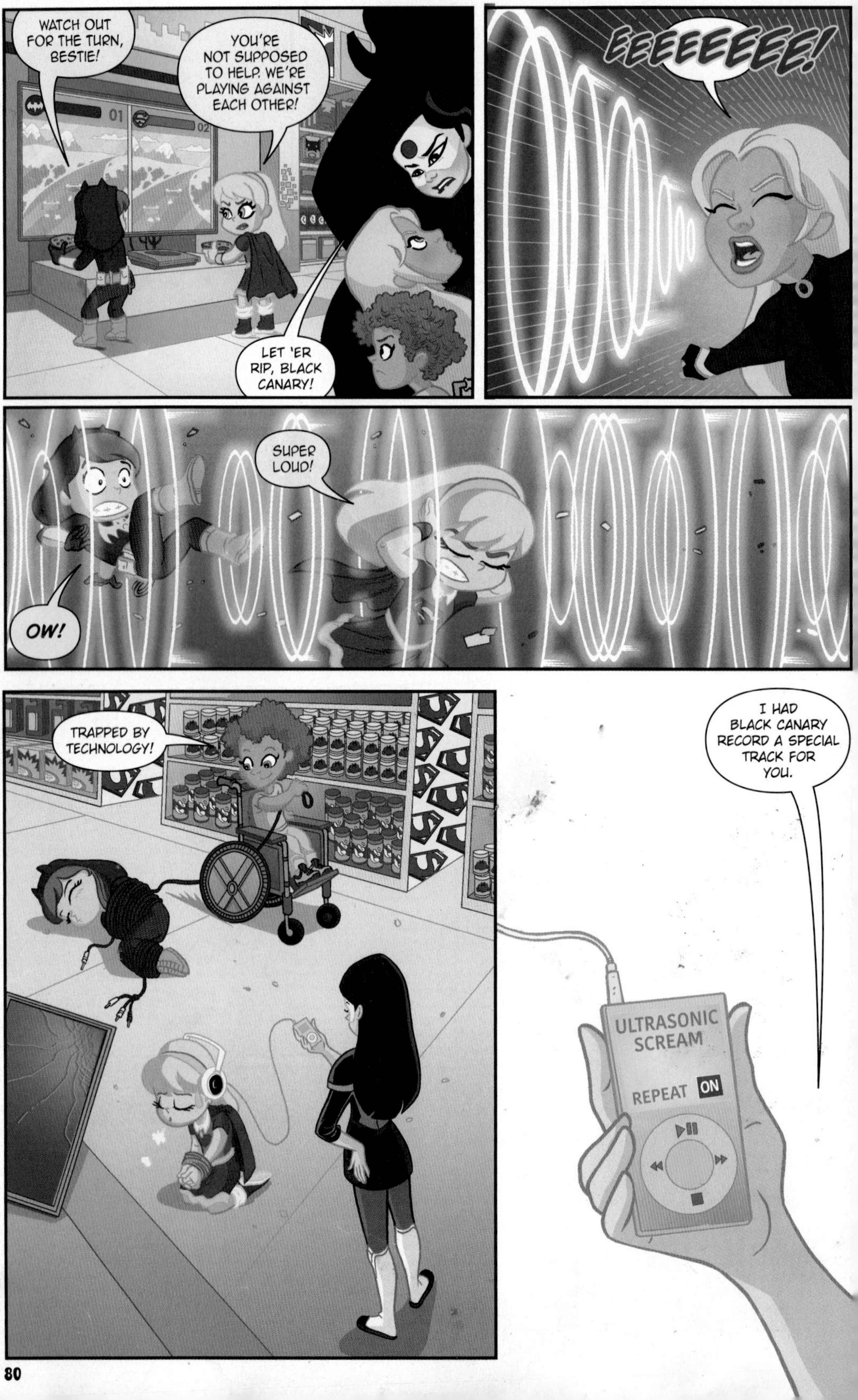
WATCH OUT FOR THE TURN, BESTIE!
YOU'RE NOT SUPPOSED TO HELP. WE'RE PLAYING AGAINST EACH OTHER!
LET 'ER RIP, BLACK CANARY!
EEEEEEEE!
SUPER LOUD!
OW!
TRAPPED BY TECHNOLOGY!
I HAD BLACK CANARY RECORD A SPECIAL TRACK FOR YOU.
ULTRASONIC SCREAM
REPEAT ON

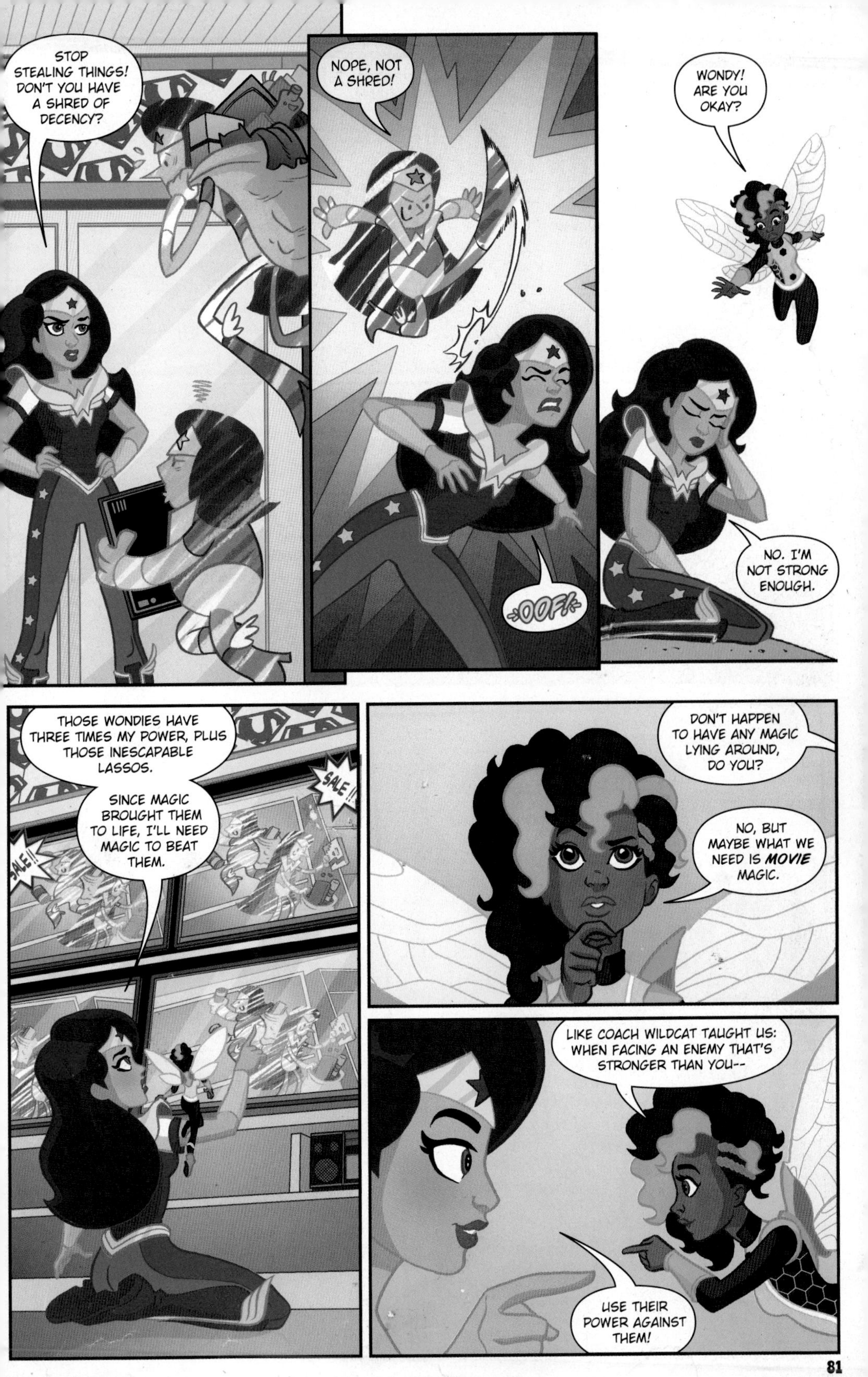
STOP STEALING THINGS! DON'T YOU HAVE A SHRED OF DECENCY?
NOPE, NOT A SHRED!
OOF!
WONDY! ARE YOU OKAY?
NO. I'M NOT STRONG ENOUGH.
THOSE WONDIES HAVE THREE TIMES MY POWER, PLUS THOSE INESCAPABLE LASSOS.
SINCE MAGIC BROUGHT THEM TO LIFE, I'LL NEED MAGIC TO BEAT THEM.
SALE!!
SALE!!
DON'T HAPPEN TO HAVE ANY MAGIC LYING AROUND, DO YOU?
NO, BUT MAYBE WHAT WE NEED IS ***MOVIE*** MAGIC.
LIKE COACH WILDCAT TAUGHT US: WHEN FACING AN ENEMY THAT'S STRONGER THAN YOU--
USE THEIR POWER AGAINST THEM!

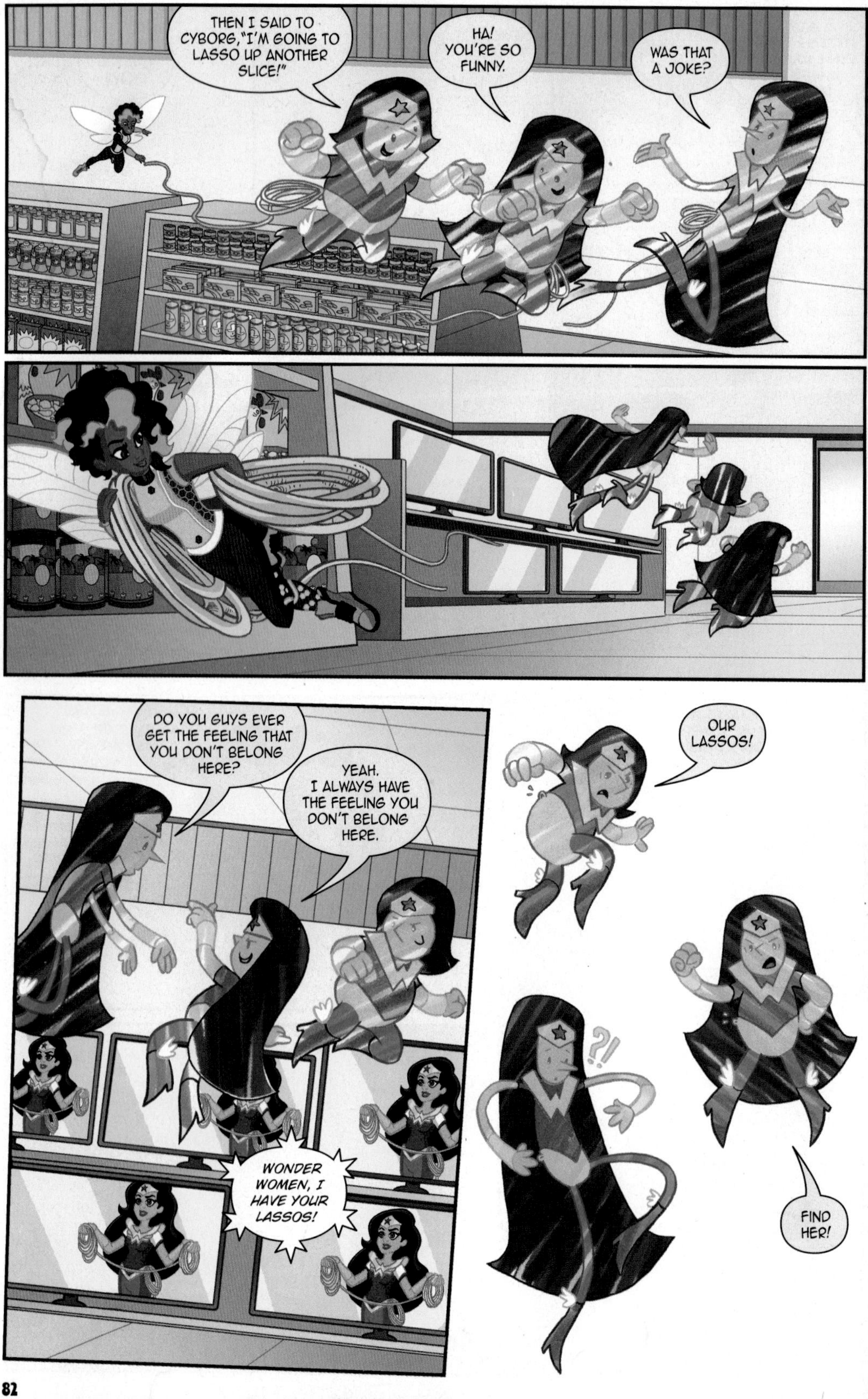

THEN I SAID TO CYBORG, "I'M GOING TO LASSO UP ANOTHER SLICE!"
HA! YOU'RE SO FUNNY.
WAS THAT A JOKE?
DO YOU GUYS EVER GET THE FEELING THAT YOU DON'T BELONG HERE?
YEAH. I ALWAYS HAVE THE FEELING YOU DON'T BELONG HERE.
WONDER WOMEN, I HAVE YOUR LASSOS!
OUR LASSOS!
?!
FIND HER!

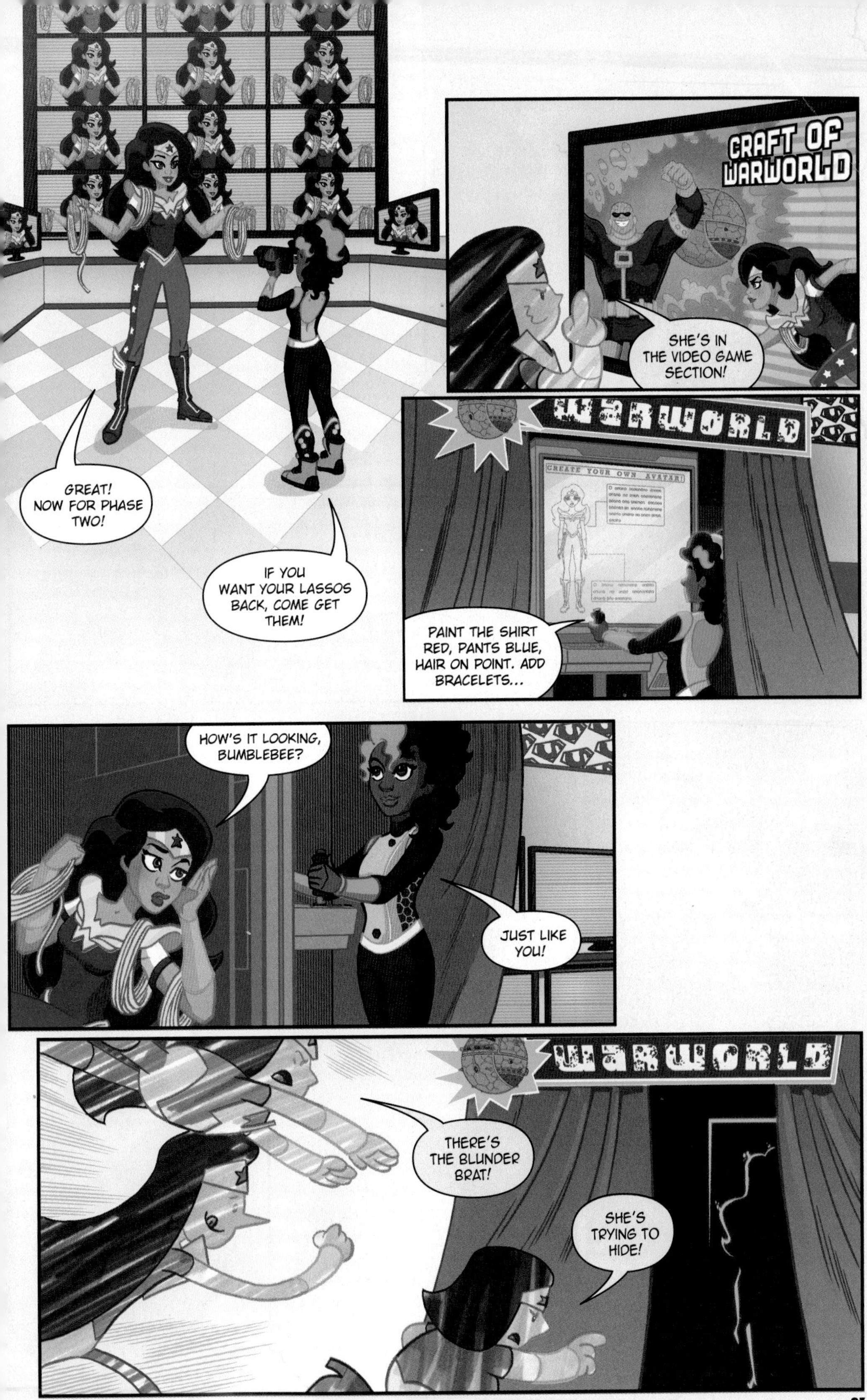
GREAT! NOW FOR PHASE TWO!
IF YOU WANT YOUR LASSOS BACK, COME GET THEM!
CRAFT OF WARWORLD
SHE'S IN THE VIDEO GAME SECTION!
WARWORLD
CREATE YOUR OWN AVATAR!
PAINT THE SHIRT RED, PANTS BLUE, HAIR ON POINT. ADD BRACELETS...
HOW'S IT LOOKING, BUMBLEBEE?
JUST LIKE YOU!
WARWORLD
THERE'S THE BLUNDER BRAT!
SHE'S TRYING TO HIDE!

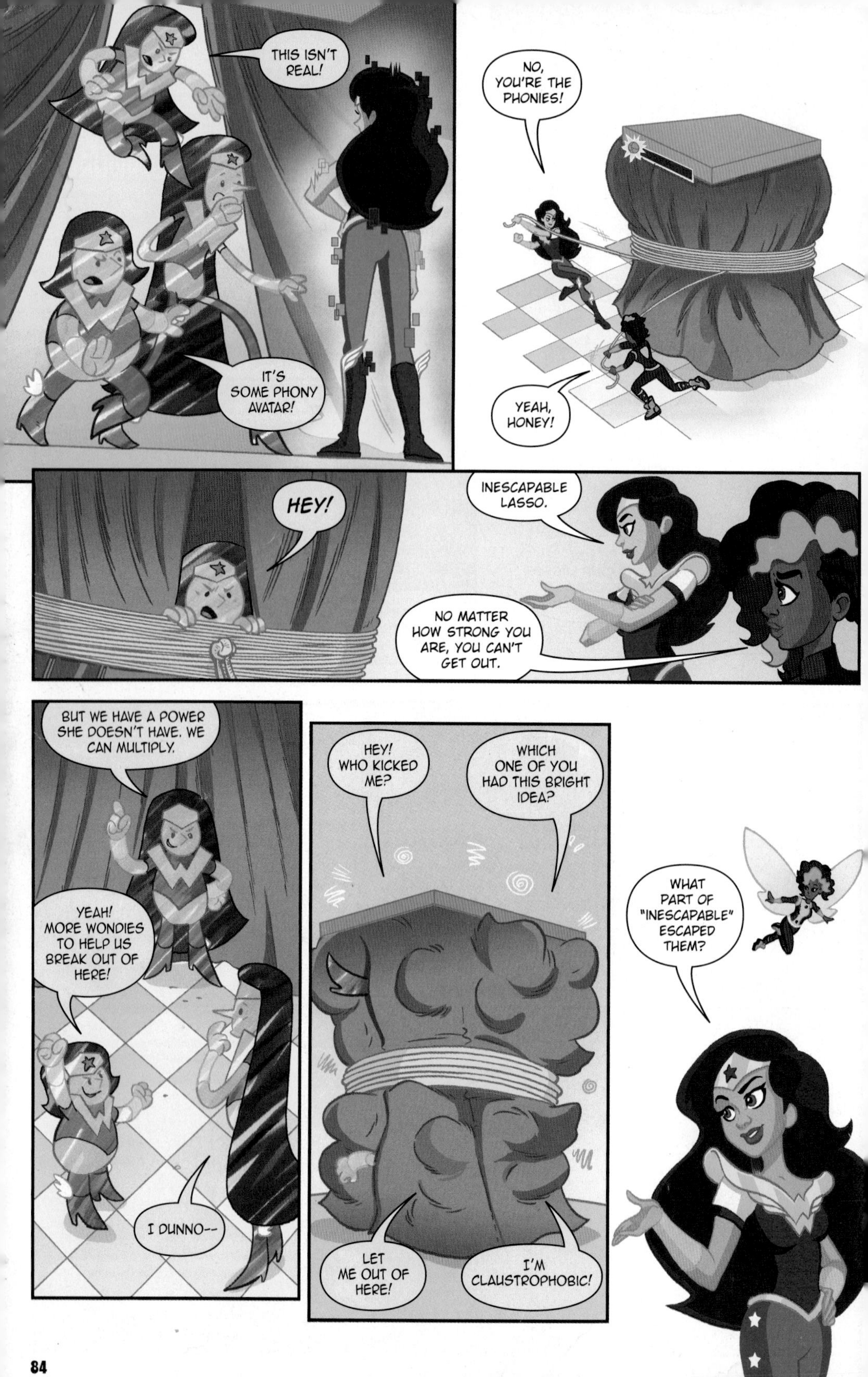
THIS ISN'T REAL!
IT'S SOME PHONY AVATAR!
NO, YOU'RE THE PHONIES!
YEAH, HONEY!
HEY!
INESCAPABLE LASSO.
NO MATTER HOW STRONG YOU ARE, YOU CAN'T GET OUT.
BUT WE HAVE A POWER SHE DOESN'T HAVE. WE CAN MULTIPLY.
YEAH! MORE WONDIES TO HELP US BREAK OUT OF HERE!
I DUNNO--
HEY! WHO KICKED ME?
WHICH ONE OF YOU HAD THIS BRIGHT IDEA?
LET ME OUT OF HERE!
I'M CLAUSTROPHOBIC!
WHAT PART OF "INESCAPABLE" ESCAPED THEM?

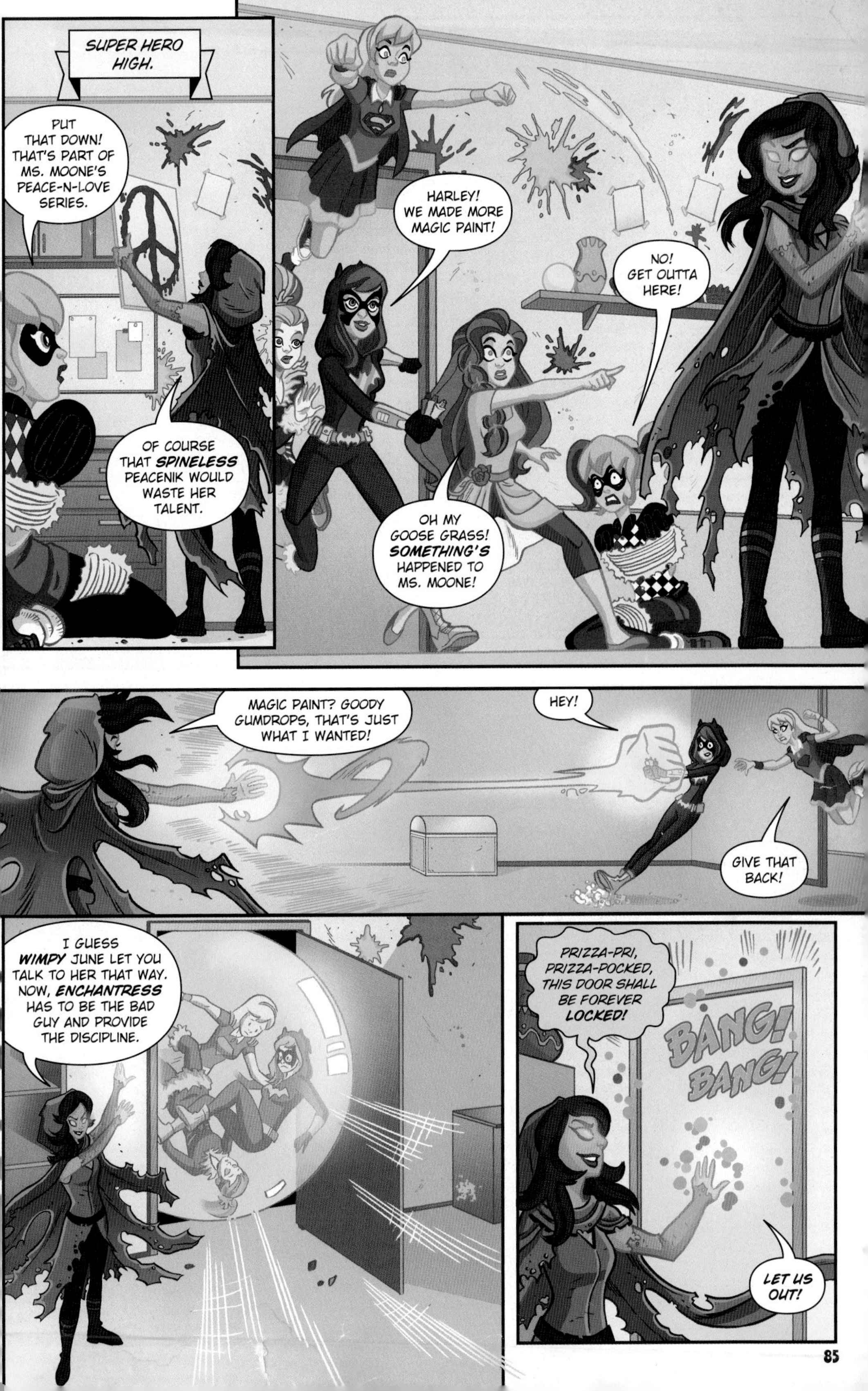
SUPER HERO HIGH.
PUT THAT DOWN! THAT'S PART OF MS. MOONE'S PEACE-N-LOVE SERIES.
OF COURSE THAT **SPINELESS** PEACENIK WOULD WASTE HER TALENT.
HARLEY! WE MADE MORE MAGIC PAINT!
OH MY GOOSE GRASS! **SOMETHING'S** HAPPENED TO MS. MOONE!
NO! GET OUTTA HERE!
MAGIC PAINT? GOODY GUMDROPS, THAT'S JUST WHAT I WANTED!
HEY!
GIVE THAT BACK!
I GUESS **WIMPY** JUNE LET YOU TALK TO HER THAT WAY. NOW, **ENCHANTRESS** HAS TO BE THE BAD GUY AND PROVIDE THE DISCIPLINE.
PRIZZA-PRI, PRIZZA-POCKED, THIS DOOR SHALL BE FOREVER **LOCKED!**
BANG! BANG!
LET US OUT!

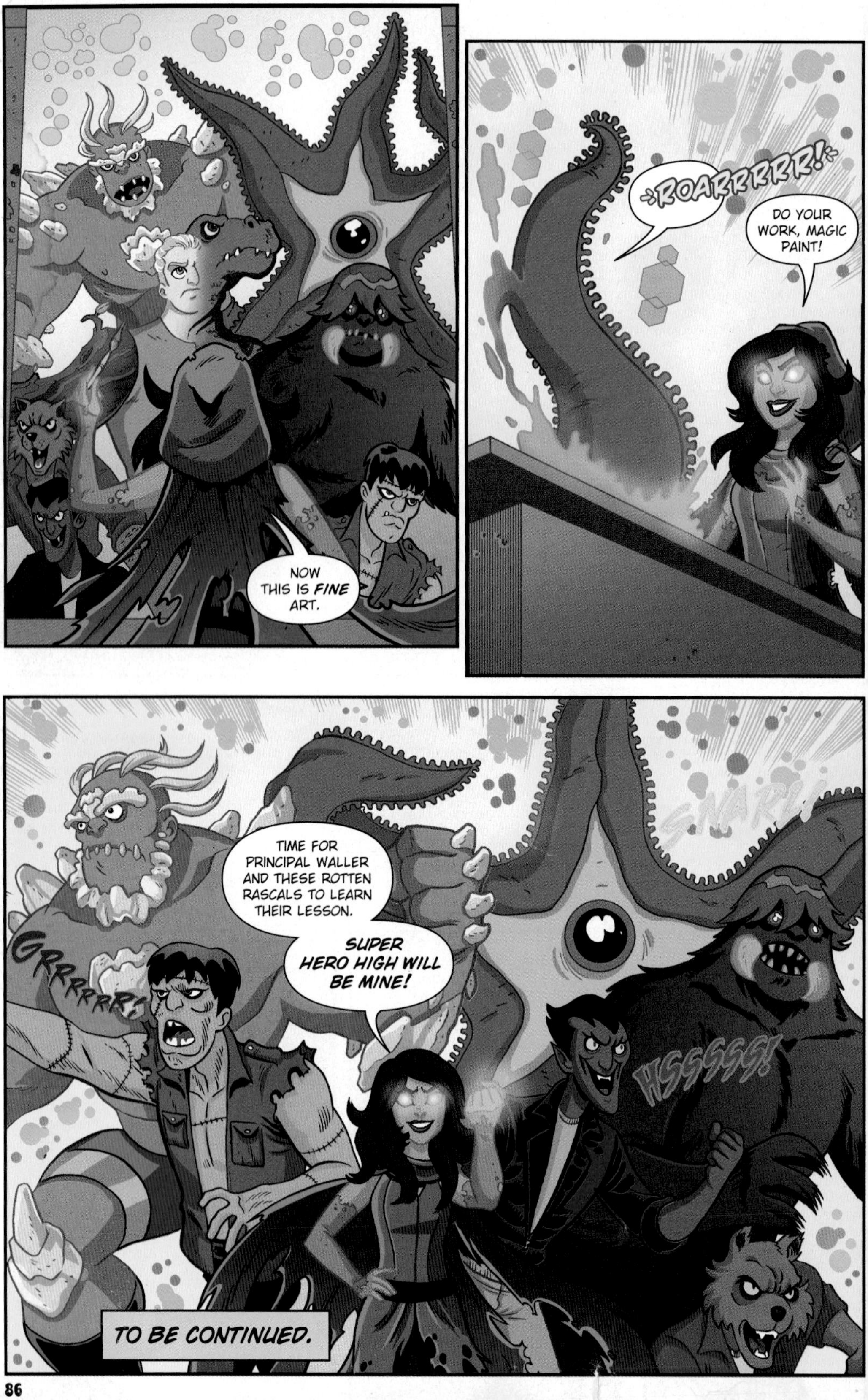
NOW THIS IS *FINE* ART.
ROARRRRR!
DO YOUR WORK, MAGIC PAINT!
TIME FOR PRINCIPAL WALLER AND THESE ROTTEN RASCALS TO LEARN THEIR LESSON.
SUPER HERO HIGH WILL BE MINE!
SNARL!
GRRRRRR!
HSSSSS!
TO BE CONTINUED.

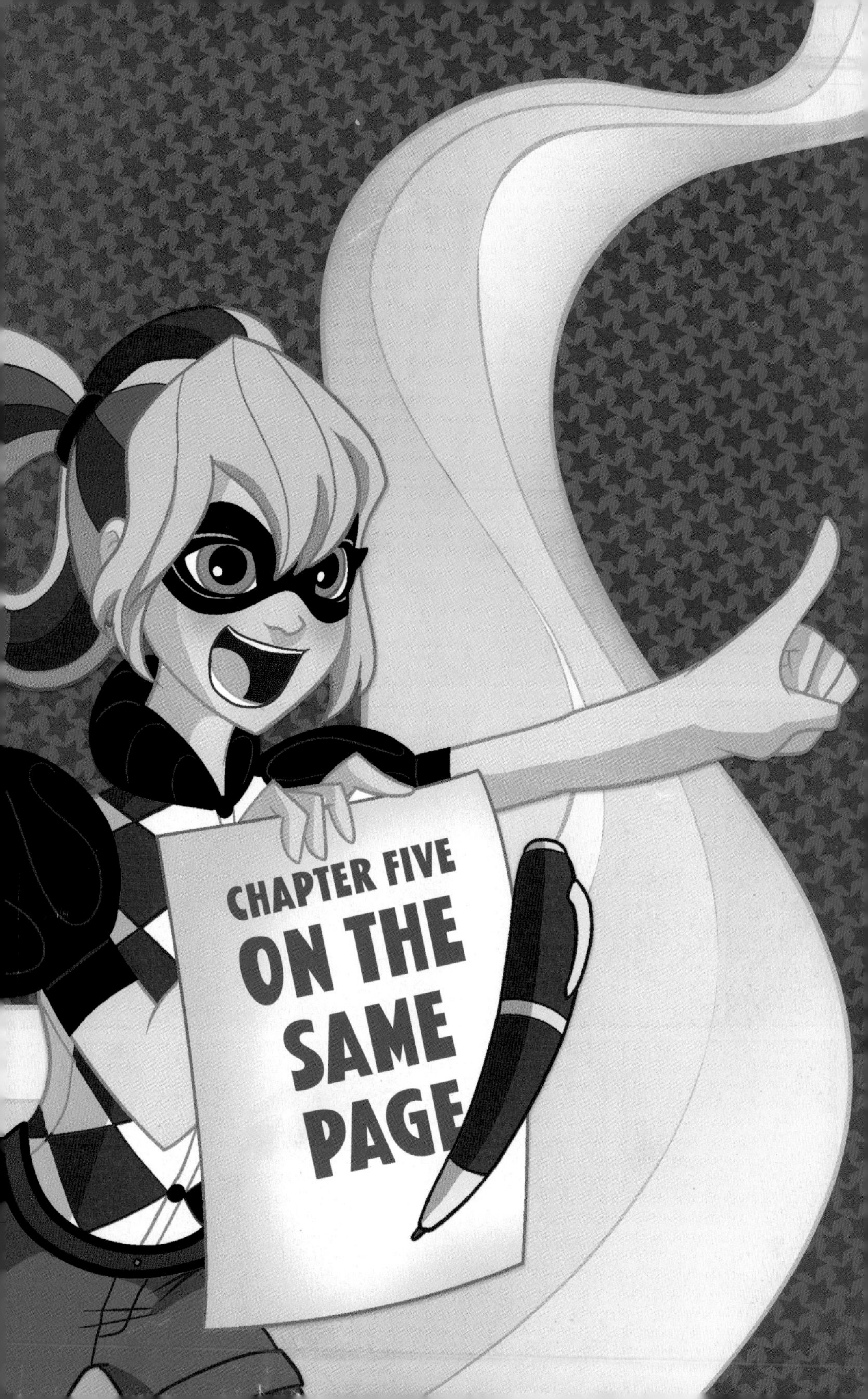
CHAPTER FIVE
ON THE SAME PAGE

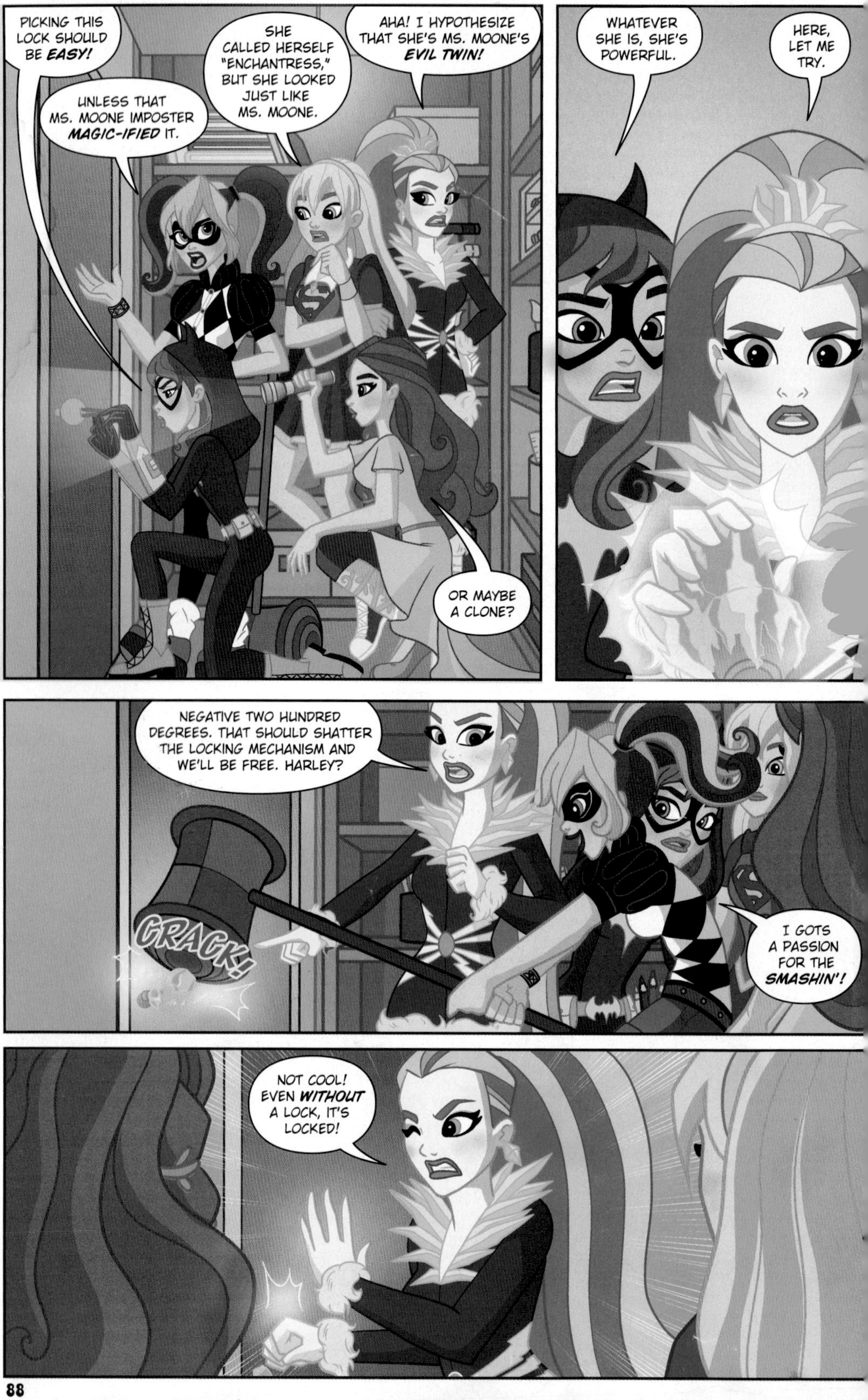
PICKING THIS LOCK SHOULD BE **EASY!**
UNLESS THAT MS. MOONE IMPOSTER **MAGIC-IFIED** IT.
SHE CALLED HERSELF "ENCHANTRESS," BUT SHE LOOKED JUST LIKE MS. MOONE.
AHA! I HYPOTHESIZE THAT SHE'S MS. MOONE'S **EVIL TWIN!**
OR MAYBE A CLONE?
WHATEVER SHE IS, SHE'S POWERFUL.
HERE, LET ME TRY.
NEGATIVE TWO HUNDRED DEGREES. THAT SHOULD SHATTER THE LOCKING MECHANISM AND WE'LL BE FREE. HARLEY?
CRACK!
I GOTS A PASSION FOR THE **SMASHIN'!**
NOT COOL! EVEN **WITHOUT** A LOCK, IT'S LOCKED!

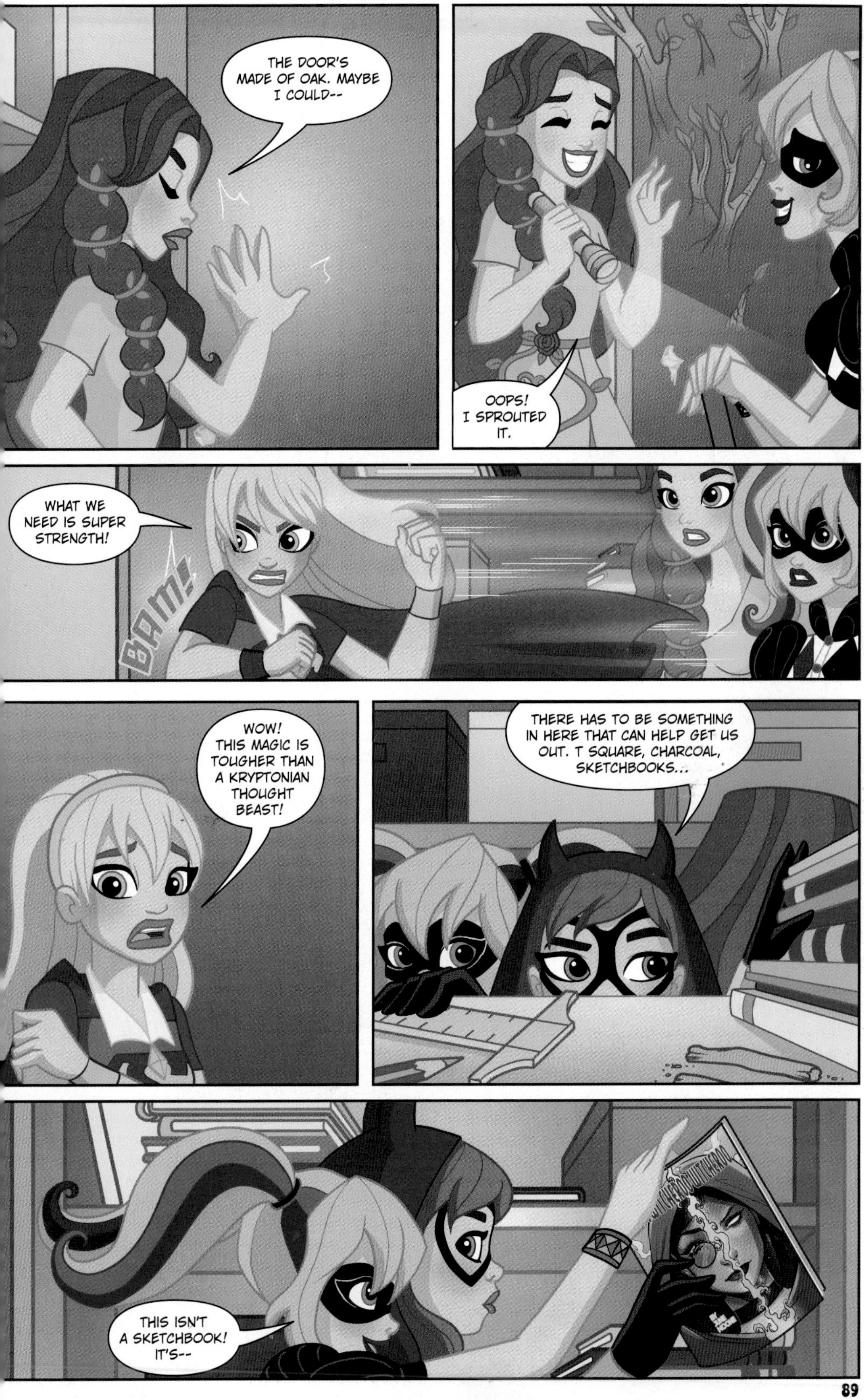
THE DOOR'S MADE OF OAK. MAYBE I COULD--
OOPS! I SPROUTED IT.
WHAT WE NEED IS SUPER STRENGTH!
BAM!
WOW! THIS MAGIC IS TOUGHER THAN A KRYPTONIAN THOUGHT BEAST!
THERE HAS TO BE SOMETHING IN HERE THAT CAN HELP GET US OUT. T SQUARE, CHARCOAL, SKETCHBOOKS...
THIS ISN'T A SKETCHBOOK! IT'S--

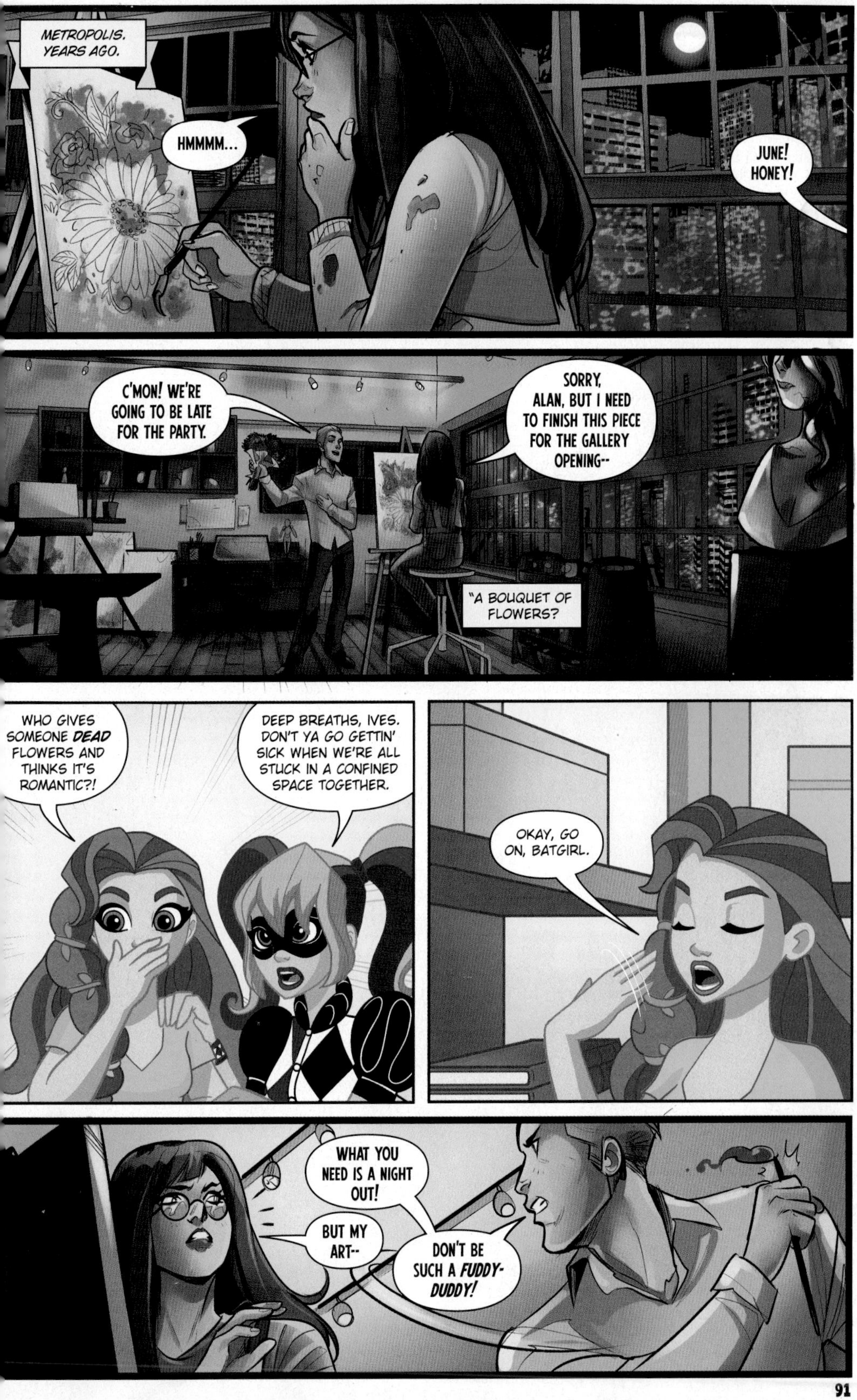
METROPOLIS. YEARS AGO.
HMMMM...
JUNE! HONEY!
C'MON! WE'RE GOING TO BE LATE FOR THE PARTY.
SORRY, ALAN, BUT I NEED TO FINISH THIS PIECE FOR THE GALLERY OPENING--
"A BOUQUET OF FLOWERS?
WHO GIVES SOMEONE DEAD FLOWERS AND THINKS IT'S ROMANTIC?!
DEEP BREATHS, IVES. DON'T YA GO GETTIN' SICK WHEN WE'RE ALL STUCK IN A CONFINED SPACE TOGETHER.
OKAY, GO ON, BATGIRL.
WHAT YOU NEED IS A NIGHT OUT!
BUT MY ART--
DON'T BE SUCH A FUDDY-DUDDY!

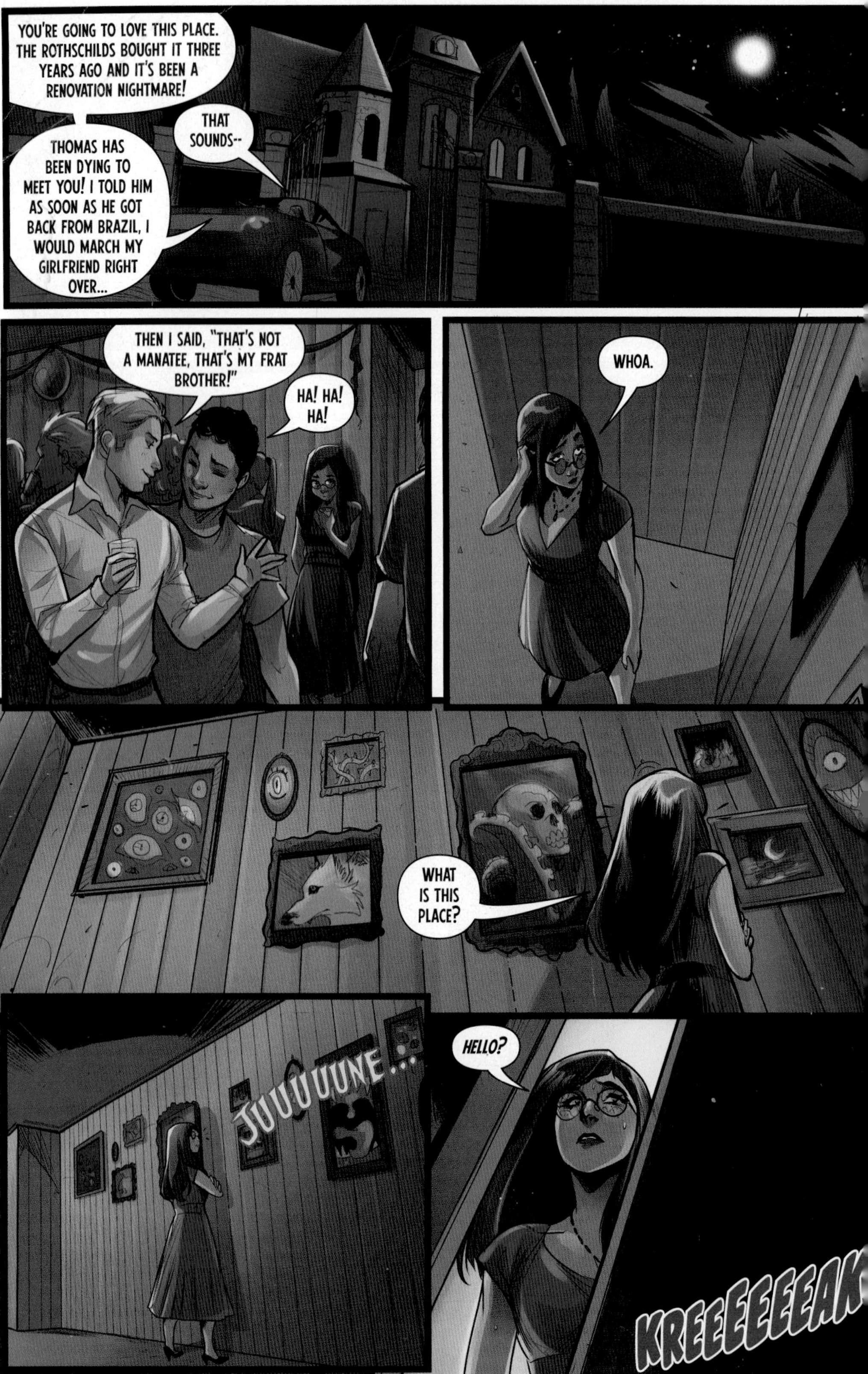
YOU'RE GOING TO LOVE THIS PLACE. THE ROTHSCHILDS BOUGHT IT THREE YEARS AGO AND IT'S BEEN A RENOVATION NIGHTMARE!
THOMAS HAS BEEN DYING TO MEET YOU! I TOLD HIM AS SOON AS HE GOT BACK FROM BRAZIL, I WOULD MARCH MY GIRLFRIEND RIGHT OVER...
THAT SOUNDS--
THEN I SAID, "THAT'S NOT A MANATEE, THAT'S MY FRAT BROTHER!"
HA! HA! HA!
WHOA.
WHAT IS THIS PLACE?
JUUUUUNE...
HELLO?
KREEEEEEAK

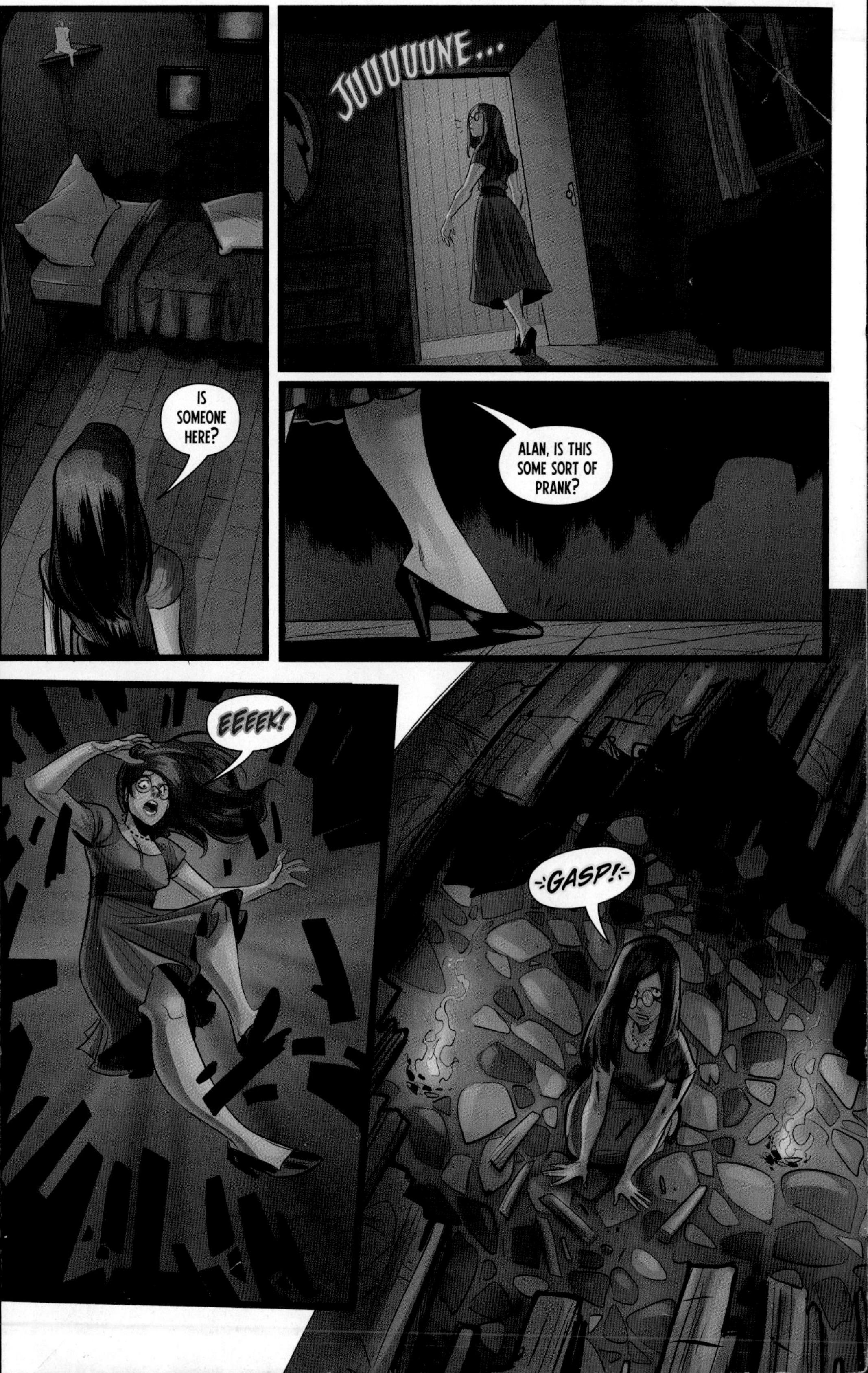
JUUUUUNE...
IS SOMEONE HERE?
ALAN, IS THIS SOME SORT OF PRANK?
EEEEK!
GASP!

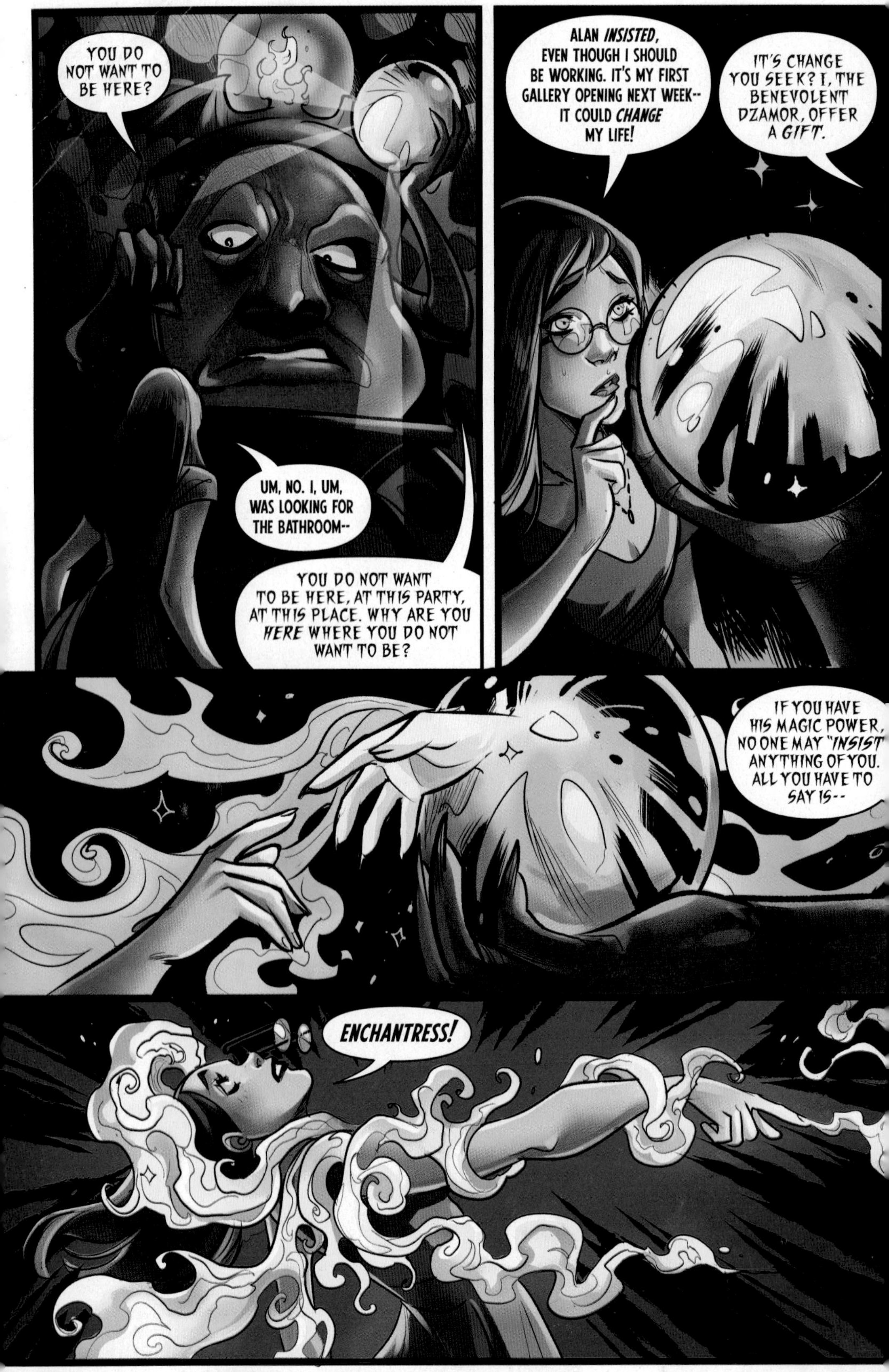
YOU DO NOT WANT TO BE HERE?
UM, NO. I, UM, WAS LOOKING FOR THE BATHROOM--
YOU DO NOT WANT TO BE HERE, AT THIS PARTY, AT THIS PLACE. WHY ARE YOU *HERE* WHERE YOU DO NOT WANT TO BE?
ALAN *INSISTED*, EVEN THOUGH I SHOULD BE WORKING. IT'S MY FIRST GALLERY OPENING NEXT WEEK-- IT COULD *CHANGE* MY LIFE!
IT'S CHANGE YOU SEEK? I, THE BENEVOLENT DZAMOR, OFFER A *GIFT*.
IF YOU HAVE HIS MAGIC POWER, NO ONE MAY "*INSIST*" ANYTHING OF YOU. ALL YOU HAVE TO *SAY* IS--
ENCHANTRESS!

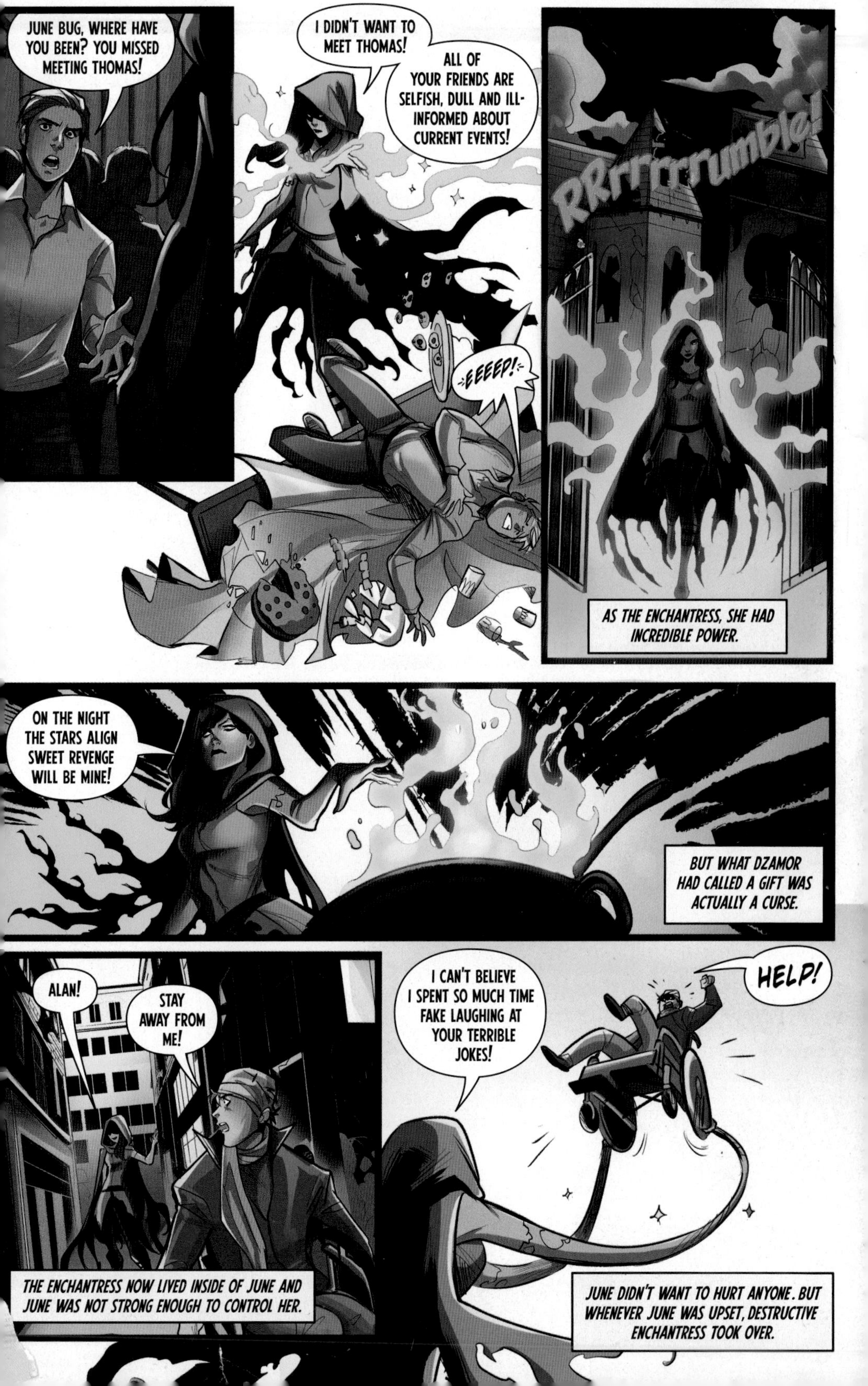
JUNE BUG, WHERE HAVE YOU BEEN? YOU MISSED MEETING THOMAS!
I DIDN'T WANT TO MEET THOMAS!
ALL OF YOUR FRIENDS ARE SELFISH, DULL AND ILL-INFORMED ABOUT CURRENT EVENTS!
EEEEP!
RRrrrrrumble!
AS THE ENCHANTRESS, SHE HAD INCREDIBLE POWER.
ON THE NIGHT THE STARS ALIGN SWEET REVENGE WILL BE MINE!
BUT WHAT DZAMOR HAD CALLED A GIFT WAS ACTUALLY A CURSE.
ALAN!
STAY AWAY FROM ME!
THE ENCHANTRESS NOW LIVED INSIDE OF JUNE AND JUNE WAS NOT STRONG ENOUGH TO CONTROL HER.
I CAN'T BELIEVE I SPENT SO MUCH TIME FAKE LAUGHING AT YOUR TERRIBLE JOKES!
HELP!
JUNE DIDN'T WANT TO HURT ANYONE. BUT WHENEVER JUNE WAS UPSET, DESTRUCTIVE ENCHANTRESS TOOK OVER.

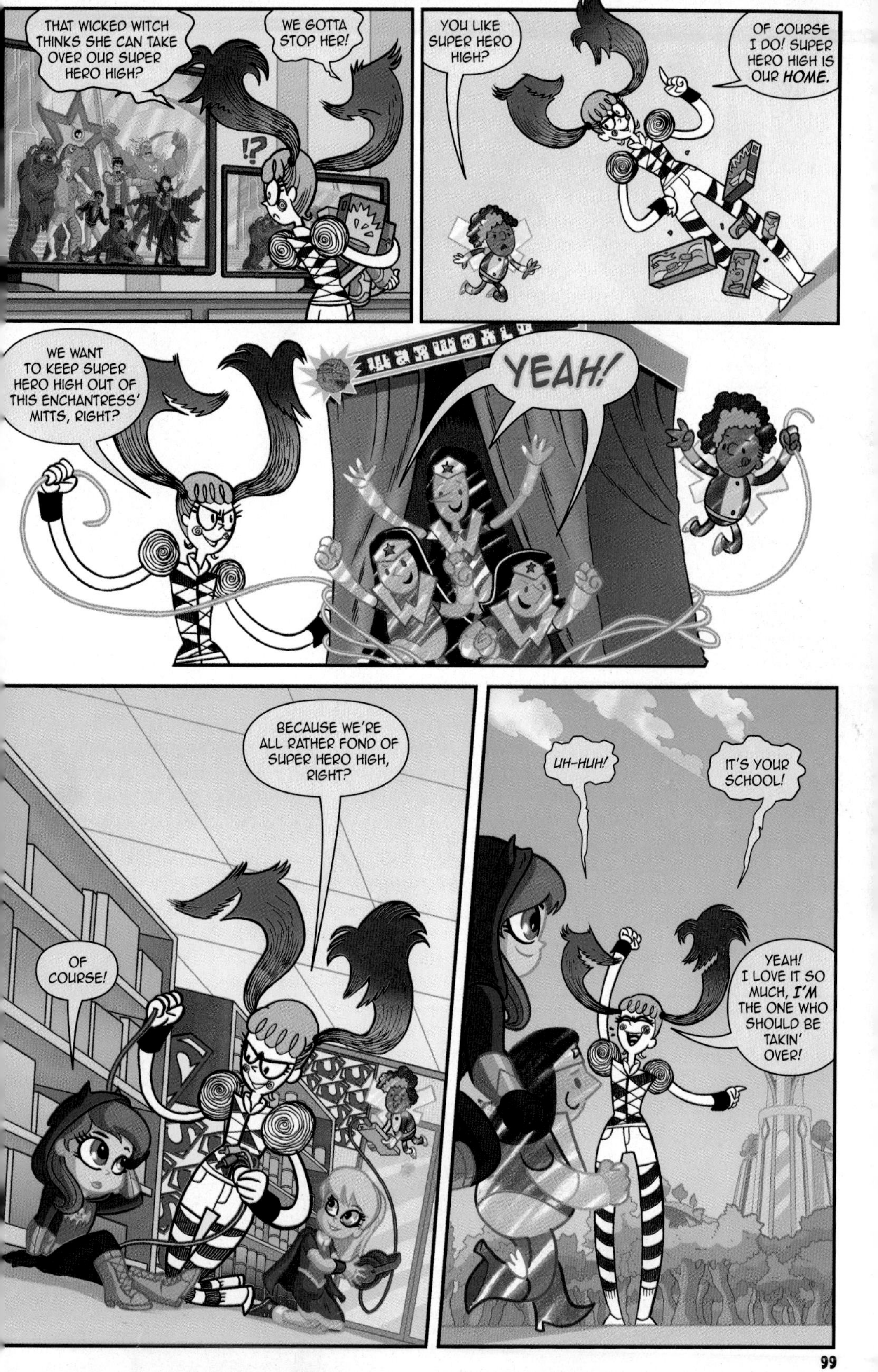
THAT WICKED WITCH THINKS SHE CAN TAKE OVER OUR SUPER HERO HIGH?
WE GOTTA STOP HER!
!?
YOU LIKE SUPER HERO HIGH?
OF COURSE I DO! SUPER HERO HIGH IS OUR **HOME.**
WE WANT TO KEEP SUPER HERO HIGH OUT OF THIS ENCHANTRESS' MITTS, RIGHT?
WARWORLD
YEAH!
BECAUSE WE'RE ALL RATHER FOND OF SUPER HERO HIGH, RIGHT?
OF COURSE!
UH-HUH!
IT'S YOUR SCHOOL!
YEAH! I LOVE IT SO MUCH, ***I'M*** THE ONE WHO SHOULD BE TAKIN' OVER!

I SENSE THE ARMIES FORMING AGAINST US. BUT THEY WILL NOT STAND.

OR ROOOOAR!

ROOOOAR!

ROOOOAR!

AWRIGHT, ENCHANTRESS! YOU'RE GOIN' DOWN!

YEAH!

UM, HOW ARE WE SUPPOSED TO FIGHT THOSE CARTOONS AND ENCHANTRESS' BEASTS AT THE SAME TIME?

YEP. BUT AS SOON AS SHE'S TAKEN CARE OF, I'M GOING TO GIVE THOSE COMIC BRATS A BEAT-DOWN.

WHEN I WAS IN HIGH SCHOOL, THEY TAUGHT US THAT THE ENEMY OF MY ENEMY IS AN ALLY.

THEREFORE, WE SHALL ALLOW THE DRAWINGS OF MUCH BADNESS TO ASSIST US IN DEFEATING THE ENCHANTED ONE!

KRACKKK!

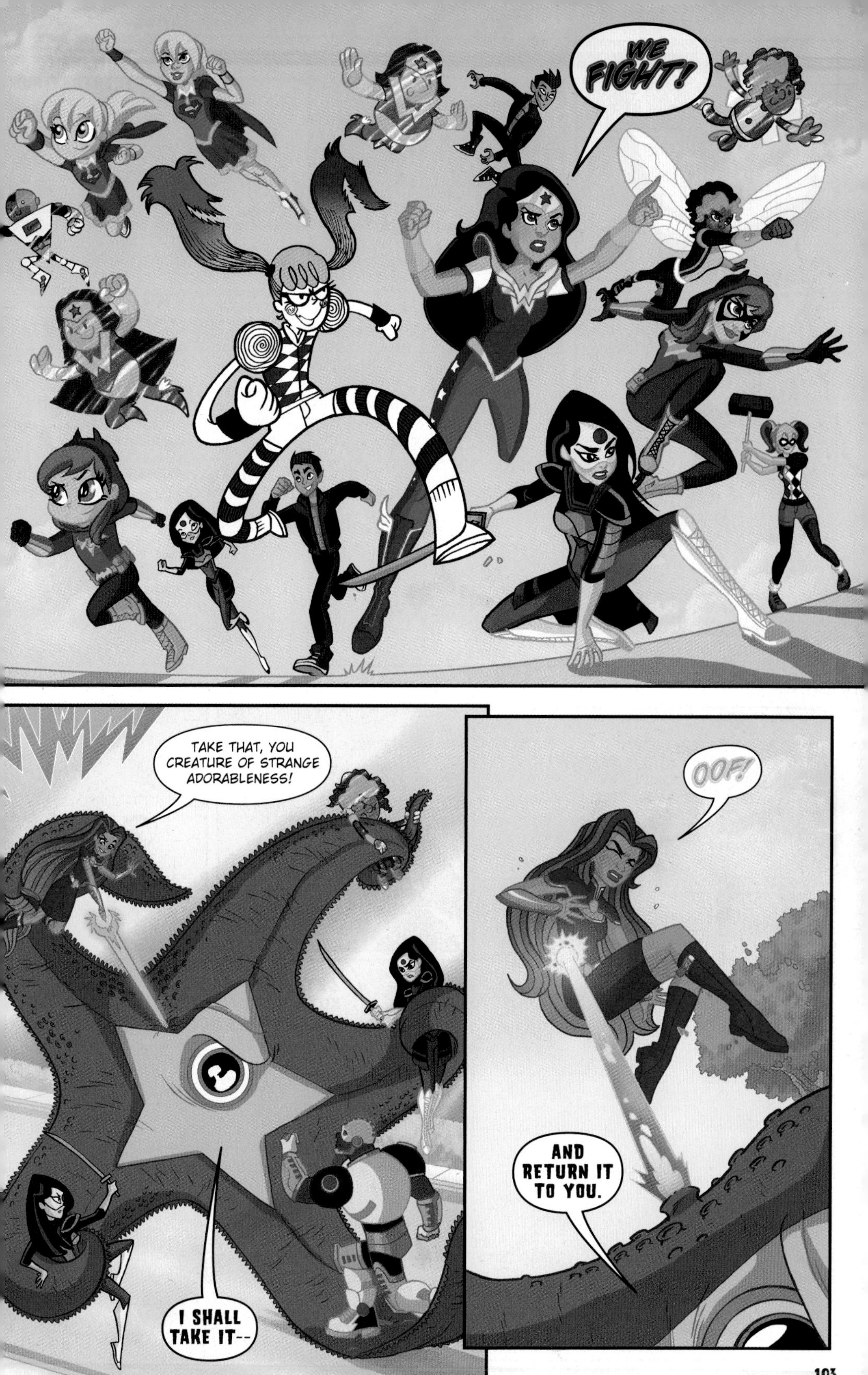
WE FIGHT!
TAKE THAT, YOU CREATURE OF STRANGE ADORABLENESS!
I SHALL TAKE IT--
OOF!
AND RETURN IT TO YOU.

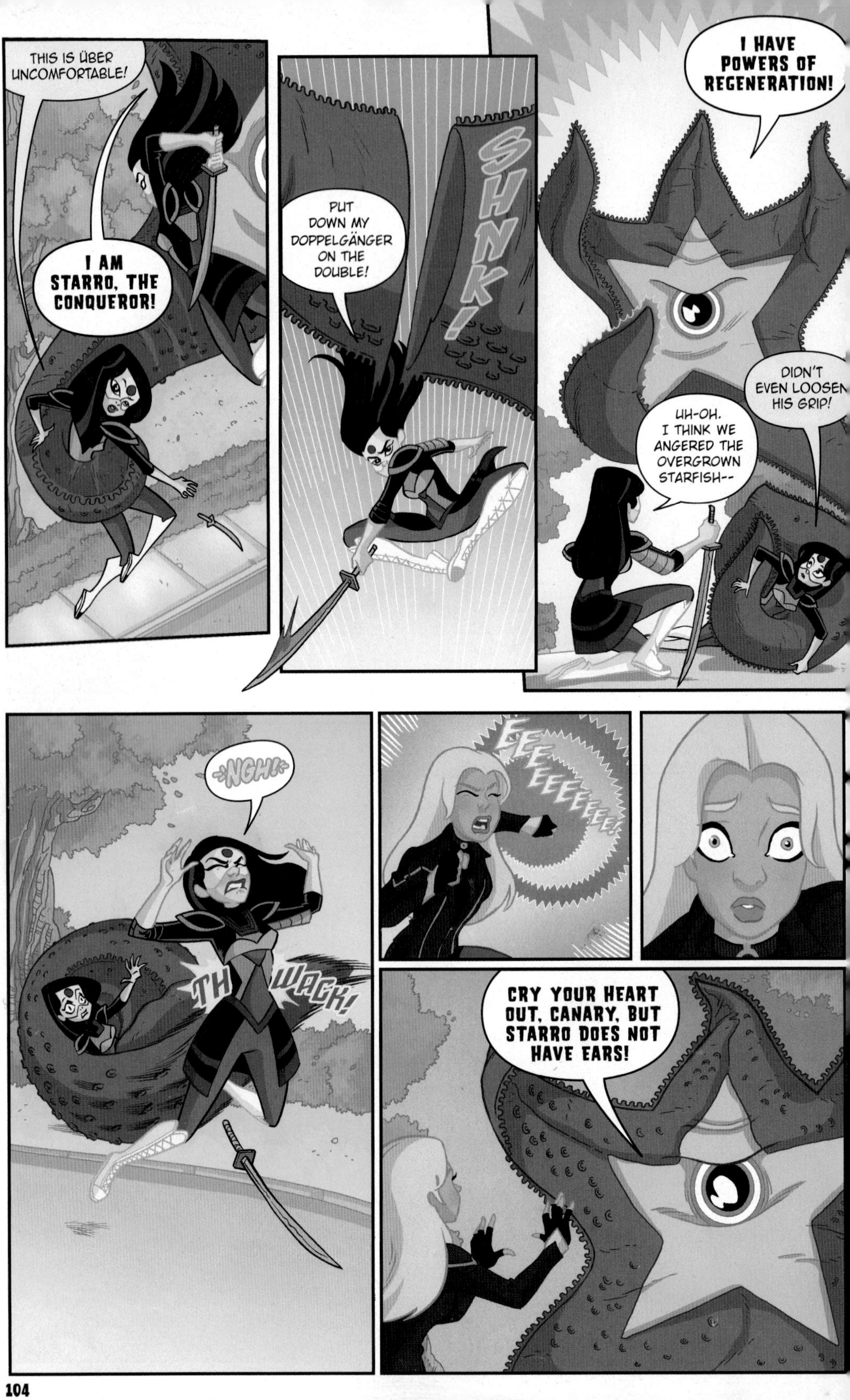
THIS IS ÜBER UNCOMFORTABLE!
I AM STARRO, THE CONQUEROR!
PUT DOWN MY DOPPELGÄNGER ON THE DOUBLE!
SHNKK!
I HAVE POWERS OF REGENERATION!
UH-OH. I THINK WE ANGERED THE OVERGROWN STARFISH--
DIDN'T EVEN LOOSEN HIS GRIP!
-NGH!-
THWACK!
EEEEEEEEEE!
CRY YOUR HEART OUT, CANARY, BUT STARRO DOES NOT HAVE EARS!

CHAPTER SIX
FINAL DRAFT

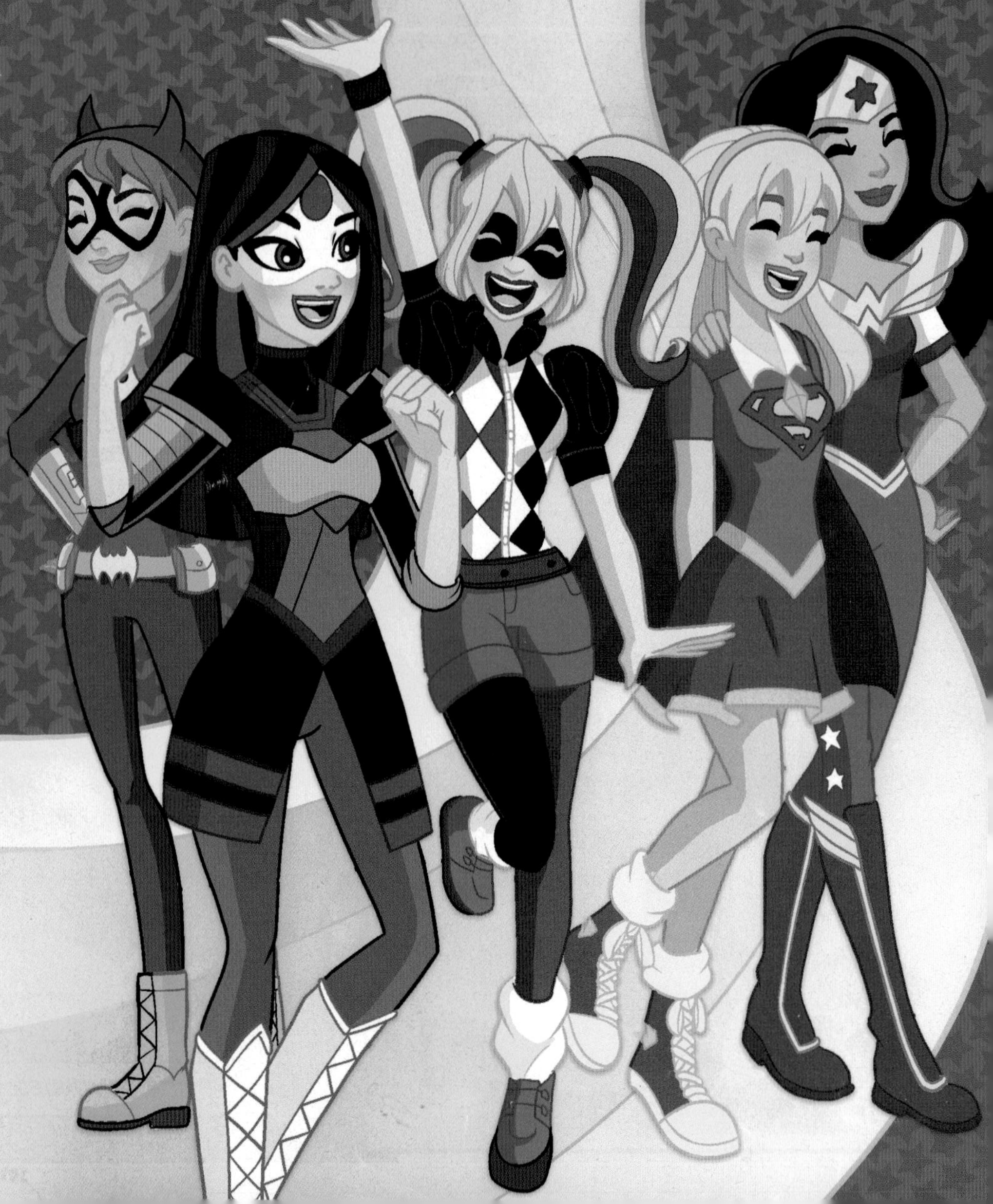

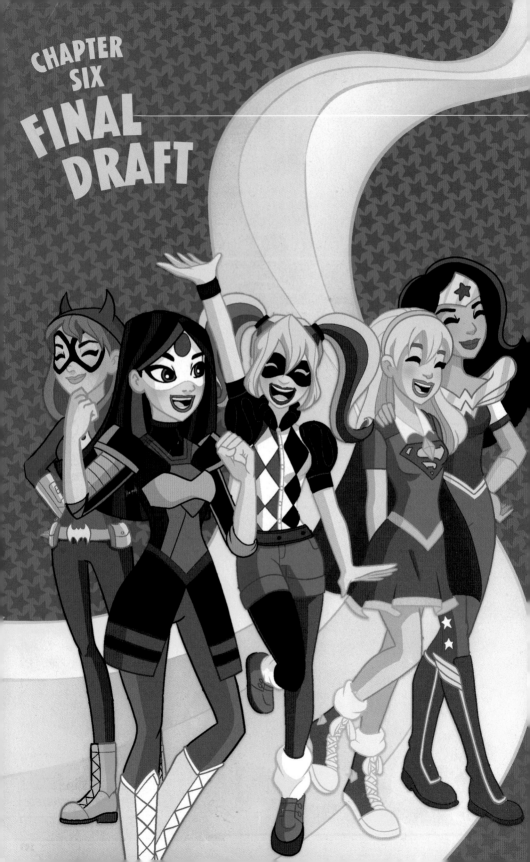

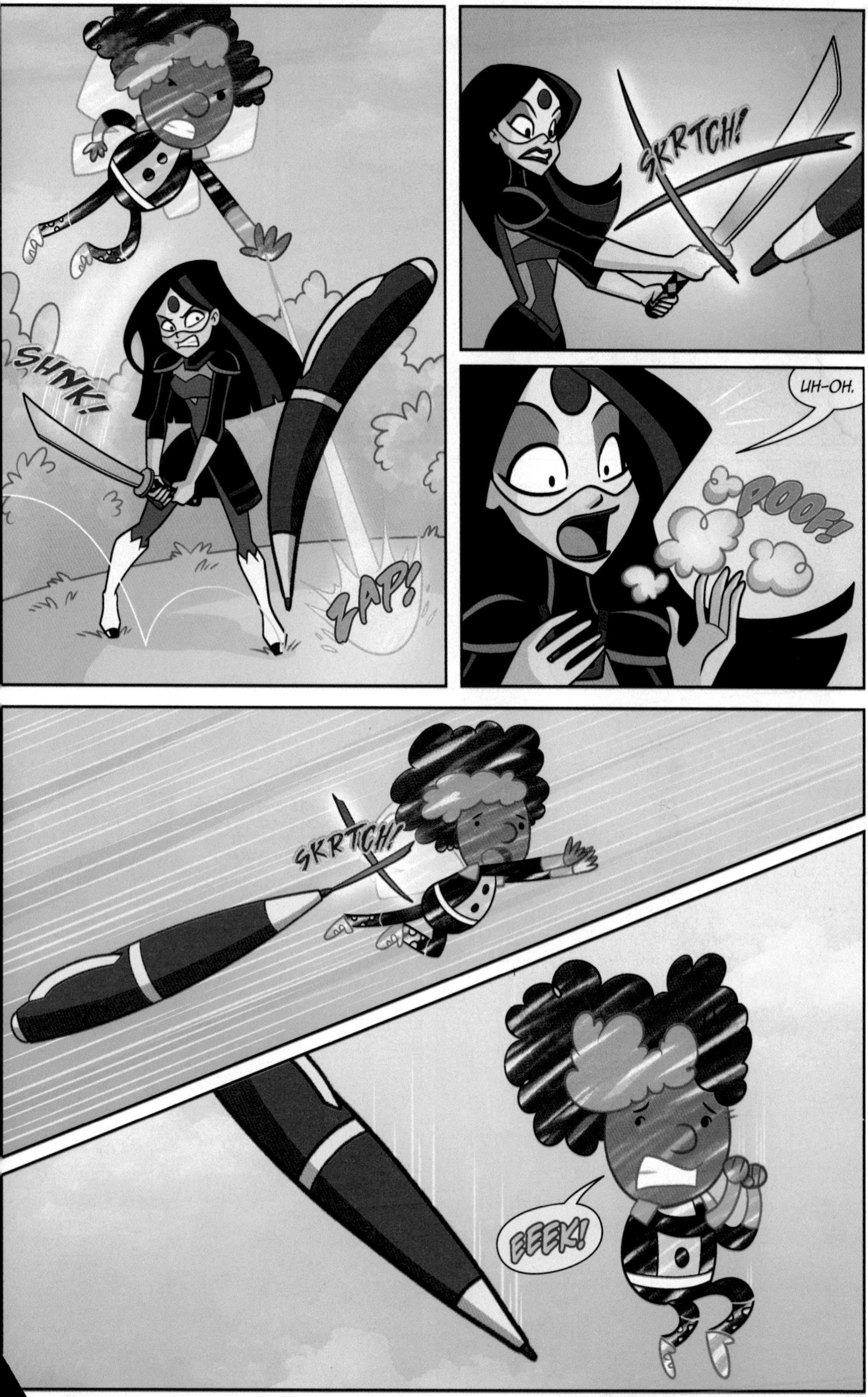
SHNK!
ZAP!
SKRTCH!
UH-OH.
POOF!
SKRTCH!
EEEK!

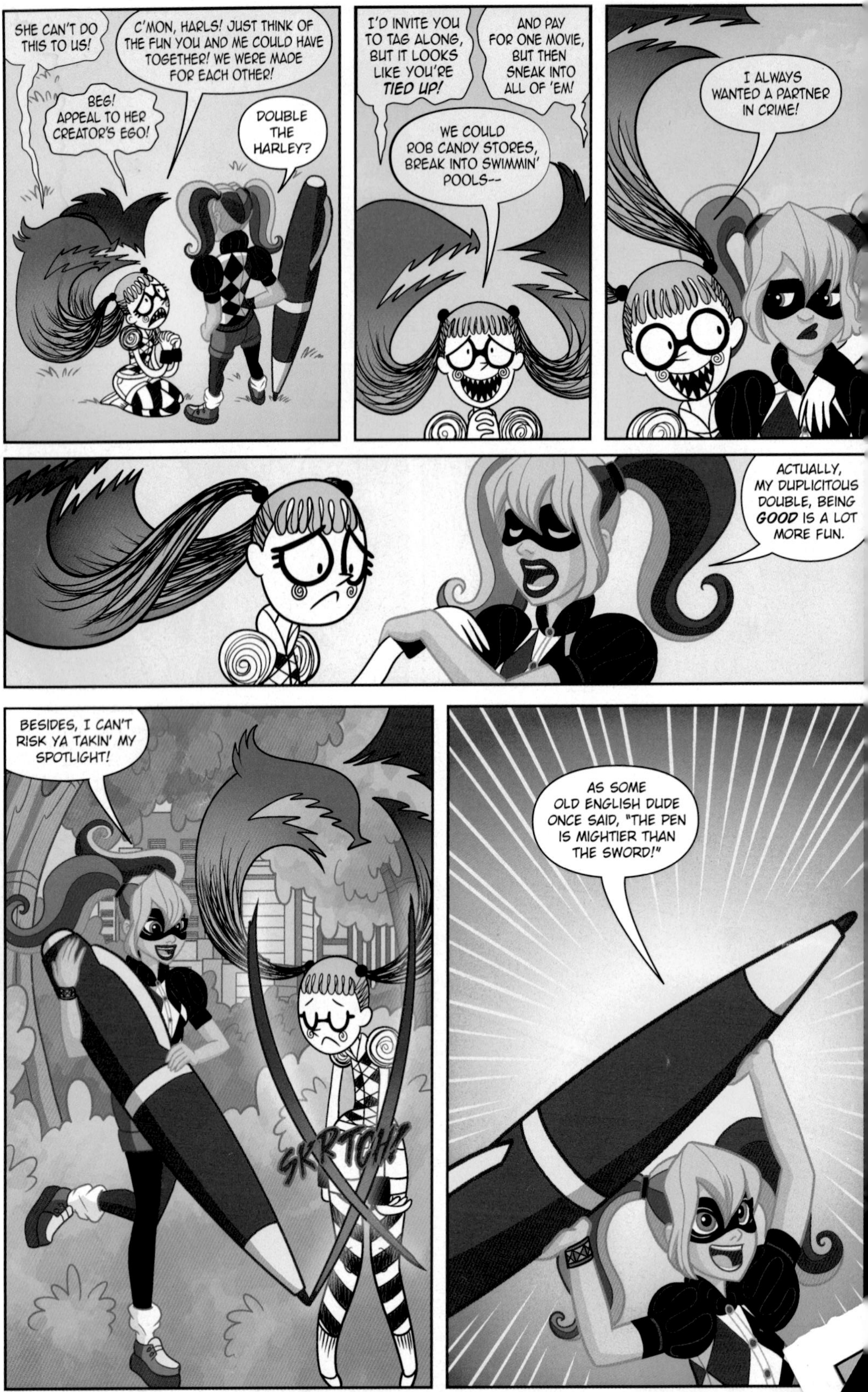
SHE CAN'T DO THIS TO US!
C'MON, HARLS! JUST THINK OF THE FUN YOU AND ME COULD HAVE TOGETHER! WE WERE MADE FOR EACH OTHER!
BEG! APPEAL TO HER CREATOR'S EGO!
DOUBLE THE HARLEY?
I'D INVITE YOU TO TAG ALONG, BUT IT LOOKS LIKE YOU'RE TIED UP!
AND PAY FOR ONE MOVIE, BUT THEN SNEAK INTO ALL OF 'EM!
WE COULD ROB CANDY STORES, BREAK INTO SWIMMIN' POOLS--
I ALWAYS WANTED A PARTNER IN CRIME!
ACTUALLY, MY DUPLICITOUS DOUBLE, BEING GOOD IS A LOT MORE FUN.
BESIDES, I CAN'T RISK YA TAKIN' MY SPOTLIGHT!
SKRTCH!
AS SOME OLD ENGLISH DUDE ONCE SAID, "THE PEN IS MIGHTIER THAN THE SWORD!"

117

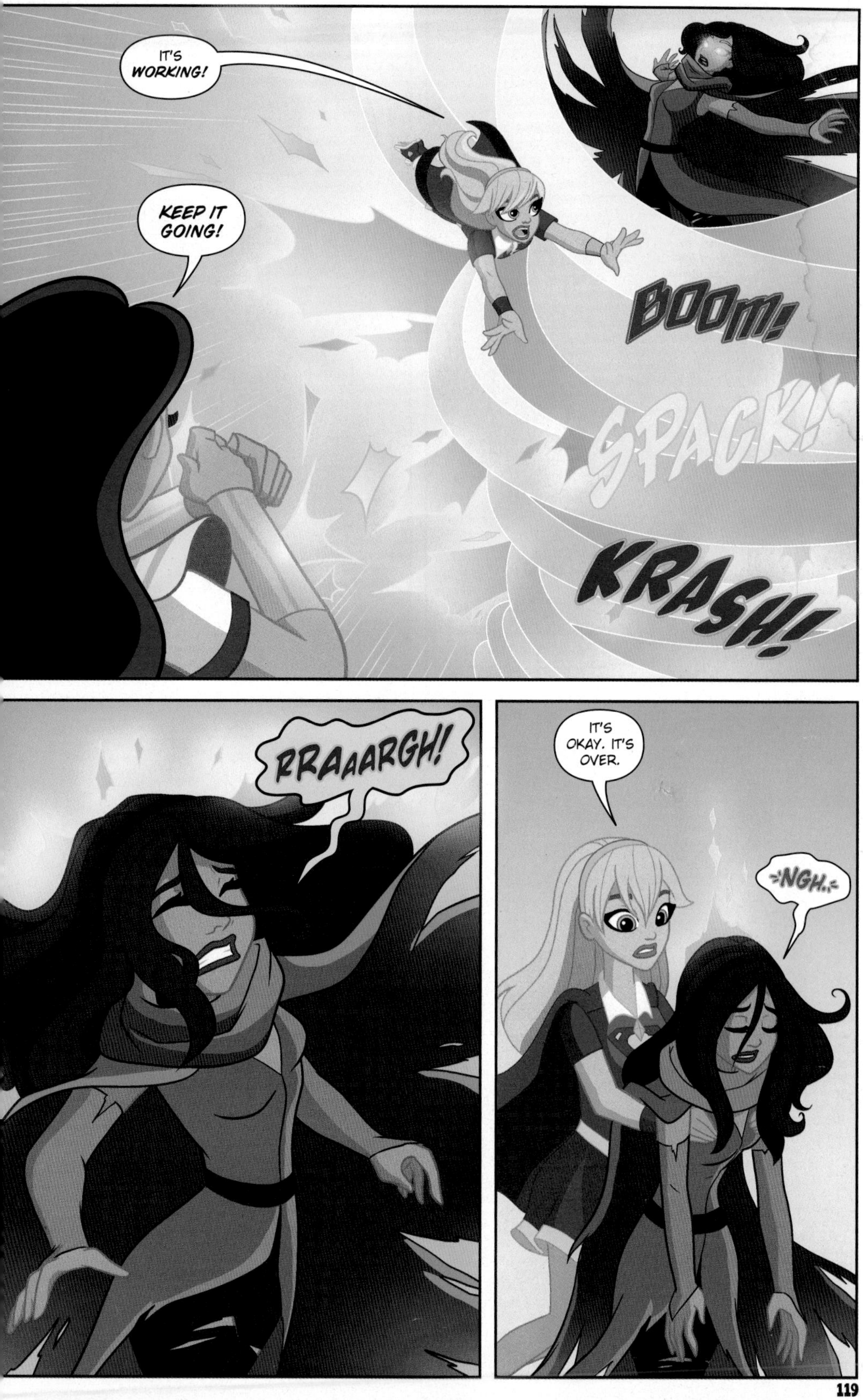
IT'S WORKING!
KEEP IT GOING!
BOOM!
SPACK!
KRASH!
RRAAARGH!
IT'S OKAY. IT'S OVER.
NGH..

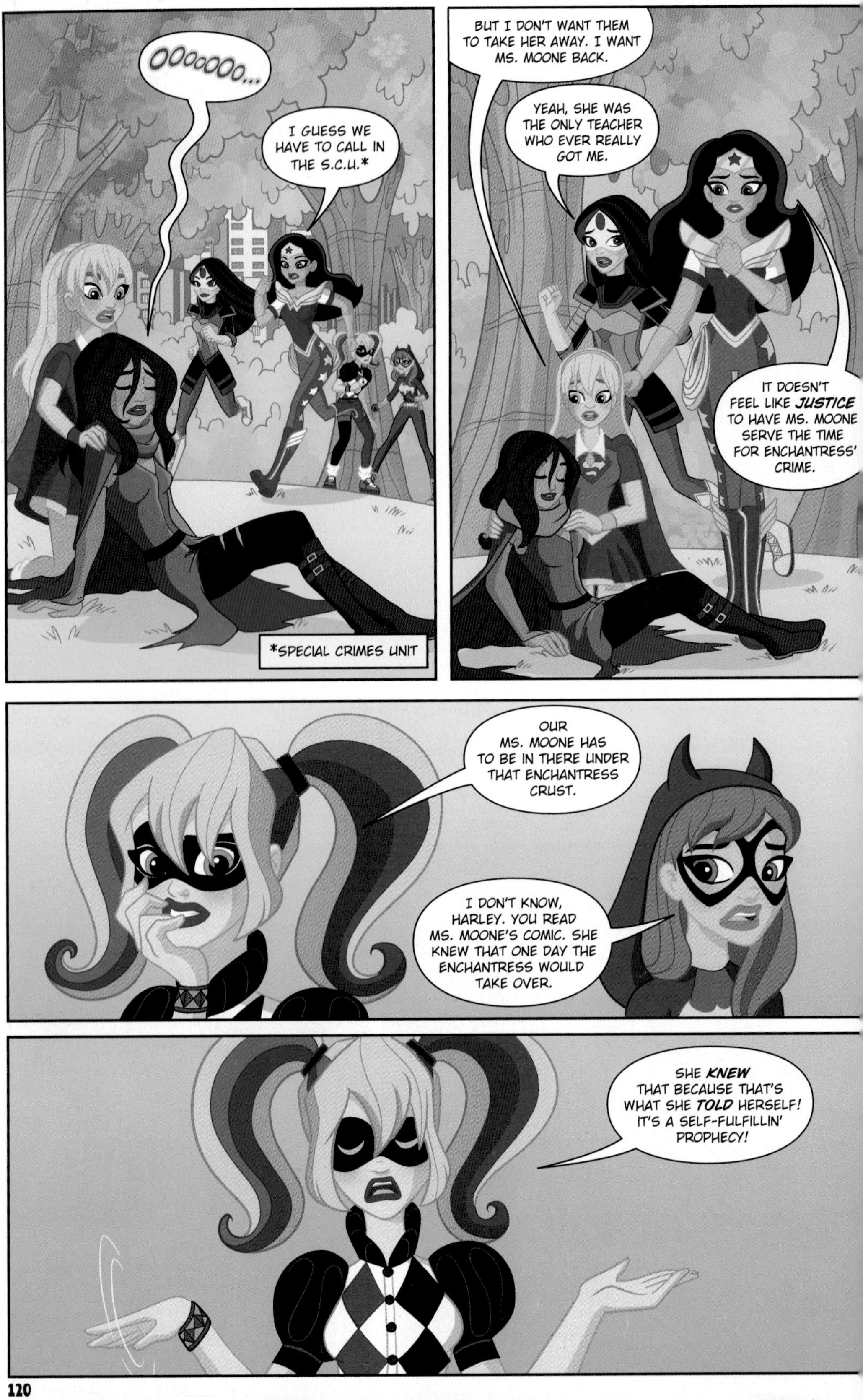
OOOOOOO...
I GUESS WE HAVE TO CALL IN THE S.C.U.*
*SPECIAL CRIMES UNIT
BUT I DON'T WANT THEM TO TAKE HER AWAY. I WANT MS. MOONE BACK.
YEAH, SHE WAS THE ONLY TEACHER WHO EVER REALLY GOT ME.
IT DOESN'T FEEL LIKE JUSTICE TO HAVE MS. MOONE SERVE THE TIME FOR ENCHANTRESS' CRIME.
OUR MS. MOONE HAS TO BE IN THERE UNDER THAT ENCHANTRESS CRUST.
I DON'T KNOW, HARLEY. YOU READ MS. MOONE'S COMIC. SHE KNEW THAT ONE DAY THE ENCHANTRESS WOULD TAKE OVER.
SHE KNEW THAT BECAUSE THAT'S WHAT SHE TOLD HERSELF! IT'S A SELF-FULFILLIN' PROPHECY!

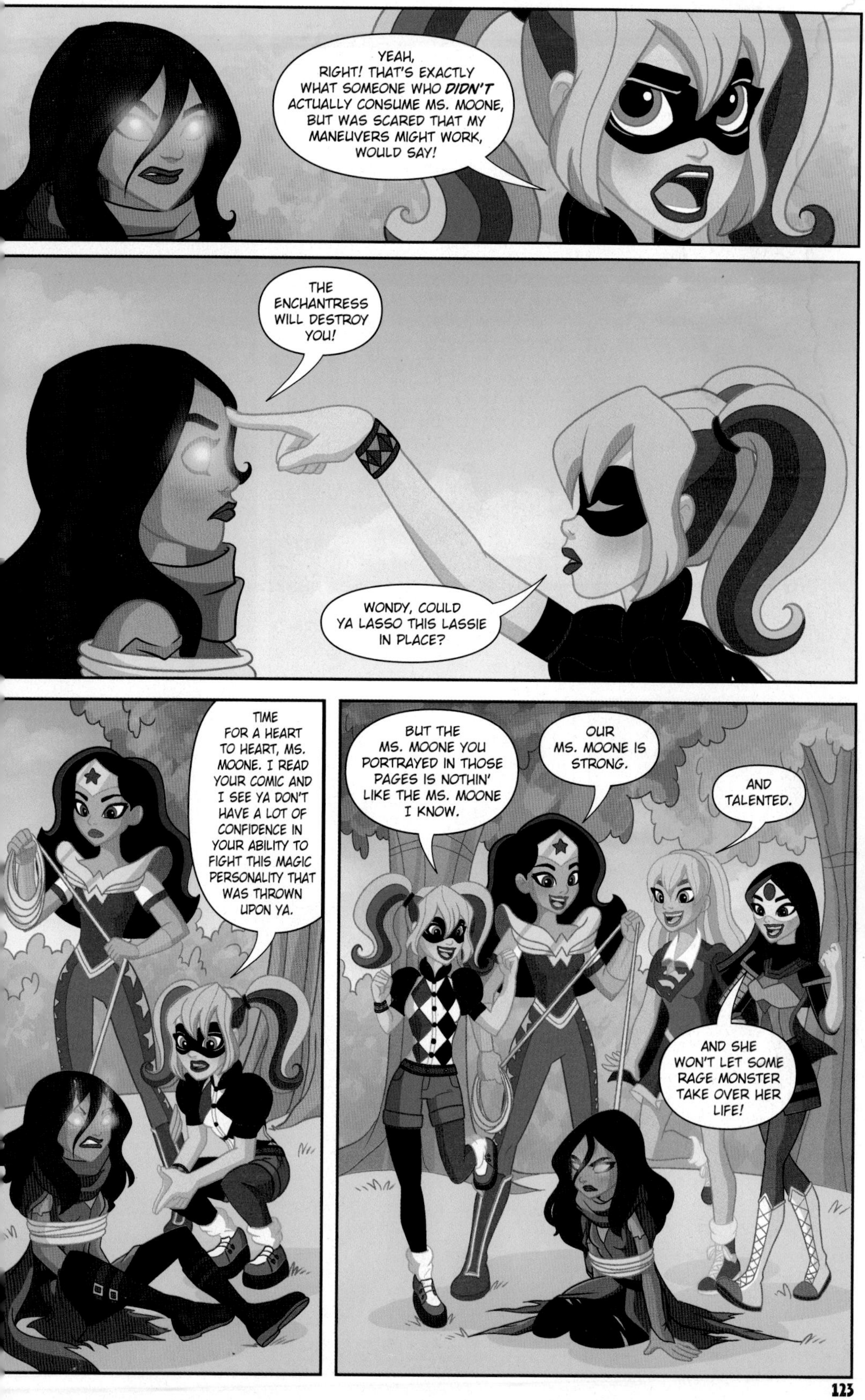
YEAH, RIGHT! THAT'S EXACTLY WHAT SOMEONE WHO DIDN'T ACTUALLY CONSUME MS. MOONE, BUT WAS SCARED THAT MY MANEUVERS MIGHT WORK, WOULD SAY!
THE ENCHANTRESS WILL DESTROY YOU!
WONDY, COULD YA LASSO THIS LASSIE IN PLACE?
TIME FOR A HEART TO HEART, MS. MOONE. I READ YOUR COMIC AND I SEE YA DON'T HAVE A LOT OF CONFIDENCE IN YOUR ABILITY TO FIGHT THIS MAGIC PERSONALITY THAT WAS THROWN UPON YA.
BUT THE MS. MOONE YOU PORTRAYED IN THOSE PAGES IS NOTHIN' LIKE THE MS. MOONE I KNOW.
OUR MS. MOONE IS STRONG.
AND TALENTED.
AND SHE WON'T LET SOME RAGE MONSTER TAKE OVER HER LIFE!

124